BLOOD, KIN, AND CURSES

BLOOD, KIN, AND CURSES

A DYSON BLAKE NOVEL

BY

HS PAISLEY

JSunley PRESS

ISBN: 978-1-9995236-5-7 (ebook)
ISBN: 978-1-9995236-4-0 (paperback)

To Sarah and Julia, who listened to me talk
about this story for fifteen years.

To all my editors, beta readers, and friends,
who helped me bring Dyson and her world to life.

Thank you for reading this long before
it should have seen the light of day.

I'm sorry for putting you through that.
Your help was invaluable.
The book is ready now.

Dyson hated that her hands were covered in blood. Again. She hated the scent of fear in the air and how it mixed with the sour tang of Magic gone wrong. She hated the ache in her swollen knuckles when she loosened her clenched fists.

She'd known she'd end up here, in this room.

Eventually.

This room, or one just like it. As soon as she'd learned how the Magical protections worked, Dyson had known it was inevitable. Only she could get through the barrier. Only she could end the war.

And she hated that too.

Her eyes traveled over a broken settee and the remnants of a table. They fell on the door to the en suite bathroom. She looked down at her hands. Some of the dark red liquid was hers. Most wasn't. Some of it had dried and crusted, looking like it would flake right off. Most of it was fresh and gleaming.

Using one hand to gather the light, flowing fabric of her black dress, and the other for balance, she walked through the vestiges of what was once a lavish bedroom. It was harder than it should have been. She stumbled twice, fell once, but finally managed to crawl to the sink in the bathroom.

"Almost like the first time I died," Dyson said, leaving a trail of deep red hand prints on the white and gold tile beneath her palms.

The first time she'd been covered in blood, about to fall into the waiting arms of death, the tile beneath her had been dirty. Too dirty to see what color it was. The first time she'd died, her blood had pooled in the fissures of the cracked subway floor.

"But I can't die again. Not yet, anyway."

With two hands on the edge of the white marble sink, Dyson steadied herself. She didn't look up at the mirror in front of her because she knew what she'd see there. Jaded hazel eyes that were once so full of hope. Blood splattered over her freckled caramel skin.

She'd stopped looking in the mirror a long time ago. She'd stopped looking because it made her sad to think of the hopeful girl she'd used to be and how everything had gone wrong.

Swollen knuckles protested when she gripped, then twisted the silver faucet. The cool water hit her cuts and they stung as she scrubbed away the blood. Then she washed her face as best she could.

The blood I can get rid of, she thought.

"But that feeling," she said, knowing and not caring that her voice wouldn't carry to the bedroom. "The feeling of bone breaking under my grip. I don't think I'll ever be rid of that."

She shook her head. The small movement made her lose her balance and she swayed. Grabbing the sink for support, Dyson flinched, as pain radiated through her body.

I need to focus on something else, she thought. I need to keep talking.

CHAPTER ONE
2014

Today, my life starts again.

Four years ago, when Dad died, everything fell apart. I inherited my childhood home. I couldn't afford it, so I dropped out of school to work full time.

My life, my goals, my dreams, were all put on hold. But today was my last day of work, of full-time work, at least. And on Monday, I would be a student again. I'd be picking up right where I left off.

"You're going back to school, you nerd!" My best friend Tina bear-hugged me, rocking me back and forth.

"I'm going back to school," I said, my eyes stinging with tears. Tina pulled back, and tucked my brown curls behind my ears.

"Oh, Dyson don't cry." She held my face in her hands. "Your parents would be so proud of you. So proud of how you handled everything. How you made it through."

I nodded and wiped away tears I'd tried not to shed.

My parents would be happy for me. I knew they would.

"Where's Roan?" I asked of Tina's partner.

"Oh, they're meeting us at the Fish and Fox," she said, starting up the stairs to my bedroom. "And they said they'll do that stupid song with you."

" 'Fairytale of New York' is not a stupid song," I said, aghast.

"It is when it's July!" Tina yelled over her shoulder.

Debatably, it's a Christmas song.

"Roan also requests 'Take on Me' as a duet," she went on. "I will not attempt the high note, so it's gotta be you." Tina walked into my bedroom and pulled a bottle of champagne out of her bag.

I smiled. I'd liked Roan a lot when I'd first met them a few weeks ago. I liked them more now. Someone who not only accepted my and Tina's obsession with karaoke, but who also wanted to join in was A-OK by me.

"Are Thomas and Kai coming?" Tina asked. I rolled my eyes in response.

I'd hoped that my brothers would get over themselves and celebrate with me today, but no. Losing Dad two years after Mom had broken something in their relationship.

"Never mind," Tina waved a hand through the air, before surveying my outfit.

As usual, I waited patiently for her to pass judgement. I wore light washed jeans and a burgundy top that looked good against my pale caramel skin.

"I love it." She popped the champagne. I gestured at the glasses I'd brought up stairs before she'd arrived. "I just think you should—"

"I am not wearing heels," I said.

Tina scoffed, then poured.

The next hour was spent drinking, laughing, and doing make-up.

"It really is art," I said as I watched her smoothly move the dark liquid liner over her cream-colored skin.

When the champagne bottle was empty, and we were thoroughly giggly, I slid my small copy of *Carmilla* into the back pocket of my jeans, and headed for the front door.

"You are not bringing a book," Tina said.

"I always bring a book on the subway," I shrugged.

"I know but . . . I just thought that . . ."

I blinked slowly at her, and she trailed off. This was an argument we'd had many times, and one she always lost.

"You're too tipsy to read!" she shouted as we walked out the front door.

"Shhhhhh," I said through a laugh.

"Sorry," she whispered. "Sorry," she said again, this time in the direction of my elderly neighbor's dark windows.

We walked arm in arm down the street, heading to the nearest streetcar stop and destination number one. Karaoke.

Roan met us there. They had a fantastic voice that got everyone in the Fish and Fox clapping and singing to their rendition of "Come Together."

"Go do that stupid song," Tina said dismissively when my name was called for the third time. Roan and I were joined by an enthusiastic Irish couple on vacation halfway through the opening of "Fairytale of New York."

"Let us buy you a round," the couple said after. We gladly accepted.

Next was Church Street and a drag show at Troops and Trollies. Tina had several friends performing. When the show was over, we danced like it was our last night on earth.

At last call, I started saying my goodbyes. With the price of metro passes, I refused to take any means of transport other than the TTC. Roan stayed behind with plans to meet us for breakfast the next morning. I told Tina to stay too, but she flat out refused to not finish the night with pizza on my couch.

She ordered just as we walked into Wellesley subway station and I smiled at my best friend.

At 1:48am, when I flopped down on one of the last trains of the night, I felt happy, tired, and still a little drunk. Tina let her head fall on my shoulder. I pulled out my book.

"You're such a nerd," Tina said.

"I love you too," I told her.

I heard the three-tone bell of the subway at the same time as I found my page in *Carmilla*. The sliding car doors started to close, but right before they did, someone stuck their foot out, triggering the motion sensor.

One of the subway platform lights flickered and died. Or was that me? Was I flickering, and dying? Everything hurt. I tried to breathe. There was a gurgling sound and I coughed.

Good that Tina got away. Better if she comes back with help. Better still if this one time, I'd taken a cab.

My vision flickered. Or was that another light?

I hadn't thought anything of the group of men that had hopped onto the train as the doors were closing. I could tell they were drunk and thought they were just being assholes by sitting so near us. When they got off at our stop, I'd thought, or maybe I'd hoped, they lived in the same neighborhood.

When one of them grabbed me, my hopes died.

I pushed away from the one who'd snaked an arm around my waist, then landed a solid punch to the guy who held Tina.

"Run!" I'd screamed at her.

I was about to do the same when the guy I'd punched returned the favor with interest. I'd never been hit like that in my life.

God, this sucks. God, this hurts. God, I should have taken that trip to Jamaica.

Tina had wanted to go this past winter. I hadn't wanted to dip into my savings.

Poor Tina. She'll think this is her fault.

I tried to roll over, to move from my side to my stomach and crawl. My vision narrowed. I stopped trying.

Blood pooled on the tile around me. It was on my clothes and covering my hands. It was on my lips and in my lungs.

I was dying, and I knew it.

Would Tina be the one to tell Thomas and Kai I died?

Blackness pushed in around me as the pain ebbed away.

How long until my brothers break their vow to never speak to each other again? How long until they sell the house?

At least I'll see my parents. I'll be with them again soon.

A figure loomed over me.

See there, that's my father now. Come to collect me. Come to take me to the other side.

My father said something and I tried to raise my hand. He touched my wrist and spoke again. I struggled to understand, to touch his face. Then everything went black.

At some point while she was talking, Dyson had sat on the edge of the claw-foot tub next to the sink.

Just for a second, she'd thought after exhausting herself looking through the bathroom cupboards and drawers. I just need to stop hurting for a second.

"As I died, I was hopeful," Dyson said. "As I died, I had faith. Faith that my parents would be there to greet me when I crossed over. Faith that we would all be together and happy. That we would wait for my brothers.

"That faith was in vain. I didn't know it at the time." She sighed. "I long for that kind of faith now."

Dyson hadn't felt like that in decades. Not really. Sure, there had been happy times, moments of light. But nothing sustained. It was hard to sustain faith and hope in times of war.

Even though that's when faith and hope were needed most.

"The next part was . . ." She remembered waking up in a small dark place, though those memories didn't come back to her right away. "It was all instinct at first. No thought. I felt, so I did. I wanted, so I took."

She looked over at the bathroom mirror. It reflected the doorway leading to the ruined bedroom.

"I was lucky it didn't last long. I was lucky someone was there for me," Dyson said, standing slowly and moving in front of the mirror. Without looking at herself, she reached for the bottom right corner of the ornate gold frame and pulled it open. Her eyes scanned the contents of the shelf she'd revealed. It was lined with small bottles, some dried flowers, and a small stack of one-inch-squared rough linen cloths.

Not here, she thought. It would be too easy if I found it here.

CHAPTER TWO

2014

You may want to slow down, said a voice inside my head, but I didn't want to hear it. I was too focused, too engrossed in what I was doing. Because a moment ago it was all black, then all dirt, then only thirst. I was thirsty a moment ago. Now I wasn't, and it was ambrosial. I wanted to keep drinking. I wanted to drink this—whatever it was—forever.

If your intention is to kill him, by all means continue, said the voice. But we don't want any of that, now do we?

Kill? No, I'm the one who's dying. Aren't I?

I paused, drew back.

There was a man in my arms. How had he gotten here? How had I gotten here?

It was no longer the hard ground of the subway platform beneath me. It was soft grass in a million shades of green.

And this man in my arms was older than those who'd hurt me, and I wasn't hurting anymore. Even the dry ache in my throat was gone.

The man's eyes rolled. They couldn't focus on anything. Not on the trees behind me, not on the stars above.

Trees? Stars? Kill? I don't want to kill anybody.

I looked around, and my eyes widened in shock. My crisp, clear vision of tombstones was surprising in the low light. To my right, I could see the bouquet of pale pink roses mixed with baby's breath in a vase on a wall covered in names. Across the lawn there was a wrought iron fence, and on the other side, an empty street. It was all so crisp, so clear, and so visible despite the darkness.

Then I looked up and swallowed a gasp. The city lights were too bright to see stars. But I could see them now. Not the bold brilliance of a cottage sky, but more. I saw more, and further than ever before.

There was a small exhalation of breath below me. I tore my eyes away from the galaxies above and dropped them to the man in my arms. I looked over the laugh lines in his pale face and the blood on his neck. His jacket and shirt were torn and blood trickled from the small and messy cuts scattered over his skin.

Did I do that? I closed my eyes and tried to remember.

An image of this man came back to me. He'd walked over from . . . somewhere. He'd seemed confused, worried, scared. He'd asked me if I was all right.

I'd tried to look at his face, I'd tried to take in my surroundings, but the trees behind him were a blur and all I saw was the pulse in his neck. Then, the sounds of the street faded to nothing and all I heard, as his eyes had glazed over, was the seducing beat of his heart.

I'd caught him as he fell. Then I—

Lick your finger, said the voice in my head. That voice that wasn't mine.

I obeyed. I couldn't help but obey. The words, so full of power, seeped into my mind and forced me to act.

My finger moved over tongue, then over the jagged cuts. They began to heal, though it would take several hours for the marks to disappear completely.

I can see his skin knit back together. How can I see his skin knit back together?

Good, said the voice.

I moved the man from my lap to the soft grass. Then, a loud crunch broke the still night air. It echoed in my ears, creating a map to its origin. It came from right behind me.

I whipped around, standing quickly. Knees bent, back hunched, and teeth bared, I growled. The growl was soft and low. I'd never made that sound before. I'd never stood like that either, but it made me feel ready, it made me feel strong.

"Oh, calm down." A man stepped out from behind a large cross-shaped tombstone. He had dark skin, darker eyes, and jet-black hair that fell in soft curls onto his forehead. He pushed the curls back with a hand and smirked. His mouth was a thin line turned up at the corner.

He threw a shovel down at his feet and I jumped at the sound it made as it hit the soft earth. Then, I heard a heartbeat. My heartbeat. Stronger and louder than I'd ever heard it before.

"What the—" I staggered backwards.

Had my heart not been beating before? Panic crept up my spine. My breaths came short and fast.

My heart should be racing. Why isn't my heart racing?

I looked down. I was wearing my favorite dress. The last time I'd worn it was my birthday party. Twenty-five years old, and neither of my brothers had come. Tina had been there, of course. She'd been determined to make sure I had a good time. We'd gotten trashed and I'd had to have the bright yellow dress drycleaned. It had been a wine stain then. It was completely covered in dirt now.

"No," I whispered. "No, no, no."

I was waking up in a small dark box. It was filling with dirt. I was swimming up and out as earth poured into my mouth and down my throat.

"No, no, no, no." I turned away from the large stone marked with my name and the pile of upturned dirt in front of it.

This isn't real, this isn't real. I have a heartbeat; I just felt my heartbeat.

"No, no, no." My voice was a soft moan as I searched my neck with two fingers. Finding nothing, I wrapped my arms around myself as the volume of the world turned up.

The sound grew and grew until I could hear everything. Every single thing around me. Birds in the trees across the street, a skateboard on pavement, and heartbeats. So many heartbeats and none of them mine.

Then the panic was gone.

It washed away like a sand castle too close to the water's edge. As if a wave came up, and pulled it back, leaving only misshapen lumps of sand behind.

I opened my eyes and looked up at the stranger.

The feeling of calm gave my brain space to wonder aloud, "Who are you?"

He smiled. His teeth gleamed white in the darkness and against his smooth brown skin. They were whiter still against the red apple he brought to his lips.

I resumed my defensive posture.

Another loud crunch ripped through the night air as he bit the apple, spraying juice in a rainbow of color. My eyes followed the droplets, so small and so beautiful, as they sprang from the apple's flesh, falling in a myriad of color. I tracked the gentle progress of lights, from the man's lips to his well-shined shoes.

Biting into an apple shouldn't be that loud. Spray from an apple shouldn't be that bright.

"I don't know you." I stated, but really, it was a question. Do I know you? I wanted to ask.

He was a little shorter than me, though it was hard to tell, leaning against the tombstone as he was. I surveyed him, trying to keep every ounce of composure I could. Trying to forget the panic that had gripped my body a moment ago.

He was well put together—grey slacks, a navy button-up, an overcoat that had two odd bulges. One over his chest, the other like there was something round in his pocket. He was handsome, with a strong jaw line and sharp eyes.

I took a few steps back, away from him, and from the man lying on the ground where I'd left him. Then I stood to my full height.

"You seem a little . . ." The words died in my throat. I'd never met him before. I would've remembered those eyes that looked right through me. I would've remembered the aura of power.

He looked at me, eating his apple, giving me time to work it all out.

When he pushed off the tombstone. I took another step back. He tossed the apple core over his shoulder. It was an easy flick of the wrist, but the core soared through the air, over the tall wrought iron fence, and into the trees.

He scared me. I wanted to run.

"Oh, stop that," his voice was lazy and it held an accent I couldn't place. English and something else. "Besides, I could catch you, and what happens next is your choice."

"What part of this is my choice?" I held my hands out to my sides. "What part of any of this has been up to me?"

"Well, I assume if you've given it any thought, you've come to some kind of conclusion."

The answer sprung to my lips. I swallowed it down. It was impossible, and stupid, and I didn't want to say it. I wanted to get home. I needed to check on Tina. School started on Monday, and I had a life to get back to.

"I was attacked," I said.

I remembered the distant echo of Tina's heels on the tiled subway platform and rough hands shoving me. My head had cracked against the hard wall and I'd seen stars. I'd tried to fight back.

She got away, I'd told myself. She's getting help. She'll be back.

But she hadn't come back.

"I was killed," I amended, not wanting to believe it. But I remembered the flickering light. The ghost of my father coming to bring me to the other side. "Was I killed?"

The man nodded, and the last light of hope in my chest went out. He motioned for me to continue.

"When I was dying," I paused, grasping for the memory.

A fist to my gut. Another to my face.

I squeezed my eyes shut, but just for a moment.

"My father was there," I said. I examined this stranger's dark eyes. They were black, but for the flecks of brown running through them.

He smiled. It was a sad smile. Pitying. I hated it.

"Oh," I said. "It wasn't him." I felt the sting of tears, the swell in my chest, the emotion begging to rip from my throat in a scream. I was about to drown in the grief of losing my father all over again, but another wave of composure washed over me and I breathed through it.

"It was you," I stated.

"It was," the stranger said.

"Who are you?" I stepped forward.

"You haven't finished yet," he said. " 'Who' is not the first question."

His eyes were searching, intense. It was like he was looking at my soul.

"What." The word fell heavy off my tongue.

"Yes," he nodded. "What are you." He said it as a statement, not a question.

"No." I stepped back. "No way, no freakin' way."

I wouldn't say it. It couldn't be real. It was too bizarre. But I had known. A part of me had known. Even if I didn't want to admit it to myself.

The haze of panic lifted with another wave of composure, and I remembered knowing.

From the second my eyes had opened in that coffin. From the moment I'd realized I didn't need to breathe. When the dirt had spilled into my mouth and down my throat. When I'd heard worms moving through the earth, and hearts beating miles away. When the panic faded and I'd climbed up, and out of the ground.

When I read my own name etched in stone.

I'd known it then. I knew it now. I denied it. I couldn't believe it. I didn't want to believe it. Because I wanted my life. My life that I'd worked so hard for. My life that I was just getting back on track. I was finally feeling like my head was above water, and now this?

"I'm dreaming," I said.

"No," said the man.

"I'm insane," I tried. "Delusional."

"No," said the man.

"I died. I'm dead, and this is some kind of you-get-what-you-wish-for purgatory." I'd always wanted more time. More time with my family. More time to save money and go back to school, and learn and grow and see the world.

"No," he said. "Well, actually," he tilted his head. "That could be. I mean, not really but . . . but I think you know the right answer."

"It can't be," I whispered more to myself than the man.

"It can." He pulled a green apple from an inside pocket of his long coat.

"It's not possible." I shook my head.

"It is," he encouraged.

"I'm not a—" I started.

"You are," he assured.

"Vampire."

"It was strange." Dyson limped out of the bathroom and toward the four-poster bed. "All those books I'd read, all the TV shows I'd loved, the movies . . ."

It was easy to think of the beginning, now that it was—

No, she cut off her thoughts. The mission first. Finish the mission.

Pain spiked up her leg with every step. She cursed not being able to find anything that might heal her in the bathroom, and she cursed her slow progress across the room.

"There must be something," she said. "Oushifa, or some other healing potion."

Her words were met by silence. She sighed, thinking back on her life. Something she rarely did.

"Sometimes I tried not to think of my mortal years, all the people I'd known, all the people who've died. Kai and Thomas. Tina. My parents. Even my old house. I thought being a Vampire would be glamorous when I was Human. It was glamorous in the movies. I thought it would be easy."

Finally reaching the bed, she used one of the posts for balance and lowered herself down. Short brown curls fell into her eyes. Her hair barely brushed her chin now, when once, it had dropped past her shoulders.

"It wasn't easy. But then," she looked around the room. She thought of how hard she'd fought to get there. "I guess nothing worth anything ever is."

CHAPTER THREE
2014

"I'm a Vampire." My tone was flat. "So, when I was—"

The memory of those men moving closer and closer to us on the train crept up my spine. The feeling of hot breath on the back of my neck when one got out of the subway car right behind us had made my skin crawl. I remembered the effort it had taken for me to spit blood in his face. The helplessness as he'd kicked me, as his friends had laughed, as I'd died alone.

"When I was on the subway platform." I opened my eyes to meet the dark gaze of this strange man lazily chewing a bite of apple. "That was you."

"Yes," he said.

"You made me this way?"

"Yes," he repeated.

"Why?" I asked. "You don't know me."

He took another slow bite. Chewed. Thought. I waited.

"To tell you the truth, I have been alone for a long time. I took a chance, a risk, I . . ." He shook his head, as if trying to clear it. "I try not to get involved in mortal problems."

Mortal problems. He means me. He means me dying. He didn't want to get involved, so I'd died.

I didn't want to think about that.

My eyes fell to the man lying on the ground. His skin was chalky and his neck was covered in jagged cuts. I didn't want to think about him either. I didn't want to think about whether or not he too fell under "mortal problems." I focused on the stranger.

"It was the blood," he continued. "And something else, I think. Maybe something beyond my control. But the blood." He looked down at the too green grass, and something flashed across his face.

Was it shame? When he looked up, his expression shifted. I tilted my head, trying to read him.

He looks like he's broken. He's looking at me like I broke him.

"Curses," he swore, as if realizing how he was looking at me. He blinked and his face became smooth and impassive again.

I was confused at the quick change of emotion, and for a moment, I just stared at him. I waited for his face to change again. When it didn't, I asked, "did you kill those men?"

I hoped he did. Or I thought I hoped that. I'd never wished death upon anyone before. I'd never intentionally caused someone pain. But the fear.

It had crept up my spine and clenched in my chest. They had made me feel so weak, so helpless, so afraid. I wanted them to feel that too.

"No." The man shook his head.

Disappointment and anger warred in my chest, but another wave of composure had me refocusing on his words.

"No, that was not my intention. Especially after I saw your book."

"My book?" I searched the ground around me as if I would find it here.

"Not *Dracula*, not *The Vampire Lestat*, not *Twilight*," he said. "You were drowning in your own blood with a copy of *Carmilla* lying in front of you. *Carmilla*."

He said it like it meant something to him. Maybe as much as it did to me.

"Stoker's inspiration," Dad had said, handing me a worn copy. One of three copies I now owned, the smallest of which I'd brought with me to read on the subway. The book had been one of my father's favorites. The genre as a whole was. That's probably why it was one of my favorites too. "Without *Carmilla*, there is no *Dracula*. And without *Dracula*—"

I didn't want to remember that either. But now I'd started thinking about my dad, it was hard to stop.

I will see my parents, I'd thought as I died. See there, that's my father now.

I don't know why I'd been so sure it was him. I was an atheist most days. My trust that God would help me had died when my father did. It had been reignited when I saw him again. But I'd been wrong. It had been this stranger.

"I bent down over you," the stranger said. "You raised your arm, and I saw—" He shook his head. "It was one coincidence too many, I was suddenly so hungry, and I needed a reason to . . ." He trailed off.

I tried to make sense of his words, of my new self, but there was so much I didn't understand.

"It was like a gift, a sign. There you were, and there I was, and I thought that perhaps you would prefer this life," he gestured to me. "Over a true death."

"And if I didn't?" The question was out of my mouth before I realized what it implied. "Not that I have decided anything yet!" I threw up my hands, palms forward. "Because I haven't."

I don't think I have.

"If you didn't want this, or were," he seemed to search for the right word, "uncooperative—"

Then his hand was on my throat, and his face was next to mine.

"I would just kill you."

As fast as he was at my side, he was gone, back standing by the tombstone, a shovel on the ground in front of him, the man lying limp on the ground between us.

I put a hand to my racing heart . . . but, of course, it wasn't racing. A pang of loss rippled through me. No heartbeat. And if the stories were true, no sunshine. Would I be able to go back to my house? To finish my degree? Would I be able to tell my brothers I was still alive? To tell Tina?

Heavy ragged breathing cut through the sound of distantly passing cars. It was punctuated by sobs that, only after my hands and knees slammed into the ground, I realized were coming from me.

It is all right, said the voice in my head.

My fingers, digging into the grass, relaxed. My breathing, harsh and rough, returned to normal.

You are all right, said the voice, that I belatedly recognized belonged to this stranger.

"How are you feeling?" he asked as I found my feet again.

"What do you mean by 'uncooperative'?" I grasped onto the last piece of information he'd given me that wasn't a death threat.

"Some new Vampires become intoxicated with their surroundings and enhanced abilities," he explained slowly, and there was a new wariness in his gaze. "You are still you, still the same person you were before, but the transition can be difficult."

He took one last bite of the apple before this core followed the last one into the trees. I heard a thud as it hit the soft earth some hundred meters away. He bent down to pick up the shovel, and walked slowly toward me.

I backed away, keeping my guard up despite the waves of tranquility I kept feeling. He stopped.

"You have nothing to fear from me," he said.

I seriously doubted that.

"Some of the young ones attack their makers," he went on. "Or Humans, or hurt themselves."

"Themselves?" I asked, still unclear of what the shovel was for.

"Oh, yes. Unfortunately, it is not at all rare," he walked around the man on the ground, over to the untidy pile of dirt in front of the tombstone I refused to read again.

"It is most prominent to those who were deeply religious in life," he said, as he started to tidy the mess of scattered earth. "But not exclusive to them, of course. Many, with and without faith alike, can't stand what they've become. Seeing themselves as all evil, true evil. They can't take it, and they end their new lives."

I listened and when the panic, sorrow, and rage was almost all-consuming, a wave of composure washed over me, and I could think again.

"For you, it was just a matter of attitude," he waved in my direction, then patted the neat mound of earth with the flat of the shovel. "Your attitude towards yourself, towards me, but most importantly, towards

Humans."

"My attitude," I echoed.

"This man." He walked over to the crumpled form on the ground. "Was it your wish to kill him?"

I only had flashes of what had happened after I'd woken up in the box.

My coffin. Of course, it was my coffin.

It seemed obvious now. It seemed like it should have been obvious when I broke the lid, and dug myself out. This all should have been obvious when I saw the man, and caught him as he fell. When I sunk my teeth into . . .

The anxious knot building in my stomach tightened.

"No." I ran my tongue over my teeth. They felt the same as always. "Of course I didn't want to kill him."

"You sound surprised," the stranger said, scooping up the man on the ground as if he weighed nothing. "Oh dear, you are naïve."

I frowned, opening my mouth to protest, but he was walking away.

"At the very least, this means I do not have to kill you," he said over his shoulder. "Bring the shovel."

I could run now, couldn't I? While his back was turned, while he was carrying that man.

I blinked. Shook my head, and followed him. I had too many questions, and right now, this stranger was the only one who could give me answers.

"That's good, right?" I picked up the shovel and jogged to catch up. I covered ground faster than I intended, and almost bumped into him. "That's good?" I repeated, not sure if it was a question I was asking myself or him.

Was nothingness better than what lay ahead?

"Yes," he nodded and stopped beside a lawn chair seated in front of a small tombstone with the name Sarah O'Lanagan. He gently placed the man in his arms on the lawn chair. "This is Sean," he gestured to the man. "He comes here a lot, sometimes falls asleep."

The stranger put a fingertip to his teeth and it came away red. I watched as he tilted Sean's head back, letting two drops of blood fall into his mouth.

"To replenish what you took," he explained. "But not enough to have any lasting effects. Shall we go?" He held out a hand.

I stared at it, then at him. I didn't trust him. I didn't trust myself. I didn't know what to do.

"The day will be here soon." His eyes went to the sky, lightening at the horizon, then back to my face. "Surely, you can feel it."

Is that what I was feeling? That fist clenching deep in my gut? Not my life being turned upside down and my world imploding?

The more this man explained, the longer he spoke, the calmer I felt. Or at least, as calm as one could feel under the circumstances.

But that feeling, that urgent pressure, the knot deep in my gut. It was the sun.

"What's your name?" I stepped forward, again, covering more ground than I'd expected to in a single stride.

"My apologies," the man gave me a little bow. "I am Sahrias Gillrana."

"Blake." I took his hand when he offered it again, because what else was I going to do? "My name is Dyson Blake."

"I know." He smiled and closed his fingers around mine. We started to run. I felt a rush of elation at the speed of our movement, and a wave of sadness as we sped out of the cemetery and into the city, leaving my old life behind.

CHAPTER FOUR

2014

Sahrias moved at a breakneck speed but I had no trouble keeping up. The empty back streets of old brick houses and new modern builds flashed by. My legs moved smoothly, eating up the asphalt beneath my feet. Wind whipped my curls around my face, and my dress swished against my thighs.

It was bliss.

I'd played sports in high school, but I'd never liked running. If it had felt like this, I would have loved it. The slit in the front of my dress provided easy movement, and for a brief moment, I felt free.

Then the ache in my chest came back.

It was slow at first, but Sahrias must have sensed it, because when I asked, "where are we going?" and he said, "I have a home on the outskirts of the city," he slowed enough to take my hand.

It should have been awkward to run this way, hand in hand. But it wasn't.

"Is it far?" I asked.

"Not far." He squeezed my hand lightly. "You will be all right."

Calm, he said in my mind. You are going to be all right.

The feeling of his voice in my mind washed over me and loosened the knot of tension in my chest.

You will be all right. We are almost there.

The wave of calm started in my hand, where I clutched his fingers like a lifeline. The sensation moved up my arm and into my chest. I sighed in relief as composure washed over me again and again.

You will be all right. We are almost there.

I was all right. But my throat was dry, and the heartbeats we passed were getting louder.

We ran. Maybe I was carried for part of it. At some point, I was taken down a flight of stairs and the next thing I was fully aware of was blood. A bag of cool liquid being pushed into my hands, then my being guided to sit down on a bed.

I sunk my teeth into the bag without thinking. I finished in moments. It left my throat feeling raw and needy and worse than it had before. I craved more. A fridge door opened and closed. A second bag appeared. A third. I lost count.

"Where'd you . . . where . . ." I felt drunk. I tried to focus on my words. "—is iss legal?"

I held up the drained bag of blood.

He handed me another. I bit into it, half-finished it, opened my mouth to speak, and it all went black.

I opened my eyes. I was afraid. Afraid I was alone again. In the box again. But I wasn't alone. A man sat feet away from me on a bed. A strange bed. A strange man.

"I'm in a bed." I heard the words aloud, but I'd meant to think them. The words were slurred. There was something in my mouth, something stuck to my front teeth.

I tried to raise a hand and feel what it was, but I was restrained. I looked down and saw empty blood bags scattered across a brown and burgundy duvet cover. A thick zip-tie held my arm against a railing attached to the bed.

"Yes," said the strange man.

No, not strange. I know him.

"Zaaaa," I remembered his name. I felt drunk and hungover at the same time. "Race car," I laughed. "Za race car. No . . . rice? Zaaarice . . . car."

"Closer than last time." His smile was warm. "We'll work on it. How are you feeling?"

I looked around the room. Bare tan walls, no windows, empty shelves. It felt cold and unlived in.

I swallowed in preparation to speak. When I opened my mouth, a sharp pain cut across the back of my throat. Every breath felt like I was swallowing razor blades.

"I'm . . ." I turned to face him. "My—" I choked on the word.

"Yes." He brought a cup to my lips.

I drank.

It all went black.

I woke up. I was in a strange bed. There was a strange man.

I was thirsty. So thirsty. A cup. I drank. A bag. I drank.

Blackness.

I woke up. I was in a strange bed. There was a strange man.

No. Not strange. I know him.

I was thirsty. So thirsty. A cup. A bag. I drank.

Blackness.

I woke up. In a bed that wasn't strange. There was a man. I knew him.

"Sahrias."

My voice was hoarse. Like I hadn't used it in a long time, or like I'd used it too much.

"Dyson," said the man in the small armchair next to my bed. "How are you feeling?"

I was thirsty. Sahrias brought a cup to my lips.

Did I say that out loud?

I drank and looked at him. He looked like he was in his early thirties, except his eyes. His dark eyes were much older.

"Dyson," he repeated. "How are you feeling?"

"Ummm . . ." What could I say? Great, the fact that I crave blood is really doing it for me? "I'm feeling a little off, I guess."

"Okay," he nodded. "Parched?"

"No." My eyes fell to the plastic bags strewn over the duvet. My face flushed. I wanted to move away from them, but I couldn't. My wrists were tied.

No, they weren't . . . or they weren't any more.

I pushed myself up, hugged my knees to my chest.

"No need for that," Sahrias said with kindness. "You don't have to be embarrassed—or afraid." He leaned forward in his chair and touched my arm.

Hot pain seared through me. I gasped, pulling away.

"I'm sorry," he drew back.

"No, you, I—" I stumbled on my words. "I just felt something when you touched me. Like a heat, like power, maybe . . ."

"Oh?" He met my eyes.

"There's something wrong with me," I stated.

"No, no, not that I'm aware of . . ." He trailed off at my confused look. "I think you might have felt my Spark, my power source."

"Okay," I said, even though I had no idea what "Spark" was.

"It shows great strength," he smiled that warm smile again. I remembered that smile. It was familiar.

I think he smiles at me like that a lot. But that can't be right . . . I haven't been here long enough to feel that way about him or his smile.

"Great potential," he said. "You are powerful, Dyson."

"I don't feel very powerful." I shrank further away from the empty blood bags I couldn't remember drinking.

"You need not worry about all this," he said, following my gaze. "It's completely normal to feed this way in the beginning."

"And what I felt," I looked at the spot on my bare arm where he'd touched me. "That's not normal."

I'm already broken. Holy shit, I'm already broken. I felt a rise of panic in my chest.

"Stronger than normal, I'd say. Though I cannot be sure. I've never sired before," he admitted. "This is a first for both of us in a way."

Vampire.

The word flashed in my mind and hot pain flared in my upper gums. The sour tang of bile rose in the back of my throat and I clutched at my chest.

My heart should be racing. I'm having a panic attack. Why isn't my heart racing?

Looking at the sucked-dry blood bags, I let out a half-sob, half-scream and tried to push them away. Scrambling backwards, I pressed myself into the corner of the room where the bed met two blank beige walls.

Vampire, Vampire, Vampire. I touched my top teeth, felt fangs with my fingertips and started shaking.

What's happening to me? What's happening to me? My life, my school, my brothers, my friends, my job, my world! What's happening to me?

I rocked back and forth, clutching my knees to my chest. My breaths were coming heavy and fast. But I don't even need to breathe.

I remembered the dirt pouring into my mouth and lungs as I swam up and out of the earth. I remembered the blood pouring into my lungs as I fought to breathe on the subway platform. They attacked me. I died. He brought me here. And now I'm a—

I squeezed my eyes shut. I squeezed them shut against the image of empty blood bags and the man who'd collapsed in my arms. I squeezed them shut against the memory of being surrounded on the subway platform. I squeezed my eyes shut against the degree I would never finish, the brothers I would never see again, their future children I would never meet.

I would never have kids of my own.

I would never see the sun.

I would never see the sun.

Never.

I leaned over the side of the bed and vomited.

Like a hot shower after a long day, composure and clarity flowed over my quivering body. I opened my eyes to see Sahrias's arms outstretched, hands holding a bucket under my head.

"It will be all right." His voice was soft and soothing, and I wanted to believe him. "It will all be all right," he said.

I burst into tears.

I don't know how long I lay there, curled up in a ball, with my head resting on Sahrias's leg. I hadn't cried on someone's lap since I'd been a child. I felt like a child now, no control over my emotions, my body, or my life. Sahrias let me cry, just like my father had all those years ago.

He stroked my hair and told me everything would be okay. My father had done that too. I must have fallen asleep like that, because the next thing I remembered was thirst, then feeling sated, then Sahrias's voice. I turned my head to the side and saw him sitting with a book open in front of him.

He was reading to me. Greek mythology.

Interesting choice. I closed my eyes and got lost in the words and the smooth rhythm of his voice.

I would sleep—and wake up thirsty. I would drink—and listen to Sahrias read. It went on like that for a while. I remembered more of what he read every time I woke.

How did he know I was into this stuff?

Roman Gods and Celtic folk heroes. The Brothers Grimm, and a book of Japanese fairy tales. And every so often he would read me *Carmilla*. The copy my father had given me. Sahrias would leave it on the bedside table, and sometimes while he read folktales, I would stare at that book. I would stare at it and think of my father. I thought of my brothers, of Tina. Then one night—

"Dyson?" Sahrias's voice was cautious. He pulled the cup back from my lips.

I looked down at the slew of empty bags surrounding me on the bed. The sheets had been changed. The duvet cover was different. I looked down at myself. My clothes were different too.

"Dyson?"

"I'm okay," I said. There was a tingling in my upper gums. Running my tongue over my teeth, I felt nothing out of the ordinary. "I think I'm okay. We are in a basement," I observed, slowly standing and walking around the room.

The bland beige walls had no windows. But they were not so bland anymore. Blood spatter stained them in many places.

"A safe room," Sahrias said. "It is not safe for us in daylight; that part of the myths is true. It's not safe for a new Vampire to be around Humans either."

Why did he say that? How did he know I wanted to see my family?

"Why are you looking at me like that?" I asked. "Like I'm going to explode or something. I'm not going to start crying again."

It was a lie. I had no idea what I would do. I had no idea about any of this.

"There is no shame in crying," he said, still looking at me like I was a bomb.

"Then why are you staring at me like that?"

"We've had this conversation a few nights in a row now," he said, looking away.

Oh. My eyebrows pulled together. That's how he'd known. But I can't remember those other conversations. Why can't I remember?

"It's not uncommon," he explained. "I have heard that it takes about three to six months for a coherent conversation."

"It's been that long?" the words caught in my throat.

Sahrias took a cautious step forward and raised his arms slightly. He didn't speak.

I swallowed.

"You've told me this already."

He nodded.

"I reacted poorly."

He nodded again.

"How long has it been since . . ." I rubbed the spot on my arm where he'd touched me, where I'd felt that scorch of power.

He kept his hand up and ready as he answered. "That was about three weeks ago."

"Oh, God." I covered my mouth with a hand. "And since that night? That first night." He took another cautious step forward. "Just tell me, okay? I'm not going to freak out."

His mouth hitched up at the corner.

"Shit." I shook my head, walked to the bed, and sat. "I've said that before too, huh?"

He nodded, then spoke. "It's been eighteen months."

"Wha—" I swallowed again. The razor dry feeling was back in my throat. I gasped, and he handed me a cup. I gulped greedily, then wiped the back of my hand over my mouth. "What's wrong with me."

"Nothing," he said. "This is not uncommon."

"But it's not common," I stated.

"Correct," he nodded again. "That doesn't mean something is wrong."

"You said before that I was strong." That sting on my skin. That power. That was his Spark, whatever the hell Spark was.

"I think you are," he said. "But I also told you I was new at this. Do you remember that too?"

I nodded.

"We've had this conversation already?"

"Yes." His eyes filled with concern. "But I am not worried about that. I just want you to—"

"How many times?" I cut him off. "How many times have we had this conversation?"

"What answer can I give you that would ease your mind?"

"That many, huh? And Tina? My brothers?" I was sure he'd told me this before too, but I didn't care. I needed to hear it again.

"Do you remember how you died?" he asked.

I nodded.

"The cameras cut out some time before I would have appeared. Enough of the attack was caught to find—and prosecute—those men. You weren't their only victim," he said.

"And Tina?" I asked.

"Safe," he inclined his head. "Officers arrived about thirty minutes after you'd . . . Tina went to the press with how long it took. Caused quite a stir."

"And you left me there on the platform?" I asked. "Seems kind of cold."

"What would have happened if you'd disappeared? I didn't know if you had family, if they would need closure. I wanted those men to be caught. Without a body . . ." He shrugged. "And the change doesn't happen right away."

"Okay," I nodded and looked at the ceiling, trying not to cry. There was blood splattered there too.

Jesus, what a mess. And he has been taking care of me all this time.

"I followed you closely when you were taken," Sahrias said. "Made sure you changed properly."

"Okay," I repeated. I didn't know what else to say.

"Your brothers started talking again when they got the news."

"I guess sometimes tragedy brings people together," I shrugged. Too bad the opposite happened after my dad died. My eyes stung.

"Yes," Sahrias nodded. "They were there for each other through everything. They buried you next to your parents."

I closed my eyes and felt tears track down my face.

God, I missed them. It had been so long since the three of us had all been together. I'd tried last Christmas. I'd tried so hard to get my brothers inside my parents' house. They'd refused. I saw them separately, going over to their respective places, and cried myself to sleep. Maybe if they knew it would have been our last Christmas together, they would have acted differently.

Sahrias passed me a handkerchief. I dabbed at my eyes and the cloth came away red.

I looked up at him, confused.

"I cry blood now?"

He smiled that same kind smile. For his sake, I hoped this was the last time we had to have this conversation.

"No," he said. "It's not blood, and your tears will not always be red. More often than not, they will be the same as when you were Human. But that is not something we have to talk about right now. Not unless you want to."

I shook my head. "In the other times we had this conversation, did I tell you that my brothers stopped speaking when my father refused treatment?"

"You can tell me again," Sahrias smiled. That same warm smile.

He did smile at me like that a lot. I'd seen that smile for the past year and a half, with no understanding of time.

"Not much to tell," I said.

For some reason, I saw my father looking back at me through Sahrias's eyes. They looked nothing alike. But in that moment, they had the same warmth.

"Especially if I've told it before. They were just hurting. Losing him so soon after mom. I think he partly died of a broken heart. And now me." I burst into tears.

Shit. I said I wasn't going to do this again.

"They are okay," Sahrias said, moving to sit beside me on the bed. "Kai is thirteen months sober. Thomas named his son Dyson three months ago."

The handkerchief slowly turned a deep, deep red as I cried.

"I was right that night, that last night I went out with Tina. I was right when I thought that day was the day my life would start again." Running a hand over her lower leg, Dyson hissed in pain when her fingers touched glass.

"Or, at least, my second life. The transition wasn't easy. It was a process. Understanding, controlling, relearning. Letting go. That might have been the hardest part in the beginning. The letting go part. But anyone who has gone through a traumatic change knows you just have to keep going. Keep living."

Knowing where the shard of glass was now, she reached down more carefully, finding it with her index finger and thumb. She grunted in pain when she wrenched the thing out of her leg and the sound echoed around the room.

I need to wash my hands again, she thought. At least this time it's my blood.

"I missed my brothers; I missed my friends. Missing my parents was nothing new, but it seemed newly difficult in the years after I was turned. I missed a lot of things."

She tossed the glass aside. It hit a metal lamp, bent and broken on the ground. Then she made quick work of shredding a pillow case into usable strips. She wrapped her leg wound, sparing only a momentary thought for its slow healing.

"That first night, what else could I do but go with him? Sahrias, I mean," she explained. "And when I woke up again, what else could I do but stay? If I hadn't, I would have been truly alone."

I don't think I could've handled that then, she thought. God, I barely can now.

"Imagine," she straightened and looked behind her. "Waking up and being told a year and a half had passed. My friends and family had grieved me. All I had left to do was grieve them."

She finished dressing the wound. It throbbed with pain though it shouldn't hurt anymore. She wasn't healing. But she couldn't die. Not yet. Not until her job here was done.

CHAPTER FIVE
2016

The next time I woke up, only a day had passed. I remembered everything Sahrias had told me, and I was ready to leave the small room that had been my home for the last year and a half.

There was a bundle sitting on the chair Sahrias usually occupied when reading. It was a change of clothes, a towel, and a washcloth. I picked it up and walked down the narrow hall in hopes of finding a bathroom. I could hear Sahrias in the room beyond, probably a kitchen of some sort, but I didn't speak.

I was happy for the time alone and soon found what I was looking for. I just ducked into the small bathroom, stripped off the pajama shorts and t-shirt, pulled back the shower curtain, and stepped into the large tub.

I stood under the hot spray for a long time. I stood there and cried silent tears for my parents, for my brothers, and for myself. The water was pink on my hands when I wiped my eyes.

I knew this wouldn't be the last time I cried for them—or for me.

If losing both my parents within two years of each other had taught me anything, it was that grief takes time. Grief makes its own schedule.

Determined to pull myself out of the sadness, even for just a little while, I turned the water as hot as I could handle. It rolled down my body and I scrubbed myself clean.

I looked for shampoo and conditioner. My favorite brands of each were sitting in a metal wire basket, hanging off the rounded edge of the tub. It was comforting that Sahrias cared enough to learn this small detail of my previous life.

He must have gone to my house. How else could he have gotten my father's copy of *Carmilla*? He must know so much about me now. Who knows what I'd said over the last eighteen months. God, eighteen months! And I know nothing about him.

When I wet the pink shampoo bar, its scent filled the steamy air. I crinkled my nose. It never smelt this potent before. The scent wasn't unpleasant, just strong, and the same thing happened with the conditioner.

I finger combed my curls, only then realizing how long my hair was.

My hair grows . . . am I alive?

I rotated the brass shower head away from my body, and turned the water as hot as it could go. Waiting until I saw the steam rising from it thicken, I stuck my arm under the scalding spray.

"Ouch!" I yelped and pulled my arm back.

"Is everything all right?" Sahrias called through the bathroom door.

"Yes!" I said, turning the temperature back to something manageable. "Good morning, Sahrias, sorry to scare you!"

That's a Human thing, right? Pain? The feeling was gone now, but I had felt it.

"Morning?" A soft chuckle came through the old wood door. "Child, it's the dead of night."

"Yeah." I was still studying my arm. "Old habits die hard. I'm never going to be okay saying 'good night' as soon as I wake up."

"Very well," he said, and I heard footsteps move away from the door.

I stepped my body out of the water before turning the tap all the way to the left. Extending my arm into the burning stream a second time, I counted to ten.

Holding back my cry of pain, I pulled my arm out of the water, and examined it. It was red and blotchy, but not really burned. It wasn't hot enough for that anyway. As I looked at the marks the scalding water left on my skin, they faded. My skin was normal. A little pale for lack of sun, but the same beige-gold tones it had always been.

Not Human. Still a person, though.

After pulling on clean clothes, I left the bathroom and walked down the hall. Sahrias was sitting on the bed in the small room.

"How are you feeling?" he asked, standing.

I dropped my towel and balled-up pajamas at the door, took a couple steps forward, and hugged him.

He let out a small "ouf" and stilled. After a few seconds, he relaxed and hugged me back.

"Thank you," I said, my head tucked onto his shoulder. I was a few inches taller than him, but I felt safe and cared for. I felt like I had a piece of my family back. "Thank you," I repeated.

I was a hugger before my parents died. Before I had to be hard and cold and take on the world alone. Right then, I needed a hug. Even though he said it had been a year and a half, it still felt like so much had changed, so very quickly.

"Are you all right?" He sounded self-conscious. "Is everything all right?"

"Yes," I nodded, then stepped back and turned to pick up my things.

What else could I say? The hair conditioner made me trust you? No. Not after I really thought about the second chance he'd given me. Not after I thought about how he'd taken care of me for the last year and a half while I was basically an adult-sized infant.

I hung my towel up on the door and plopped my pajamas on the small arm chair. Other than the bed and a side table, it was the only piece of furniture in the room.

No, I couldn't tell him the conditioner made me trust him. But it did make me wonder—

"My hair is in really good condition." I ran my hands over the damp curls. "Like, maybe better than it was before. How did you know how to do that?"

A smug grin curled his lip.

"I didn't want to be one of those fath— people," he changed the word midway, "who didn't understand a Black woman's hair," he explained. "I share a property with a biracial woman. She has hair just like yours. I called her to ask for advice."

That was a level of dedication I'd never received from . . . anyone. It almost set me off crying again. My parents did the best they could, but what were a Black man and a white woman to do? They didn't know and had no one to ask. But Sahrias did. He'd asked, and that meant a lot.

"Thank you," I croaked, then swallowed hard. My throat felt hot and dry. I tried to ignore it.

"I think I did pretty well, hmmm?" He handed me a mason jar.

I nodded, took the jar, drank a large swallow, and immediately spat it out.

"Oh, God!" I covered my mouth with a hand in horror at what I'd just done.

Sahrias squinted through the blood I'd just spat in his face. It slowly dripping over one eye and down his cheek. He reached into his pocket and pulled out a handkerchief.

"I am so sorry." I put the jar down and looked for something bigger for him to use. All I saw was my wet towel which would not improve the situation.

"I am so, so sorry," I said. "But also, gross, what is that?" I pointed accusingly at the jar as though my actions were its fault.

"Pig's blood." He wiped his face. "You will get used to it."

"I'm really sorry."

"It's quite all right," he smiled and gestured for me to follow him. I picked up the traitorous liquid and trailed him down the narrow hallway, past the bathroom and into a small kitchenette. It had a sink, a white mini fridge, and a wood cabinet that looked about three hundred years old.

I guess you don't need a stove when you don't eat.

Sahrias soaked the handkerchief in the little sink, and finished cleaning off his face. "At least you're not trying to take a bite out of me anymore."

"Did I do that?" My eyes went wide.

"It's normal behavior for a new Vampire."

"Oh." I tried the pig's blood again and nearly spat it out a second time. I forced myself to swallow. "Why don't I remember anything?"

"For the young ones," Sahrias rinsed off the handkerchief, and hung it to dry on a metal rack screwed into the wall above the sink, "there is an adjustment period. Your mind is so focused on survival; your body is a slave to the sun. Your senses are overloaded. It is too much for your brain to process and store information."

"Oh," I repeated, taking another sip. This time it wasn't so bad. I downed the rest.

"And as you can see," he handed me a second jar, then nodded at the square dark wood table with a straight-backed chair on either side, "the lack of memory doesn't last forever."

"No more Human blood?" I sat. The thin cushion did little to make the chair more comfortable. I felt a mixture of heartache and gratitude as I realized Sahrias had lived in this tiny basement apartment for the better part of two years to care for me. That couldn't have been easy.

"No," he said.

"Will I always need this much?" I finished the second jar. He sat down across from me and slid a third jar past a neat stack of what looked like letters on the table and into my hands.

"No," he said. "I feed once every few days when I am out of the city. A little more when I am consistently around Humans."

"Is it hard?" I wasn't sure what I was asking.

Was it hard to be a Vampire? Was it hard to be around Humans? Was it hard to live only off blood? Was it hard to be alone? Always outliving everyone you meet?

"It is a life-long battle," he told me, somehow answering all of my questions, and none of them. "It can never be won, only fought. Every day."

"And no more Human blood?" I put my now empty jar on the table between us.

"No."

"Ever?"

"Not for a good long while."

"Why?" I asked

"For starters," he said, taking the jar to the sink. I turned in the chair to face him. "Right now, you don't have the control to drink from a Human and not kill them."

"But the man—" I started, thinking back to that first night.

"In the first few days of a young Vampire's life, their makers can share their own control with great ease. This is why you were able to stop."

I remembered the composure that had washed over me again and again.

"As you get older," he continued, putting the newly cleaned jar on the drying rack above the sink. "It becomes more strenuous, but the connection, the ability to push thoughts—it never really goes away."

"When will I be able to control myself?" I asked.

When can I be around people again? That's what I really wanted to know. When can my life return to some version of normal? Or whatever the new normal might be.

"I'm sorry, Dyson," Sahrias shook his head, and my heart sank.

How had he known what I was going to ask next? I hadn't even fully formed the question.

"You will not be able to tell your friends and family you are still alive." His smile was sad, pitying almost. "It would not be safe for them. For the most part, it is forbidden. And for the exceptions, it's always a risk."

"I think I knew that already," I sniffed. I didn't want to cry again. "I just wanted to hear it from you."

"But your control will grow. In time." Sahrias took off a necklace. He stepped forward and handed it to me. Thin gold wire criss-crossed over and around a small fragment of stone. It hung on the end of a fine chain and seemed to hum with power. Then the hum was gone.

"It's beautiful," I said, not sure why I thought so, or why he was showing it to me. "There isn't much to it, but it is beautiful."

"Yes," he said. "It was a gift from a friend. I am not sure where he found it, but there is something about it, isn't there?"

I nodded, still looking at the contrast of the fine smooth gold strands and the ancient-looking stone.

"There is a light inside all living things. For some, that light shines brighter. For others, it just shines differently," he said, and I looked from the stone to my maker. To someone who might be another father. "To us, to Lumankind, we call it Spark. It is intention and power and positivity. It's love and life."

I was confused at what this had to do with the necklace, but I was interested enough to not ask questions.

"As it is given away, with a spell, or even a hug or a positive thought, it is replenished immediately. Some think it can even be stored in an object. An object of significance." He gestured to the stone.

It hummed in my hand again, but only for a moment.

"Keep it."

"Oh no, I couldn't." I tried to hand it back. I stood and stepped forward when he wouldn't take it. I'd never been good at accepting gifts. It made me uncomfortable.

And this one—one that seemed so special—I couldn't.

Sahrias reached out a hand. Instead of taking the necklace, he closed his fingers around mine, the small stone still in my palm.

"Keep it," he repeated and I felt a zing of energy flit between us. Or was that the stone? "It has been dear to me for a very long time. Perhaps, if these theories are right, it holds all of those positive feelings. All that good will. Keep it," he said again, "for you are dear to me too."

My father had given my eldest brother a ring once. It had been his grandfather's. I'd never received a family heirloom. Until now.

"It might help my control?" I asked, putting the chain around my neck.

Sahrias shrugged. "It very well could. We will start hunting animals when we go to my home in the mountains. Your control can take anywhere from six months to a year, maybe more. It varies."

"But I'm behind," I said, lifting my hair out from under the chain. "Like, over a year behind."

"That is not uncommon," he repeated his earlier words.

It was a non-answer to my non-question. I left it alone.

"So, we will be hunting," I said. "Where?"

"We have a home in the Rocky Mountains. We'll leave in the next few . . ."

But the rest of his words were drowned out by the thought of the hunt, the kill, hot fresh blood.

A sharp pain in my mouth brought me back to the moment and had my hand flying to my upper gums.

"Holy shit." This was the first time I was feeling them without having a panic attack. Thin and long and . . .

I had to see them.

I stood, barely registering Sahrias speaking, and sprinted to the washroom.

"—move so quickly." His words ended on a deep sigh.

I looked at my teeth, my fangs, in the mirror. They were slowly retracting, the point dulling. Within moments, they looked normal.

"How the hell does that even work?" I asked, still staring at where my fangs used to be.

Then I looked at the rest of my face. I hadn't done that in the last day or so, which meant I hadn't done it in the last—

"Eighteen months," I said to my reflection.

I wondered what had happened to my parent's house. I hoped one of my brothers moved in. I wondered how Tina was doing, and how things with Roan went. I'd liked them.

God, it didn't feel so long ago that Roan and I were singing together at the Fish and Fox. But it had been. So many things would have changed. But not me. I was still here. The same, and different.

I had the same hazel eyes. The same wild curly hair. The same freckles. The same full lips. My skin was a little paler than usual, but similar to how it was in the winter.

And I looked tired. Really tired.

Dark circles drooped under my eyes.

"You're still you," Sahrias said from the doorway, hands full of letters and what looked like bills.

"What are you doing?" I asked.

"You don't have full control of your speed." He smiled. "These were blown off the table when you ran in here."

"Oh," I said. "Sorry."

"You're still you," he repeated. "Nothing about your personality, your likes, your dislikes, nothing about your soul has changed. Just your diet." He shrugged a little. "And your routine. But you are still you."

"I need something longer for this one," Dyson examined the gash on her side. Luckily, the bullet wound in her shoulder had partially healed. She must have received that wound before she'd lost so much blood.

"I need to feed," Dyson said.

Impossible right now though, she thought.

Her eyes flicked from the barricaded door to the heavily curtained windows. She wasn't worried about someone coming in that way. No Human could make that climb. Not without her hearing.

I can find something to wrap this with, she thought. And I can keep talking. That's what I can do.

The fabric of her dress had been caked with dried blood. Removing it meant reopening the wound. She did it anyway.

"The mountains were great, at first. I got stronger, and I got restless," she said, shredding the bed sheet despite the screaming protest of her arms. "I was challenged every day—and I loved it. I was learning so much so fast, but . . ."

It changed.

She remembered the day everything went sideways. Dyson paused and lifted her hand in search of the stone that hadn't hung around her neck for decades. Her fingertips found a pair of rings instead.

"I was challenged every day," she said again. "But it only took a year for the isolation to get to me. I got a little stir crazy. I got cocky." She turned to speak over her shoulder. "Live and learn."

CHAPTER SIX
2017

I slammed my fingers on the keys of the grand piano, and looked around the living room. One of three living rooms in the massive house I'd lived in for the past year. The other two living rooms of the old mansion were considerably more comfortable. One had a large fireplace and was full of big squishy armchairs. Sometimes I'd read in there instead of the library— yes, this house also had a library.

The third living room was more of a sunroom, and no, in daylight, the sunroom definitely would not be comfortable. But at night, lying in the reclining patio lounger, and looking up through the glass ceiling at the night sky above, the sunroom was my favorite.

All these rooms, all this space, and it was only me and Sahrias.

I'd already been in the sunroom, trying to escape my boredom. That, and every other room in the house.

My fingers climbed up to the high notes and back down slowly as my eyes moved over several Victorian-style couches, the kind that were pieces of art before they were pieces of furniture, a pair of large French doors, and a cello Sahrias had never touched. It must have belonged to one of his two housemates, neither of whom had made an appearance in the time we'd lived here. I wish they had. It would have been a nice change of pace.

I'd been playing piano for the past hour, and Sahrias still wasn't home. Usually, I didn't mind the nights he went out. Usually, I loved them.

A night alone meant a break from my relentless lessons. We worked on power control, learning how to not rip a door off its hinges when I was just trying to open it. We'd read about religion and mythology, more of which was real than I'd thought. We studied physics, which I hated with the fire of a thousand suns—and that is, almost, a direct quote.

Sahrias had called it quits with physics last month and I'd nearly cried for joy.

Usually, a night alone was spent catching up on TV shows and reading, or playing piano and star gazing in the sunroom. Usually, I cherished the time.

Tonight, I was lonely, antsy, ready for more.

I was getting stronger, gaining control, and I wanted something beyond lessons and the odd trip to a nearby town day after day. Last week we'd hunted and I hadn't even killed the deer. Just took what I needed, and let it go. I was in control of my abilities, I was ready for more, and I was bored.

So, so bored.

I was bored of living in the woods, and having just one person to talk to. I was bored of only wanting to eat the same thing every day, and never having anywhere new to go. I was bored of the one path Sahrias and I would walk through the woods. And no matter how much I loved to run, I was getting bored of that too.

I wanted a job, I wanted friends, I wanted a life.

When I'd first expressed this, we'd started going out. The nearest town wasn't far—and that helped a little. But I wasn't allowed to get close to anyone. I wasn't allowed to go out alone. I wasn't allowed to do anything. He didn't think I was ready.

I'm ready. I know I'm ready for more.

When I'd woken up that evening, there'd been a note on my bedside table.

I'll be back before dawn.

Don't leave the house.

-Sahrias

My fingers slid to the low notes and sat there, unmoving, a deep eerie chord echoing through the room.

It had been almost three years, and I still felt like I was going through a strange growth spurt. But instead of size, I was gaining strength and speed. I hadn't had to replace a door in months. I was gaining control. I was better.

I lifted my fingers and the chord died.

"I'm going out for a walk," I told the piano.

Just the yard, and along the path. Just the path.

Once the decision was made, I was excited. I ran upstairs to my room and grabbed a copy of *R is for Ricochet* by Sue Grafton.

Maybe my focus would be better with a change of scenery. I'll walk to the end of the path and back. Then I'll try to read my book. That will be safe. Responsible. Sahrias can't get mad at me for that.

I was at the front door in moments, and made a very conscious effort to slowly turn the knob and pull. I stepped outside and breathed in deep. My body relaxed at the scent of the forest around the house, then stiffened as I scented a buck.

My mouth watered. I breathed in again, and my heart sunk. It was three kilometers west, well off the path.

Disappointing, since I'm being responsible. I'll find a spot to sit. The path is over a kilometer long. I'll read and wait for an animal.

I took another deep breath of cool night air, tried to shake the desire to hunt, and walked across the wide lawn.

Not being side-tracked by my enhanced sight was something Sahrias and I had worked on. It only took a few weeks of practice to no longer get distracted by the grass. It took longer than that to stop spontaneously bursting into tears at the thought of Tina or my brothers. I still did that sometimes, but those times were now few and far between.

Sahrias gave me small updates, when he thought I could handle them. Thomas had moved into my parents' house. Tina and Roan were going strong. Kai was still sober, and back in school.

Learning to control my emotions was harder than learning to control my abilities. But I had done it, for the most part. I was doing it now.

"I am in total control," I said to my sneakers.

I gently kicked a rock forward as the ground changed from well-kept lawn to well-worn path under my feet. I kicked it again.

"I am in total control," I told the rock.

Clouds shifted and the path grew dark. They shifted again and light spilled through the branches above, decorating the trail in front of me.

The buck was moving north. If the path had been five kilometres long instead of one, we'd intersect. But I was being responsible.

Thick trees reached up and over me. Sahrias had taught me their species. Douglas fir and juniper. Big leaf maples, western hemlock, and—

I looked up.

Was I at the end of the path already?

Walking like this didn't take the ache out of my legs. I wanted to run. Fast and far and chasing prey. The scent of blood on the air called to me. I wanted to answer.

"Keep going?" I asked the darkness. "Or go back?" I looked in the direction of home. "Keep defying Sahrias and for sure catch that buck?" My eyes went to the dense trees, to the hunt. "Or play it safe."

I turned again to look at the path well-traveled. I sighed deeply and started to walk back to the house.

I'll play it safe.

Then the wind changed. I should have held my breath. The thick scent of blood filled my senses more than it had a moment ago.

"All right, Robert Frost." *R is for Ricochet* slipped from my hands and I turned my feet towards the densely knotted trees. "You got me."

I shot like a bullet into the trees, towards the hunt, and the road less travelled.

The run was exactly what my body craved and I felt a rush of freedom as the trees whipped past me. When I caught up to the buck, I slowed and followed it to a small lake.

I watched it dip its head to drink. I waited for my moment. My mouth watered. The air seemed to still with my focus. All was quiet.

A loud crack echoed across the water. The buck took off.

Maybe, if I hadn't been so absorbed in the hunt, I would have realized how far I'd run. I would have noticed there was a path leading up to this lake. Maybe then, I would have heard the couple walking up that path.

Maybe, if my hunt hadn't been interrupted and if I hadn't been so hungry, I would have been able to stop my instincts from taking over.

Maybe, if I had not been overconfident, and if I'd listened to my maker, I would have been able to avoid the situation entirely.

But I hadn't listened. I was overconfident. I'd been enthralled by the hunt, and when the smell of Human blood reached my nose, I realized just how very hungry I was.

A low growl rolled in the back of my throat.

A couple ran splashing into the shallow lake. The girl shrieked and laughed as cool water hit her feet. The boy tugged lightly on her hand to pull her close. She smiled up at him. He smiled back.

For a moment, they just stared at each other. He pulled her close, wrapping his arms around her. She did the same. He leaned down to kiss her, aiming for her lips. He got her cheek instead.

She'd turned away when she heard something behind her.

Something in the trees.

Dropping his hand, she took a step toward the treeline. He followed.

Recapturing her hand, and taking the lead, the boy moved towards the forest's edge. He pulled aside a branch, stumbled backward, and his mouth opened in a scream. Then he crumpled at the girl's feet, out cold.

She looked down at him, shocked. She was about to bend over and see if he was okay, when something stepped out of the trees.

A deep rumbling sound seemed to shake the very ground they stood on. The girl stepped back. The figure stepped forward. The girl tried to yell for help, but the sound died before it left her mouth.

Cold water on her heels made her gasp, as did the figure stepping into the moonlight. It was a woman. A tall woman, with thick brown curls that fell over her shoulders, and dark black eyes. The woman's full red lips curled back over white teeth. White teeth with canines larger than normal.

Larger and sharper.

The girl tried to yell again. Again, no sound came. She wanted to run. Her feet wouldn't listen. She wanted to cry out. Her voice wouldn't obey.

Run, run, run, the girl shouted in her mind.

The woman drew closer.

Scream, scream, scream, she silently pleaded. But her body would not, could not, respond.

The woman was right in front of her now. The girl looked up into her eyes and lost herself.

Run, the girl thought feebly. Scream . . . scream.

But she didn't want to go anymore. She didn't want to run. She wanted to stay. Stay right there with this frightening yet beautiful woman.

"Oh, God," the girl said aloud.

"Not quite," the woman replied.

As she had been with the boy, moments before, the girl was with this woman. Pulled tight to her chest, heat flooding her cheeks, want filling her mind.

The girl thought, hoped maybe, that this woman would kiss her. She felt lips on her cheek, on her neck, and arousal swept through her body. She shivered in anticipation.

The girl felt pressure on the soft skin of her neck. There was a kind of pop. A feeling of lust rushed through her. She shivered and uttered two words, seemingly pulled from the mind of her attacker.

"Sweet surrender."

CHAPTER SEVEN

2017

Savage pleasure rushed over me as teeth broke skin. The gush of hot liquid hit my tongue, and I groaned into the girl's neck.

A pair of hands grabbed my shoulders.

"Dyson, NO!"

I was ripped away before I'd even had a chance to swallow. A fist landed hard in my gut. I fell to my knees. The reddish haze of the hunt, and of hunger lifted as a wave of composure washed over me.

"Sahrias?" I felt disoriented.

"Get that out of your mouth, spit it out!"

"What?" I wiped the back of my hand across my lips. Lips still wet with blood.

"Don't swallow it! Did you swallow any of her blood?" His voice rang with power. I felt the strong push of his words. "Spit it out." He spoke in my mind and out loud. "Now. Get everything in your stomach out."

I didn't have a choice. My body convulsed. I vomited.

"Did your heart beat?"

It was a horrible feeling. Having your body listen to some outside force instead of your own desires.

"Get everything in your stomach out," he repeated, pushing the words into my mind. He sounded frantic, panicked.

I convulsed and threw up again.

"Stop doing that to me!" I yelled up at him from the ground. He leaned down and shook me by the shoulders.

"Did your heart beat?" he demanded again.

"No!" I pushed him away. "What's wrong with you?"

"What's wrong with—how could you be so—" He sputtered in his anger. "Why would you, can't you, can you not smell it? Can you not taste it?"

Sahrias stood over me. I shrank under his gaze.

"You just drank bad blood."

"What did you think you were doing?" Sahrias dragged me through the large front doors and threw me to the floor. The ornate red and gold rug did little to soften my landing, but that small pain was nothing compared to the fear and confusion welling up inside me.

"I'm sorry!" I stood cautiously.

Shit, I messed up. I didn't even know what happened. One minute I was following that buck, and then . . . Oh, God, I could have killed that girl. I would have if Sahrias hadn't shown up.

He paced back and forth. I'd never seen him this angry. Not when I'd broken almost every door in this house by mistake, and not when I'd accidently broken his arm when we were training. Never. But now, he radiated power.

"Are you a child?" he spat. "As if I thought you were ready for—" His hands were balled into fists at his sides. "For anything! Anything beyond these walls, if there is not a collar around your neck. Eating whatever crosses your path like a dog!"

"I'm—" I cut off, flinching at Sahrias's furious gaze.

"You." He stepped towards me like a predator, showing teeth, fangs sliding out in his anger. "You will stay here while I go clean up your mess, and so help me God," he emphasized the last word by thrusting a finger toward the heavens, "if you are not here when I get back . . ." He stepped closer to me.

I was three or four inches taller than him, but I didn't feel like that now. He loomed over me.

"They won't have to compel me. I will hunt you down and kill you myself."

I flinched again, closing my eyes. I felt the truth in his words. It hurt.

When I opened my eyes again, he was gone.

I didn't move an inch from where Sahrias left me. Was this still his hold? Or was I so scared it just felt like I'd be struck by lightning if I moved a muscle? But I didn't have to get struck by lightning to know what it felt like. I felt that way now. Burning from the inside out.

I'd messed up. I would have killed that girl and I would have gone after the boy next. I was sure of it. I had been totally out of control.

"Are you a child? Eating whatever crosses your path . . . So help me God. . . Like a dog . . ."

The words ran through my mind. A song stuck on repeat. It was dark and ugly and became more grotesque the longer it played.

The words were punctuated with the scream of the boy when he saw me in the trees, and the sound of his body hitting the soft earth. I could still hear the light sound of the buck's hooves as it ran away, and the crack of the branch that spooked him.

I still felt the hot soft body of the girl as she fell into my arms.

"Sweet surrender."

I can't remember if those words came from me, or her? Maybe I never knew.

Through the blur of trees and heartbeats, of rushing water and rushing blood, I remembered those words. I remembered my lips on the soft skin of her neck, and the hot blood flowing beneath it. I remembered my teeth sliding long at the sight of the buck drinking at the water's edge. The concentration I'd had shifting. My fangs breaking skin. The sweet reward.

Standing in the high-ceilinged front hall, my mouth watered.

"They won't have to compel me," Sahrias had said. "I will hunt you down and kill you myself."

Who is they? Who could be strong enough to compel Sahrias? And why?

Bad blood . . .

The words drifted back to me.

The pull on my shoulders, the fist in my gut.

"Bad blood." Sahrias had said. "You just drank bad blood."

Those words pulled at something in my memory. They meant something. I knew they did. But how could the girl's blood be . . . bad?

"One day, when your control is better, you will be able to feed from Humans," Sahrias had said a few months after we'd come to the mountains. We'd been sitting at the dark wood dining room table. He'd been splinting his arm.

I'd had to help him set the bone, a horrifying experience. For me. It was old hat for Sahrias. He'd been perfectly calm when he'd said he'd healed in a couple of hours.

"When that day comes," he'd looked up from his arm, tucking the bandage in around the splint. "I will teach you where to bite and how much to drink. How to compel and how to smell bad blood. Some of it will be instinct—"

"Wait a minute," I'd interrupted, and he'd winced when I'd jostled his arm. "Sorry. Umm . . . compel?" And the topic had changed.

Bad blood. You just drank bad blood.

Anger and fear mixed with my hunger. He should have told me. He should have taught me. I should have asked for more information.

"You will stay here . . . like a dog . . . Are you a child? So help me God . . . clean up your mess . . . kill you myself."

I shuddered at the memory of his words and my eyes flicked to the lightening sky. A different type of fear came over me.

What if he doesn't come back? What if something happened to him while he was cleaning up after me? Cleaning up after me? What does that even mean? What if he's hurt? What if he's . . .

I felt panic creep up my spine.

If something happened to him, I would be alone. I would be alone in this new world where I knew nothing and no one.

Oh, God. How could I survive without him?

The sound of footsteps stopped my panic, and relief almost brought me to my knees.

Sahrias walked through the front door, slamming it shut behind him. The noise made me jump, even though I knew it was coming.

He stopped a few feet inside, then took off his gloves and long jacket. Walking right past me into a small alcove to the left of the front door, he reached an arm high on the wall and flipped a switch I'd never noticed before.

"Follow me," he said.

I'd explored every inch of this house over the past year. Or so I'd thought. The wall in front of Sahrias slid to the side to reveal a narrow carpet covered staircase. Humility washed over me as I realized for the second time the last few hours, I didn't know as much as I thought I did.

The staircase was pitch black, but I could see. When we reached the bottom of the steps, he turned the lights on, ignoring the enhanced night vision that came with being a Vampire.

I'd expected the basement space to be damp and dank. Concrete floors and cobwebs. It wasn't. After ducking through another small doorway, I was in a crisp, clean, windowless basement apartment. High ceilings. Classic decor. Nothing particularly new, but nothing outdated either. I opened my mouth to ask what this place was, but Sahrias spoke before I got the words out.

"Sit," he said, pulling out a chair and settling at the head of a rectangular oak table.

I walked slowly towards a chair and pulled it out. The table was a large slab of wood that looked like it was a six-inch slice of a thousand-year-old tree, bark still attached to its sides. I sat in the high-backed chair and looked at my clutched hands in my lap.

"Explain." Sahrias's voice was flat.

I felt his eyes on me, but I didn't meet them. My eyelids felt heavy. The sun pulled me to sleep. I started talking anyway.

The longer I did, the more I realized how stupid I'd been. How arrogant. I tried to convince Sahrias that I had really believed I could handle anything. When I looked up, I was startled at what I saw.

Sahrias, normally so calm, so composed, looked defeated, broken.

Like I was the one who broke him. I remembered him looking at me like this only once before, and just like that time, he blinked, and the look was gone.

When he spoke next, his tone was gentle.

"There is a—" Sahrias paused. "A man coming tomorrow night. He will—" He paused again, and now I saw what looked like sadness in his eyes. "Run some tests."

"Okay." My words were small. "What kind of tests?"

"Making sure you didn't ingest any of the girl's blood. The results will be more conclusive if you do not eat anything between now and then."

I waited for him to elaborate. He didn't.

"I'm sorry, Dyson." He looked at me for a long moment. "It's going to be a long day for you, and an even longer night." I opened my mouth to ask another question, but he kept talking. "The day is already here; you must feel it."

I could. The never-relenting pull of sleep when the sun was up. I felt powerless against it.

"This apartment is safe." He spoke like every word cost him some great price. I couldn't tell what, or why. "We are safe from the day here," he repeated, standing slowly. "There are several rooms. I'll show you to yours."

I didn't stand. Not right away. He walked along the table and stopped beside me. Placing a shaking hand on my shoulder, he met my gaze with soft eyes.

My eyebrows drew together, confused at what this gesture meant. He shook his head once, then dropped his hand and walked down the hall. I followed.

The sound of an engine revving echoed through the small room, and I jerked awake. Rolling over, I tried to go back to sleep.

Th-thud th-thud th-thud.

When I was a younger, newer Vampire, I would have slept through a house being demolished. Now, I would wake during the day to noises near and far.

Damn, I looked over at the clock on the bedside table. It was just past eleven. I would have been happy to wake up, and have all of this be over.

Instead, images of Sahrias and the young couple played in my mind. I tried to close my eyes against the memories.

They intensified.

Over and over again, I saw the young couple arm-in-arm. I saw the boy pass out. I saw blood moving under his skin. I stepped over him to the girl because her blood raced faster. It called to me like a siren song.

The images were made all the worse by the ache in my stomach and the dryness in my throat. I threw my legs out of bed, determined to distract myself.

I stood too quickly. The room swam.

"Holy," I whispered to no one and sat back down.

How long had it been since I'd eaten?

One hundred birds called out. One hundred answered. Th-thud th-thud th-thud.

I clapped my hands over my ears.

God, that was loud. And I am so, so hungry.

Over the past several months I'd been able to go longer without feeding and still maintain my control.

Why did I think I could leave the house? Why did Sahrias leave me alone?

But thinking about how long it had been did nothing for my current situation. I glanced around the room for something to occupy my mind. There was nothing. Not even a book or a TV. Just a bed, a small armchair, a table, and a clock. It reminded me of that first room. The one I'd woken up in over and over again, remembering a little more each time. The difference was, Sahrias had been with me then. He wasn't here now.

I'll see if he's in the kitchen and maybe he can explain what's going on with me.

I stood, slowly this time. The room didn't spin. I breathed a sigh of relief and walked to the door. I turned the knob and pulled.

It was locked.

Seriously? I looked over at the clock. Only six minutes had passed.

"Great," I announced to the room.

Sound crashed in around me. I flinched away from it, bringing my hands to my ears, but it was everywhere.

Why was the wind so loud?

Then it stopped.

Hooves scrabbled across asphalt. A bag of chips opened. Th-thud th-thud th-thud.

When would this mystery guy be showing up? What kind of tests would he run? Who was he anyway?

I should have asked more questions. Sahrias hadn't really told me what was going on. I had been too worried. Too scared. He could have left me a note in here, or something. What is he keeping from me?

I felt hot anger rush through my body.

Who the hell was he to decide what I have the right to know? I took a step back from the door and looked down at my hands. They stung, like I'd slapped something.

Had I slapped the door? What was—

"Ahhhh." I collapsed as sound crashed on me again and again. Over and over like waves breaking on rocks.

I stood slowly, clenching my eyes shut as if that would somehow keep the noise out of my ears.

This is his fault. His fault! Not mine! What kind of maker leaves his progeny alone and hungry? No explanation. A vague note. Who would do that?

Someone who thinks he's always right, said a voice in the back of my mind. A control freak who uses you like a dog.

Like a dog. He'd even said that to me.

"You aren't so perfect," I hissed. "You don't always know what's best, what's right! Why the hell do you get to make all the decisions? It's my life! It should be my choice how I live it! You stole my life!"

I reached up to grab the chain around my neck. To wrap my fingers around the stone that meant so much to him, rip it off my neck, and throw it in his face.

But it wasn't there.

He must have taken it off me. He had stolen it. The only family heirloom I'd ever received and he'd taken it back. He was no father of mine. He'd stolen my life, my brothers, Tina, and now he'd stolen the stone!

I was pacing back and forth yelling over the noise of the world in my mind. Yelling at Sahrias as though he were right in front of me.

"Who cares about some stupid Human! It was one girl! And she would have been fine!" I spat on the ground. "She wanted it. She wanted me to. She fell into my arms—I felt her desire for me. I know she wanted it!"

I rushed the door and slammed my fists against it. It stood fast.

"There are literally billions of Humans!" I pounded on the door.

A plate broke on a hard floor, a woman screamed, th-thud th-thud th-thud.

Fury at Sahrias for not explaining, at the girl for crossing my path, at being locked in this room, at not being able to eat anything—it all came crashing down onto that door.

The door yielded nothing but a small bruise on either hand. Instead of lightening and fading away, as was normal for Vampires, the marks remained.

I'm not healing. Why aren't I healing?

A stiff breeze rustled through a thousand leaves and the noise in my mind became a background to the pounding sound of my hands on the door.

Th-thud th-thud th-thud.

I hammered on the door until my hands hurt too much to continue. Turning, I slid down and sat on the floor. I felt a consistent throb on my hands as if they were still beating the unyielding wood.

Why aren't I healing? I looked at the bruises. I gave my head a little shake. What was I saying? What am I saying?

"What the hell is wrong with me?" I said to the small blotchy spots on my palms. "Why would I, what's . . ." I let my head drop into my hands, ignoring the very Human ache they gave off.

I'm so thirsty, so thirsty, why can't I have something to drink? Why did I get so angry? Why aren't I healing? Why did I go out last night? What happens if I did swallow some of her blood? What's going to happen to me?

The questions ran in a loop through my mind.

A car door slammed, an angry man yelled, th-thud th-thud th-thud.

I curled into a ball in front of the door.

What's wrong with me? What's going to happen to me? On and on, questions and more questions. Never any answers.

A TV turned on, a fridge opened, th-thud th-thud th-thud.

I put my hands over my ears as a world of sound grew louder. It pushed into my mind. It suffocated me.

A pair of hands typed, a pair of feet walked, a pair of lips touched, th-thud th-thud th-thud.

Sound bombarded me and I couldn't keep it out. I rocked back and forth trying to force myself to focus on something, anything.

A door slammed, a baby cried, th-thud th-thud th-thud.

Th-thud th-thud th-thud.

TH-THUD TH-THUD TH-THUD.

But I couldn't. I couldn't take it anymore. I lay there, curled up and helpless, waiting for the night.

The sound of rushing blood and heartbeats echoing in my ears all the while.

Dyson blinked, looking up at the canopy of the bed. She couldn't remember lying down. She couldn't remember the sun pulling her to sleep. She was old enough now that she only slept when she wanted to. She was old enough now that the sun had little power over her. But in her current condition, Dyson had to work hard to resist the tiredness.

Feeling something dig into her back, she shifted and reached behind her. The movement hurt and she grunted in pain. She needed to feed, or to find some oushifa. If she didn't, she'd die before the mission was over. And many more would die with her failure.

The thing digging into her back was the clip of a gun from an old-school Beretta. Dyson tossed it aside and lay back down. The small movement had exhausted her. She looked back up at the canopy. The clean cloth seemed to be the only thing in the room not broken or soiled.

"I didn't realize then what Sahrias was struggling with," she said, not knowing where she'd left off. "He'd never sired before. Had never been responsible for another life before. Not like that, anyway. And, in his mind, my mistake was his mistake. My failure was his failure. I didn't realize then, when he saw me with that girl, that he really thought he would lose me."

Dyson braced for the pain and pulled herself up. First, she pulled using the sheets beneath her, then with the bedpost at her side.

"He was like that later too," she grunted as she regained a seated position. "After everything happened . . . of course. He saw my choices as his fault." She gingerly pulled herself to stand, not bothering to put the top half of the dress back on. It hung around her waist. "I hope when he hears about this, if I succeed, I hope he knows it was needed."

She looked over her shoulder.

"He'll know you wouldn't have stopped otherwise. I needed to do this, to be here . . ."

Dyson's heart sunk when her eyes discovered the grand piano, so similar to the one she'd once played, now smashed nearly to pieces. She turned away, pushing that out of her mind, determined to find some oushifa, if there was any here.

"Sahrias was always trying to protect me, trying to be the one to shoulder the burden. And the result was the same." She waved her hand around the ruined room, gesturing to the blood-spattered walls. "I still ended up here, but now, I'm trying to protect him."

CHAPTER EIGHT
2017

At some point I stopped rocking back and forth, and gave in to the chaos in my ears. I had little choice. It pushed and pushed and pushed until I surrendered.

Time passed. Someone lifted me onto a bed and I was alone in a loud silence.

A needle pierced my skin. Something was pulled from inside me. There was a whispered conversation.

Time passed. I came back to myself. Then I tried to hear.

No, that's not exactly right. I tried not to hear. I waited, braced for the impact of crushing sound, but it never came.

How long had I been out? Who cares. It's all working now.

I opened my eyes and blinked slowly around at the room. I had a feeling, a word, a thought.

Hungry. Sitting up, I threw the covers off, and felt something around my neck.

The necklace. He gave it back . . . or maybe it was never gone. What happened?

I tried to grasp the fragmented flashes but couldn't piece anything together. Then I heard something that had my head snapping to stare at the bedroom door.

It was laughter. Sahrias and someone else. I took that as a positive sign and I stood. I was still wearing the torn and tattered clothes from the night before. I didn't want to wear them. It was a mark of my mistake, of my shame. I wanted to change out of these clothes—and out of the person I'd been.

As if my thoughts made clothing appear, I spotted a neat pile on a small navy-patterned armchair by the door. Stripping quickly, I pulled on the sports bra and underwear. Then green-plaid dorm pants, and a white long-sleeve t-shirt. I left the pair of thick wool socks on the chair, and looked at the door again.

Was it still locked?

Cautiously, I turned the handle. It clicked. I pulled the door open. I slowly made my way down the narrow hall towards the light and laughter in the kitchen.

"She lives!" a high-pitched voice squeaked.

"Indeed," Sahrias responded.

"Hi," I said, stopping just inside the light given by the simple black chandelier above the wood table.

I wasn't sure how I was supposed to act, how I was supposed to be after fucking up so royally.

"Sit down." Sahrias gestured to one of the high-backed chairs. "You must be hungry."

I looked at my maker. I was hungry, but more than that, I was wary of his attitude. His ease.

"Oh, stop that, Si!" the unfamiliar voice squeaked. "You're torturing the poor girl, and we've done that enough."

I looked around for a speaker, and assumed "Si" was a nickname for Sahrias. All I saw was Sahrias sitting alone, and a chair moving away from the table by itself.

That's weird.

I heard the sound of small feet on the floor and the fridge opening. Unlike the vintage fridge upstairs, this one was new with a stainless-steel finish. Looking around the kitchen, I realized everything was new except the dining set.

Feet padded across the floor again and the smallest man I had ever seen, hopped up into a chair.

"Here you are, my dear." The little man stood on the seat to push a mason jar across the table.

He was two and a half feet tall, if that, with wiry hair that seemed to hover around his head. I thought it must be a trick of the light, but his hair was green. A pale, pale green.

Sharp pearly blue eyes peered at me as he pushed the jar in my direction. His smile was warm and his skin was the light brown color of untreated cedar.

I walked the last few steps towards the table, taking the jar, I sat in the nearest chair.

"Thank you," I reached a hand across the table. "I'm Dyson."

"Oh, yes, I know, dear," he squeaked as he shook my hand. "I am Tarinsalus Day, but you may call me Tarin. I am a Healer of sorts. For Lumankind."

We released each other. To my surprise, instead of returning to his chair, Tarinsalus Day sat cross-legged on the table beside me.

Sahrias made a disapproving sound, and Tarin ignored him.

"Oh, don't mind him." Tarin leaned forward, starting in a stage whisper. "He sometimes forgets what he was like when he was a new Vampire!" He yelled the last part down the table.

I covered my smile by bringing the jar to my lips.

I drained the jar and sheepishly ran the back of my hand across my mouth. I felt, as much as heard, the loud th-thud of my heart.

I sighed. Instant relief.

"Two more, Si," Tarin said.

After sliding both down the long table to me, Sahrias returned to his seat. I drank the second almost as quickly as the first. My heart wouldn't beat again for a while, but it still felt good to drink. I approached the third jar with less vigor.

"You're a Healer," I asked. "So, I needed healing?"

"Oh, no. You are fine, my dear," he nodded quickly. "A little thing like that—"

"Little thing?" Sahrias cut him off. "I do not think we should call what happened 'little.' "

"If you really felt like this was no 'little thing,' " Tarin put very sarcastic air quotes around the words "little thing," "you would have educated her on it sooner."

"She was not ready sooner," he said. "Her control around Humans wasn't enough that she would be able to smell the difference."

My eyes followed the back-and-forth conversation. Seeing him interact with someone else, with a friend, sent a pang of longing through me. I missed other people, I always had. But watching Sahrias with Tarin made me realize he did too.

"You are angrier with yourself than you are with her," Tarin said, waving away his explanation.

"Of course," Si bristled. "Of course, I am."

I blinked and looked at him.

Was he?

"As if this is normal," Sahrias muttered. "As if you were a perfect father. And as if my early years were anything like hers."

Tarin sighed. "That is true, old friend. I am being unkind."

There was a beat of silence.

"Are you an Elf?" I asked without thinking. My eyes widened in horror and I covered my mouth with a hand. "Sorry," I said through my fingers.

"Oh, no need to apologize, deary," Tarin chuckled. "You don't let her out much, do you?" he said to Sahrias.

"Understatement," I said, not quietly enough.

"I am not an Elf. If I were, I would be much taller—or much smaller, depending on the type. I am a Sanatorum. A Healer, a Cedrus Dryad, if you want to get specific."

I tried to remember if I'd read that name in my studies with Sahrias. Cedrus, cedar. With his yellow-brown skin and green hair, he'd blend right into a forest setting.

"A sort of wood nymph," he said.

"Sahrias said something about tests?" I asked.

"Well, my dear, I ran a few tests on your blood to be sure you did not ingest any of that poor girl. You may have been infected," Tarin's gentle words did nothing to soften the intensity of his gaze. "I may have been able to give you something—oushifa perhaps, though that's more for strictly healing—or a potion that would help your body, oh—" He moved his hands in the air in front of him searching for his words. "Clear up the problem, I guess you could say."

"And bad blood?" I asked.

"There are different antibodies produced by your Spark that fight and kill most diseases," Tarin explained. "But you can be a carrier for some things, and the girl you fed on last night has HIV."

"But Vampires don't get sick," I said. Tarin opened his mouth to speak, but words poured out of me. "And Humans can live totally normal lives with HIV. Surely Vampires have found a way to cure it by now? Hell, Humans will within the next fifteen years."

"Drugs don't work on us in the same way," Sahrias said. "I agree with you, it will soon be considered curable. But never for us. Which means that if it is ever eradicated in the Human population, we will likely be responsible for any resurgence. God forbid any mutation."

"But what—"

"You can pass it on," Tarin said. "Not just HIV, of course. Malaria, Ebola, Hepatitis B and C."

"And we are carriers for the rest of our lives," Sahrias said. "You would never be rid of it. You would pass it on when you fed. Every time you fed, unless you killed. Then again, you might be killing anyway."

"We are very lucky, though," Tarin said. "The Starlit Shield will not be involved."

"Very lucky," Sahrias said on an exhale. His eyes moved to me, then dropped to my necklace. I reached a hand up to touch the stone. It hummed in my hand, then went still.

"Who is the Starlit Shield?" I asked, and Sahrias's shoulders stiffen.

"A group of high-level Luman," Tarin said. "They help manage our impact on the human population."

"Among other things," Sahrias muttered through gritted teeth.

"Manage our impact?" I asked, though I thought I already knew the answer.

"Kill any potentially problematic Luman," Sahrias said.

"Quite draconian, if I do say so myself. Sometimes they don't even allow testing to—anyway," Tarin waved his hands through the air. "An older or perhaps less hungry version of yourself would have been able to smell the strange difference in the girl's blood. It would have been a warning to avoid her. It's subtle, but it's there."

I looked down at my hands. I felt embarrassed. Ashamed.

"Si told me you have been just spectacular. That's part of why it was so hard for him, why he was so scared."

"Scared?" I didn't look up. "He isn't scared of anything."

The little man threw back his head and laughed. I looked up to see Sahrias's face soften.

"You, my dear," Tarin said. "You scared Si horribly last night. I mean to say, if the Starlit Shield had caught wind of—"

"I am happy," Sahrias cut Tarin off, "that I got there in time."

"Yes," Tarin said. "Quite."

"And that you were able to come so quickly." Sahrias nodded at Tarin, who waved him off. Then he looked at me like he wanted to say something, but couldn't find the words.

"And?" Tarin looked pointedly at his friend.

"And I should have handled the situation better," Sahrias said looking at me. "I should have explained more. It was because I was so very scared of losing you that I acted the way I did. I beg your forgiveness, Dyson."

Not knowing what to say, I just nodded.

"I suggest you two have a long discussion about bad blood after this— and mad blood too. Did you hear about Brandon?" Tarin said turning to Sahrias with a pained look. "The Shield led him to the light, after everything he did, all his work." He shook his green-haired head and sighed.

"Well, the risk he posed? They weren't likely to find a cure before he found a way out and destroyed another city," Sahrias said, his face unreadable. "I'm surprised they let him live as long as he did."

I zoned out the conversation about Brandon and his research. My half-empty jar of blood sat forgotten in front of me. All I could think about were the what ifs.

What if I'd been infected? What if Sahrias hadn't stopped me in time? What if I'd swallowed that girl's blood? What if the Starlit Shield had learned? Would they have let Tarin test me? Would they have killed me?

What if, what if, what if, what if, what if.

"Dyson," I heard, but I was still lost in the thoughts of the worst possible outcomes.

"Dyson." I was snapped back to reality by Sahrias's voice in my head.

"Yes," I said. "Yes."

"Bed?" he asked.

"What time is it?" I looked around the kitchen for a clock. I was exhausted but found comfort in the company. Even if I wasn't listening to the conversation.

"You still have a few hours until sunrise," Sahrias said. "But you need some rest."

I thought about arguing. I knew it was no good. My mind was overwhelmed. My body was lethargic.

"Okay," I said softly.

"I'll walk you," he said.

I relaxed at his words. I wasn't ready to be alone just yet.

"It was nice to meet you." I extended my hand to Tarinsalus Day again. "Thanks for your help."

"Oh, no problem at all! Happy it turned out for the best." He smiled and shook my hand vigorously. "Lovely to finally meet you. I've heard so many wonderful things. You have no idea."

I smiled, sure I didn't. I'd never thought of Sahrias speaking of me to anyone, let alone saying "so many wonderful things."

"Rest well, dearie," Tarin said.

I looked over my shoulder at him and just managed to catch a wink before Sahrias led me around the corner and up the stairs.

"You really did scare me," Sahrias said when we reached my bedroom door.

"I thought you weren't afraid of anything," I teased and tried to smile.

"Well," he nodded. "Now you know better."

"I'm so sorry, Sahrias. I really am." My eyes stung with unshed tears.

Sahrias stepped forward and hugged me.

"I know," he said in my ear. "I know."

Sahrias pulled away first, but not before I felt a wave of . . . something. I felt better.

"You need to sleep," he reached out and wiped away a tear. "I will explain more in the next few nights. I promise."

"Okay," I nodded. "Good night."

Sahrias rolled his eyes and smiled. In the early days, he'd tried to explained it would be more appropriate to reverse the two greetings. Every time, I'd say the same thing. Old habits die hard.

"Sleep well," he said.

CHAPTER NINE

2017

For the second time in as many nights, I woke to the sound of laughter, and immediately tried to limit my hearing. Not that the exercise in control had done me much good at the lake.

Tension and uncertainty gripped my body.

"Get over yourself," I whispered to my ceiling. "You are better than what happened. You are not your actions."

I rolled my eyes and got out of bed. My mental pep talks were as generic and uninspiring as my throat was dry.

And my throat felt very, very dry.

I swallowed hard and walked down the hall to the bathroom.

Turning on the silver tap, I watched the water run into the marble bowl. The sound was soothing. It always had been, and now, the rushing water seemed to loosen the knot of tension in my chest.

I touched the cool liquid with my fingers and brought it to my lips. It tasted the same as it had before I'd been turned. Or at least, it tasted the same as it did in my memory. It wasn't the taste of water that was the issue. Swallowing it had been nearly impossible since I was turned.

I'd tried a few months ago, and it had been like drinking wet cement.

Believe it or not, wet cement was miles better than my first attempt.

I brushed my teeth, washed my face, and went back to my room to change. Moments later, I was standing at the top of the stairs.

I'd been gearing up to ask Sahrias if I could get a job in the nearby town. Maybe take a class. Pottery, knitting, anything. I needed something else, something more. I didn't know exactly what, but I needed connection.

Could I still ask for that after what I'd done? I didn't think so.

Taking a slow breath, and ignoring the burn in my throat, I opened my hearing enough to catch the conversation below.

"Yes, yes," squeaked a small voice. Tarin. "Oh, yes, he was furious!"

"Niloc was always furious with me for one reason or another," a deeper voice said. Sahrias.

His laughter washed over me. It loosened the knot in my chest more than the sound of running water had.

"Well, you know he had a soft spot for you and Rayyan and—oh, stop that," Tarin said. "It's been long enough, come now."

"I don't know that it will ever be long enough, Tarin. After what she did? After what she still tries to do? I just . . ." Sahrias trailed off.

Rayyan? I'd never heard that name before. Sahrias didn't really talk about his past, so it wasn't surprising.

"I know, old friend, I know. But she may yet change. She is—" Tarin stopped when my foot hit the top stair and the wood creaked.

Damn. I guess I won't be learning more about Rayyan today.

The only reason Sahrias hadn't already heard me was because he hadn't been listening. I gave myself one last internal pep talk, then walked down the stairs and into the kitchen.

Both men turned when I entered.

"Hi." I felt awkward, like I was intruding. Tarin was sitting on a very tall bar stool, elbows resting on the wood-topped island. Sahrias stood on the other side, leaning back against the counter.

"Dyson!" Tarin squeaked. "You must be famished!"

I smiled at his enthusiasm.

"Good morning, Tarin," I said.

"My dear, it's not even the afternoon anymore." He glanced at Sahrias.

"She knows," Sahrias said, meeting my eyes and smiling.

"Old habits," I shrugged.

"Well, at any rate, you need to drink. Go into the fridge and get something," Tarin said as if I was a guest in his house. Sahrias had told me he had two roommates. Maybe Tarin was one of them.

"Tarin," I asked, walking towards the vintage refrigerator. "Are you one of the people who helped Sahrias build this house?"

"I'd say he and Lala, our other housemate, did most of the building," he waved his hands through the air. "But yes, the three of us share it. I am more responsible for the spell work."

I knew it. I knew there was Magic for this house to work the way it did. The plumbing alone must have been a nightmare.

I pulled open the fridge, took out a mason jar with a hand-written label reading 'deer' on it, and settled myself next to Tarin on the free barstool.

"The media room is my favorite part," he said. "That is a project Lala and I shared, whom neither of us have seen in a lifetime or more?"

"There were media rooms a lifetime ago?" I raised my eyebrows in question.

"No," Tarin said, giving me a confused look.

"But she's been here," Sahrias clarified. "I came back about ten years ago and the gaudiest contraption I've ever seen hung on the wall."

I looked to Tarin for translation.

"A flatscreen television," he answered.

"Ohhh," I said, taking a large swallow from the jar. "I do love the flatscreen."

There were few things I enjoyed more than sharing a show I loved with someone, and Sahrias rarely, if ever, watched anything with me. He let me tell him about them, though, and he was a good listener. He would let me talk and talk and sometimes he would get invested in the show's stories, but only in my retellings. Never enough to actually watch.

"What's your favorite movie?" I asked Tarin.

"As if I could choose just one," he squeaked in indignation.

"I knew I liked you." I smiled.

"I can already tell you two will be insufferable," Sahrias groaned, and that made me smile wide. He seemed more relaxed than before. Not just before yesterday, or whenever I had gone out. He seemed more relaxed than I had ever seen him.

It must be because Tarin was here. I hoped he'd stay for a while, because I was loving this version of Sahrias.

I finished half the jar and heard the single beat of my heart. My shoulders relaxed and I refocused on the conversation.

"Si," Tarin stood on the bar stool and leaned forward, his little hands on the island. "You have no taste for entertainment."

"Excuse me." Sahrias's eyebrows rose in mock outrage.

"What was the last film you watched? Honestly," Tarin said. Sahrias just lifted his mug to his lips. Tarin clapped his small hands. "Exactly."

"I prefer the opera," Sahrias said imperiously, tilting his nose up.

"Yes, yes, Si. We know you are very sophisticated," Tarin waved away

Sahrias's words. "Opera, fine art, liberating lost gemstones . . ."

"Tarin," Sahrias said in a warning tone.

"You're a snob," Tarin replied. "Own it." Then he leaned toward me and whispered, "Have you seen *The 39 Steps?*"

"God." The word left Sahrias's mouth like a curse. "I remember you dragging me to that in '32? '33?" He squinted at the ceiling.

"1935," Tarin said, sitting on the island.

"I was born in 1989," I looked skeptically at him.

"So?" His tone was accusatory. "You have never seen anything made from before you were old enough to go to a movie?"

"No. I mean, yes. I have. Of course, I have."

The longer I rambled the higher his bushy green eyebrows went.

"Then?" he asked, eyebrows almost getting lost in his hair.

"You're right," I said with my hands up in surrender. "*Star Wars* is one of my favorites."

"Has he seen them yet?" He hooked a thumb in Sahrias's direction. Sahrias was watching our conversation with a smile.

"No, he refus—"

"To the media room!" Tarin interrupted in a yell. He hopped off his chair, and vanished into the hallway.

I looked at Sahrias. His smile broadened, and he nodded his agreement. Rushing after Tarin, I called out, "please let this be a normal field trip!"

Sahrias groaned and walked slowly behind me.

"With the Frizz?" Tarin called back. "No way!"

"What!" Sahrias sat up in his recliner when the credits started to roll.

"That's it? But what happens to Han?"

"There's still one more, Si," Tarin smiled. His feet barely reached past the edge of the black leather chair he was sitting in. "Keep your pants on."

"There are actually five more," I corrected, from my sprawled position on the plush grey carpet. "And more to come."

"Let us not speak of them," Tarin turned his head away. "I'm a purist."

"Oh, come on! They had their moments," I tried, sitting up.

"Please, as if it's just that easy to turn a Jedi to the—"

"SPOILERS!" Sahrias yelled, making us both jump. "Can we please just see what happens to Han!"

"Wooah," I said, standing. "It's okay." My tone was soothing, like I was talking someone off the ledge of a building. "I'm going to start *Episode VI* right now. Remain calm."

I walked slowly to the VCR. Tarin really was a purist. He had the ones where Han shoots first and Jabba isn't in it until *Episode VI*.

"Just nod and smile," I stage-whispered to Tarin.

"Oh, shut it!" Sahrias lobbed a pillow at me.

I dodged it easily and hit play.

The sun was minutes away from breaking over the horizon when Sahrias walked me to my bedroom door for the second night in a row. Tarin had gone to bed right after we'd finished *Episode VI*, muttering something about sleep schedules and how we would have to repeat any conversations or debates we had when we woke up.

I was reaching for the handle of my bedroom door when Sahrias spoke.

"Dyson," he said, and I turned to face him. "I want to apologize again for the way I behaved. I don't think it is possible to overstate how important you've become to me."

I looked at him, unsure of what to say.

"I have not done a good job of sharing my past with you," he said. "The truth of the matter is—" He took a deep breath. "Someone hurt me very badly a long time ago. And I shut down. I think I've done a poor job of not being that way with you."

"It's okay," I said.

"It's not." He shook his head. "You deserve more than that, and I will try to be better."

"You don't have to," I told him, and I meant it.

When my mother had died, my older brother Thomas had had all these expectations of how Kai should act, how he should feel. Kai, the youngest, had crumbled under the pressure and loss. Their relationship had never really recovered. Then Dad had died, and they'd cut each other out of their respective lives. Being caught between them had been horrible.

I honestly don't think they would have ever spoken to each other again if I hadn't died. Sahrias still updated me on them sometimes. And on Tina too. We agreed it was better I didn't know too much. Not yet. I was still grieving them, and my old life, in a way.

I knew all too well that grief took time. Sahrias could grieve his loss any way he needed to.

"You don't have to," I said again when he opened his mouth to protest. "Would I like it if you were more open with me? Yeah, of course I would. But that doesn't have to mean talking about things you're not ready to talk about. I can wait. We're going to live forever, right?"

He sighed. "So young and yet so wise."

"Only sometimes," I smiled.

"Well." He took a deep breath. "I will start by telling you something I should have said to you a long time ago. That night, on the subway platform, when I found you?"

I nodded, not likely to forget the night I'd died.

"That night saved my life. You saved my life." He cupped my cheek for a moment, before letting his hand fall. "You gave me meaning, and purpose, and hope."

I blinked, stunned at this declaration.

"I had been a shell of a man for decades," he went on. "I never wanted to sire, for many reasons, but when I saw you there . . ." He took my wrist and ran his thumb over my small ankh tattoo.

Thomas had taken me to get it when I'd been eighteen. My parents had been furious.

"You remember what I told you?" Sahrias asked.

"My book," I smiled. I'd never told him, but Sahrias seeing meaning in one of my father's favorite books had made me trust him more than I would have otherwise. His making sure I had my father's copy only increased that level of trust. "*Carmilla* made you do it."

"That wasn't the only thing," he said. "I am, more often than not, an atheist. But that night, I thought I felt the hands of Fate. And I am so grateful I went where they pushed me. I am so grateful I have you." He dropped his eyes from my face, to the floor. "I've never had a daughter before. I don't think I could lose you, Dyson. I don't think I could survive losing you. It's no reason for my behaviour. I know I was wrong. And I will be better. But I just, I—"

He looked back up at me, eyes shining with unshed tears.

"I love you too, Sahrias," I said, and hugged him. "I love you too."

CHAPTER TEN

2018

My eyes snapped open. I gasped for air—it felt like I'd just run a marathon. My breath was coming hard and fast and I was hot. So hot. I sat up as heat built in my chest. I felt light.

Light as air, hot and bright as the sun.

I moved my hands from my chest to the mattress below me, but it wasn't there. Looking down, I tried to scream. I hovered inches in the air. I reached for the mattress and tried to lie down. I couldn't.

I tried to scream again. The sound caught in my throat. Heat grew in my chest. Bright white-gold light filled the room.

Gasping, I tried to scream a third time. It worked.

"Sahrias, Sahrias!"

I was drifting higher. My back arched as hot pain coursed through me. I opened my mouth and screamed in pain.

"I'm here." Sahrias skidded into the room without a hint of his usual grace. "I'm . . ."

The words died on his lips.

My chest was fire, my eyes burned from it. I closed my mouth to stop the scream, but as soon as I did, it tore through me again.

I was burning. It felt like my skin was on fire. I threw my head to the side and reached for my maker.

He stood in the doorway, bathed in brightest gold.

"No, no, Gods, no." Sahrias lifted his hand to shield his eyes from the light as it grew brighter.

I tried to say his name but couldn't. I couldn't even scream anymore. It hurt too much. Unable to control my body, my eyes opened wide. Light pulsed around me.

Wind from nowhere and everywhere blew my long curly hair in a tangle and stole the sheet off my body. Flat on my back in the air, my mouth open in a silent cry, I saw Sahrias drop to his knees.

"Dear God," he said, as the wind roared. "How do I protect her now?"

I woke but kept my eyes shut. I wiggled my fingers and toes. There were sheets on top of me and a mattress below.

Everything seemed normal.

Had it been a dream? It felt so real . . . but no, it couldn't be. I popped open my eyes just for a second, then squeezed them shut again. It had been so bright. Hell of a dream . . .

Sliding out from under my covers, I sat on the edge of the bed.

"Dyson," Sahrias said.

My head snapped up as if he were in the room with me. I knew he wasn't.

"Would you come down?" he said. His voice was quiet, but my ears picked it up all the same.

"In a minute," I said softly, knowing he could hear me too. Sometimes

I would yell back, just to annoy him.

Tonight, I wasn't in the mood.

"Good morning," I grumbled. Sahrias sat at the kitchen island with an empty glass and a half-full jar in front of him. He didn't look up.

"Hello." Sahrias's voice was hollow as his eyes scanned the newspaper in his hand.

I went to the fridge, pulled out a jar, took off the cap and took a big swig.

"What's going on?" I asked. He looked up at me, and his face fell. "I look that bad, huh?" I smiled. "I don't think I slept very well."

"Oh?" Sahrias said. He sounded off too.

"Do you put any stock in dream interpretation?" I asked and leaned my elbows onto the island. He blinked, clearly confused. "Like dreams about teeth mean death, and dreams about rivers mean you're in denial— or maybe that was something else."

"Why do you ask?" he said, the corner of his mouth twitching at my bad joke.

Hmmm. I'd been expecting a hard no. Sahrias was always good for a straight answer to a simple question. Unless the question didn't have a simple answer.

"Last night I had the weirdest dream. I was hovering over my bed," I said. "I think it was bright."

"You think?" Sahrias asked.

"I don't remember," I shrugged and made my way to the empty bar stool and leaned back. The stools were more like tall chairs, with their decorative back and well cushioned seats. "I guess it was nothing. I just feel off."

"Well, if it comes back to you and you deem it noteworthy, feel free to tell me about it and we can . . . ahhhh, interpret?"

I smiled and asked again, "What did you want to talk about?"

"I think it is time we leave the mountains."

My mouth dropped open in surprise.

"Are you serious?"

A few months ago, I worked up the nerve to ask Sahrias if I could get a job in town. He dismissed it out of hand. No go for a knitting class either. It wasn't until I'd told him how lonely I was that we started talking about a real change. I started an online class in psychology.

It helped, but it wasn't what I needed.

"When? Why? Should I go pack now?" I pushed away from the island and started to stand before Sahrias put a hand up to stop me.

A broad smile split his face. I loved it when he smiled like that, wide and open. It happened sometimes when he forgot to be Mr. Serious.

"Not right now," he chuckled. "But I take it you want to leave?"

"Does the pope sh—"

"Dyson!"

"—in the woods—sorry, I mean, yeah, yes. I do."

"I have to make some calls, but since you are so eager—" He looked at me. I put an elbow on the island and propped my head up in my hand.

"I'm eager." I batted my eyelashes at him.

"Compelling," he rolled his eyes, smile still in place. "Where would you like to go?"

"Germany," I said without hesitation. Finally, after what felt like hundreds of failed tests, finally last month, I'd drunk water, and it hadn't felt like cement. It felt closer to honey than what I remembered but over the last month it had gotten better.

Today, water. Tomorrow, beer.

"I want to go to Germany," I reiterated, "and drink beer."

"I almost died in Germany once. It's kind of soured my taste for it. But I could try again. And you are managing water now, so perhaps in the next few years."

Years? I mentally groaned. Really?

"Where will we stay?" I asked, thinking that a hotel might not exactly be safe. "And how do I pack? Do I bring everything."

"Goodness no," he laughed. "Pack for a week and wear something comfortable. There are companies that cater to beings like us," Sahrias explained with a lazy wave of his hand. "Retrofit apartments, they rent out some of their own."

"A week," I said, eyes going wide. "But—"

"Dyson, we will come back at some point. Your things will all still be here. This house is yours too now." He poured the remainder of his jar into a tall glass, and drank. I had no idea why he did that, but I'd stopped asking a long time ago. "You're still thinking like a Human," he said.

"Well, how else am I supposed to think?"

"Like you are going to live forever and will own houses all over the world."

"Own houses all over the—Sahrias!" I rolled my eyes. "I haven't had a job in four years, and even assuming I got one in the near future, how the hell am I supposed to afford—" I put air quotes around the words, "'houses all over the world?'"

"Well, you are now a part owner of this one," he said, but I was already lost in thought.

I would have been finished school by now. If I hadn't died. I would have been twenty-nine years old. I kind of still was, but it didn't feel the same.

I would have been two years out of school, and working. I would have had a life. I would have been able to do all the projects in my childhood home. The ones my father never had the chance to finish.

But instead, I'm stuck.

I will never look older than I do right now. I have no purpose, no goals, no—

Stop it, I cut off that line of thinking. A house, a car, and a white picket fence was never what I'd wanted in life. It wasn't even a real alternative.

It was this or death. This or nothing.

Given the choice to do over again. I would choose to be here, even if I felt adrift in the universe.

"Dyson?" Sahrias asked, looking at me in the way he sometimes did. Like I was someone else, like I'd done something else. The worry for him was enough to push my longing for a life I'd never have out of my mind.

He searched my face for a moment and I almost asked him what was wrong.

"Sahrias," I said his name as if I was the one answering an unasked question. There was a beat of silence before he smiled and said, "I'd prefer to not start in Germany, even if we do go there eventually."

Maybe one day I would ask him what that look meant, but not today. Today, I had something else I needed more.

"I'd like to go somewhere where . . ." I paused, not sure how to say the next part.

"Yes," Sahrias prompted.

"I'd really like to have some, I mean you're great and all, but—"

"You want friends," he finished for me.

I nodded.

"I am surprised it's taken you this long to ask." His smile was warm. "I'll make some calls."

I'd never experienced such luxury. There was a small fridge beside my seat in the light-proof private plane. I popped it open once we were in the air, and pulled out a bottle of blood. I drank it slowly, thinking of the bittersweet feeling I'd woken up with, and the feeling that I was leaving something important behind.

When the sun rose, two hours into our flight, I did nothing to stop its pull of sleep. Eight hours later, I felt groggy, and off, and sure I'd forgotten something. I'd dreamed of it, light and love and something else. But I couldn't remember what it was.

I heard a groan from across the small aisle of the plane. We'd left around 4 a.m. It was 2 p.m. British Columbia time now.

"The time change never gets easier," Sahrias sat up, adjusted his seat, and looked at his watch. "The sun just set here."

I grabbed another bottle from the small fridge and drained it.

"I feel like hot wet garbage on a sunny day," I said.

"Indeed," Sahrias opened the mini fridge next to his seat and pulled out a bottle of his own. "That sums it up rather well."

"What now?" I asked, waking up a little. My excitement for what was coming pushed away the groggy haze.

"Now," he smiled, "we go for a drive."

Once the sun fully set, we gathered our things and headed off the plane. Just as Sahrias had said, a car was waiting for us. I put my bag in the trunk and looked up at the small plane. That feeling I'd had when I'd woken up washed over me again.

What did I forget to bring? I racked my brain. What did I leave behind?

Dyson unrolled the parchment she'd found in the second bedside table and read the short message.

"Your people have sent reinforcements," she said, skimming the scribbled ink. "Better late than never, I suppose. There will be scouts ahead of the rest, I'm sure of it. I wonder how far they are now?"

She scanned the parchment for a date.

"Two days ago," she whispered. "They will be here soon. A day. Two at most."

Shit, she thought. She knew a scouting party was already there, or very nearby. One of the scouting party would venture up to this room and report back. And when they did, she wanted to be ready.

Maybe I can turn this to my advantage, she thought. Maybe now I won't have to go looking for food after all. Someone will come to me. But I'll have to be in better shape when they arrive, and the oushifa will only help so much.

No matter what, I'll need to feed.

Slowly, painfully, she put the top of her dress back on. Dyson looked around, thinking where to search next.

The desk, she thought. The broken, splintered pieces of desk littered one corner of the room. She moved slowly toward it.

"We started in England," Dyson said, thinking back to simpler times and trying to ignore the pain. "We stayed in a small northern town. I practiced. I was impatient, but I wasn't going to slip again. Ireland was next, and after a few years I could drink." She smiled and shifted aside some of the desk with a foot.

"That's where I really got the hang of drinking liquids other than blood, I mean. Alcohol has a sharp kind of—" She brought her fingers to her lips. "Tang. Ireland was also where I started working again. Short shifts at a local bar. I wasn't around enough to make real friends, but it was nice to be with other people.

"After Ireland, we went through France, Switzerland, Italy." She paused. The effort it took to kneel down momentarily stole her words. "Not Germany, although I wanted to. I wanted to swim to Libya, spend some time there, then swim to Greece, but Sahrias didn't think we could beat the sun."

She looked over her shoulder.

"I'm getting ahead of myself," Dyson said, before returning her gaze to the ruined desk. "I'm getting out of order . . . something very strange happened when we were in Paris."

CHAPTER ELEVEN
2031

"I want to have sex."

Si looked slowly up from the book he was reading. Equally slowly, he placed his glass of wine on the small round table beside him.

"Come again?" he said.

I raised an eyebrow.

"Poor choice of words." He smirked, shook his head, and looked out over the city. Our little veranda had a perfect view of the Eiffel Tower twinkling in the distance. He looked like a movie star, sitting on the white painted metal chair in black slacks and a dark navy button up. Even after all this time, I was nowhere near as poised as he was without trying.

"I want to have sex," I repeated.

"I actually did hear you the first time. I am assuming you do not mean with me . . ."

"Of course not, Si," I whined. "I'm just confused and I don't really have anyone else to talk to about this."

"Why are you confused?" he looked at me like I was asking why two and two didn't make five. "I am confused at your confusion."

I wasn't in the mood for Si's jokes tonight. They were rarely funny, and I was already worked up.

"I haven't thought about my vagina in almost fifteen years," I said. Si winced, and it was my turn to smirk. "But tonight, at the bar, this guy came in and—I don't know what happened. All I could think about was sex."

"Okay," Si said.

"With him," I specified.

"Yes."

"Not you."

"I understand that, thank you." Si rolled his eyes.

"So?" I asked, pulling the matching patio chair over to the table and sitting down.

"I am still confused," Si said, and I was sure he was being intentionally obtuse.

"Are you trying to hurt me?" I asked.

"Why didn't you just go home with 'this guy' from the bar?" he countered.

"Well, that's the dumbest question I've ever heard," I said. "You have noticed that our hair still grows, right?"

"I am not convinced that Human males really care about that." His eyes flicked down and back up.

"I'm not convinced of your sanity," I squinted at him. "Yet here I am asking you for help."

"Help with what, exactly?" he leaned forward, putting his elbows on the table.

"Well, not personal grooming," I nearly shouted and he shushed me.

"Sorry," I said. "Understanding. I need help understanding."

"You want to have The Talk?" He smiled a little and his eyebrows rose high on his forehead.

"If it's a different talk than the one for Humans," I said, meaning it. "Yes! I mean, I haven't had my period in fifteen years, but my hair still grows . . . so, I don't know."

There was a beat of silence.

I looked out over our view. Though the city wasn't somewhere I would want to live forever, Paris had a beauty few places did.

"Did I ever tell you about when my father gave me The Talk?" I said.

"Not your mother?" Si leaned back, picking up his glass of red and taking a sip.

"Not my mother," I laughed. "I actually got most of my 'Talks' from my dad." I shook my head. "I never did ask them why."

We fell into silence again and a cool breeze fluttered the pages of Si's book.

It was a comfortable silence, despite the potential awkwardness of the conversation. We could have sat like that until just before the sun rose, and we sometimes did. Sometimes I would come home and find him out here, and we would sit in silence for hours. Si told me it was a vampiric thing. That our relationship with time was different than other beings.

We'd had that conversation in Italy after two years had passed, and I'd barely noticed.

"It's the routine," he'd said. "Sometimes, when we get into a routine, when we sleep, when we are focused on something, time just slips by."

Not tonight though. Tonight, I needed an answer, and what was happening to me was not routine. I looked from the twinkling tower to my maker.

Si took another sip of his wine and started to speak.

"The cases of vampiric pregnancies are, more often than not, Magical. Other than that, sex with a Human is what you would expect."

"But Si, this is why I'm asking," I said. "I don't know what to expect."

"It's not so different than before," he told me. "Your control has improved so much in the last ten years that I think it highly unlikely you will kill a lover."

My eyes opened wide in surprise.

"I might fuck him to death?"

"Language," Si warned.

"Nuh-uh, Si, you can't casually throw around killing lovers and then be mad at a curse word."

"Of course I can," he said imperiously.

I pushed my sleeves up to my elbows, took in a deep calming breath, then said, "Please explain."

"Not much to explain," Si tilted his head. "Younger Vampires who feed during intercourse—"

"God, don't call it that."

"—lose control and don't know how to stop themselves."

I blinked slowly at him.

"But, as I said," he continued, "I think it highly unlikely that you will do that. You've been working around Humans for over three years. You have friends."

"I have co-workers," I corrected. "They don't really call you a friend if you always turn down day trips to the beach."

"What about that nice boy in your dance class?" he asked.

An odd warmth spread over me. Tristan. I hadn't thought about him since this whole ordeal started a couple hours ago. But now that I did, I had a hard time stopping.

I remembered when we'd danced last class. The feel of his hand on my back, of how we moved together. I stifled a groan at the memory, experiencing it differently than I had when it actually happened.

I thought about running my fingers through his blond hair and pressing my body along his—

"I'm pretty sure he's gay," I said, the image of the two of us faded from my mind.

"Hmmm." Sahrias picked up his book. "Well, I'm sure you'll find someone."

"Thanks," I said sarcastically. "This was no help at all."

"I'm sorry," he looked up sharply. "What exactly would you like me to do here? Go on a dating app, why don't you? You're in Paris, for god's sake. Paris, France! I hate to be stereotypical, Dyson, but of all the cities you could have rediscovered your sexuality in, your timing is impeccable."

"But why now?" I didn't like not understanding my body. And just when I was starting to feel I had everything under control. "What happened to make me feel this way now?"

Sahrias sniffed.

"Wait." I pointed an accusing finger at him. "What aren't you telling me?"

"I'm not not telling you anything."

"A double negative?" I accused. "Really? That's supposed to convince me that you're telling the truth? The whole truth? I'm going through some weird vampiric puberty here. Help a sister out."

He sighed, finished his glass of wine, and poured himself another.

"Nothing about you can ever be simple can it?" he said. "I suppose it's just not in your DNA."

"What do you mean, Si?" I said.

"Our relationship," he gestured between the two of us, "is unusual."

"Why?" I asked.

"It's familial."

"Well spotted, Daaaad" I said, dragging out the 'a'. I pulled Si's glass of wine across the table, tried a sip, and wrinkled my nose.

"Wasted on you," he grinned. "Your pallet will come back in time."

I loved this new version of us. The one that had developed over the last decade. The one that started after I'd gained enough control to go out on my own. He had relaxed a little, though I'd still never seen him in a pair of jeans. He'd started treating me like a sister, almost. Still taking the roll of father when I needed it, like tonight.

He laughed more now. He joked more. Even Tarin mentioned the change when he'd come to see us in the Alps.

"Vampires often change their lovers over, so they can be together forever," Si told me.

"Does that usually work?" I asked. "Are they together forever?"

"Nothing lasts forever, Dyson. Not even us. But I know a couple who have been together for over a millennium."

"Wow," I said. "I bet they have a great therapist."

He chuckled. "I do not think they are exclusive, but they are each other's primary partner."

"What about you and your maker?" I asked.

His eyes went dark. A shadow of the colder harder version of him I used to know flashed across his face. I didn't think he'd answer. He'd never talked about her before. But to my surprise, the guarded look of apprehension left him, and he told me about his past.

"Yamini and I were together for a long time." He closed his eyes for a beat, before looking out over the balcony. "It felt like a long time then.

It wasn't. Not really. She found me in South India in the time of the Middle Kingdoms. I was born into what you'd now call a low caste. I never knew why she picked me. Because I needed her, I suppose."

He said the last part with a bitterness I wasn't used to hearing from him. I knew he was old. Really old. But he seldom spoke about the beginning.

"She took me away from my life, fed me, clothed me, took care of me. I fell in love with her. When I learned what she was, I begged her. For months and months, I begged her. I wanted to be with her forever and I told her so."

He sipped his wine, then stood and walked into the apartment. He returned a moment later with a glass and a bottle of white he knew I liked.

" 'Love won't feel the same after,' she'd said. 'You won't love me if I change you over.' I promised her I would. I swore I would love her until the day I died again."

Si poured a glass.

"And then, one day, she did it, while we were making love. She drank my blood and I drank hers. And it was bliss knowing the gift she gave me. Knowing she would be mine for the rest of time . . . and all the while she made it seem like it was my idea."

"Thank you," I whispered, when Si slid the sweet Bordeaux over to me. My pallet for wine was that of a teenager's. I liked the sweet stuff and couldn't taste the undertones of anything yet.

"You're welcome," he said, and settled back into his chair. "At first it felt no different. I still loved her as much as I had when I was Human. But bound to her as I was, and in the height of my bloodlust, I lost more than I realized."

I wanted to ask how long his bloodlust had lasted. I wanted to know if it was as unusually long as mine. But I stayed silent.

"She was my lover before she was my keeper," he squeezed his eyes shut against the memory. "She taught me little to nothing about being a Vampire. About being a good Vampire. We traveled where we wanted and killed who we fed on. Sometimes we'd bed them first. She didn't care. She didn't care how many bodies we left behind us. And she never taught me to care, so I didn't either.

"When my bloodlust faded, it was just life. All that death, all the blood. I knew nothing else for so long. Then one day, I realized what she'd done. How she'd used me, controlled me. I realized that she'd gone mad long before I met her. For a while, I had unknowingly joined her in that madness. I was just a pet to her. A distraction."

"Distraction from what?" I asked.

Sahrias's eyes met mine. His eyes seemed so sad. I wanted to take his pain away. But I knew nothing I could do would help. This was his past, his baggage. I knew now why he was reluctant to share it.

"She had loved someone once," he said. "She had loved someone so deeply that, when he died, she'd broke."

"Oh," I said, quietly.

"He died and she found me. Eventually I got away."

"How?" I asked.

"I met someone," he said. "Someone who showed me there was another way to be. Someone who treated me as an equal and showed me a new world. Who believed in helping those who could not help themselves."

"Rayyan," I said.

He nodded. Decades old words resurface in my mind, and something clicked into place. Something about shadow of an expression on Si's face.

"I have not done a good job of sharing my past with you," he'd said some fifteen years ago in the mountains. "The truth of the matter is someone hurt me very badly a long time ago. And I shut down."

Which of them had he been talking about, Yamini, or Rayyan? I didn't know much about Rayyan. Just that she was a woman from Si's past, that she'd been important to him, and that she was gone.

"Where is Yamini now?" I asked.

"She is long dead," he said, the corners of his mouth turning down. "And the world is a better place for it."

Sahrias stared into his wine, seemingly lost in memories. But of exactly what, I did not know. All I could see was the depths of sadness in his eyes.

"Do you want a hug?" I asked. "I want a hug after hearing that. I can only imagine how you feel."

He laughed a little. "Yes. Yes, I would very much like a hug."

CHAPTER TWELVE
2038

"I think you'll like it here," Si said. "At Erroin. I think it will be good for you."

"I could go to night school anywhere." I said. "Why here?"

He stopped his trek through the forest and looked at me the way he did when he was wearing his "dad" hat. "What did you tell me when we left the Rockies?"

"Ummm. . ." That had been some two decades ago. It didn't feel that way, but it had. Sahrias was right when he'd said time moved differently for us. Sometimes so fast, and other times so slow. The decades had felt like nothing. "That I wanted to go to Germany?"

"After that," he said.

I thought in silence for a moment before it came to me. I rolled my eyes, putting on my "petulant child" hat. The transition was seamless. It was one we'd done many times over the last twenty years.

"That I wanted friends," I said.

Sahrias started walking again, and I trudged through the trees behind him. I wouldn't call what we were walking on a path, but the trees were spaced enough that it wasn't difficult to find my footing. Clouds covered and uncovered the moon. Patches of light came and went through the tall trees.

I remembered the first time that the transition from adult back to child had happened in my Human life. The moment when my parents realized their kids were adults—and the moment my mother realized she could still put on her "big boss" hat. My brothers and I would crumple under her gaze, no matter how old we were.

"And when you were Human, where did you make all of your friends?" Si asked like he already knew the answer.

"At school." I smiled. "But—"

"And what did you say about the friends you had in Paris, and then in Bern, and then in Istanbul, and—"

"I get it," I said, cutting him off and catching up to him. "That I didn't have any because they didn't know what I was."

"Exactly. At Erroin, you can openly be a Vampire and be honest with the people around you."

"You're doing this all so that I can have friends?" I asked.

God, I am pathetic. Si has to take me to a school in India just to make a single friend. What if I don't make any? What if I live forever and never have friends ever again?

"Believe it or not, Dyson," Si said, breaking me out of my downward spiral. "Not everything I do is for you." His grin was small. "I like it at Erroin. I used to live there. It's a different kind of normal. One where everyone is like us, more or less."

"Okay," I said.

He must have been able to read the fear and worry in my eyes because he said, "When you left university, how many new friends did you make?"

"I don't know. Not many," I lengthened my stride to match his change of pace.

"It's hard." He smiled at me over his shoulder. It almost seemed like he was reading my mind. "It's hard to make new friends. I wasn't sure about your control until a few years ago. By then, you'd gotten into a rhythm. I didn't want to break it."

"Yeah." I nodded and breathed out my anxiety.

He was right, I had gotten into a rhythm. I would work, occasionally go out for drinks. I'd even had a few boyfriends . . . if you could call them that. They didn't last and I never really knew any of them. They never really knew me either. How could they when I had to lie about who I was?

"If for whatever reason you don't like it, we can leave," Sahrias said. "But you can finish your degree here. You can work with kids who need help here. You can teach here."

I can have purpose again. A community.

Sahrias stopped walking and waited for me to meet his eyes.

"Niloc Erroin, the founder of this school, is a very old friend of mine. I've not seen him in a long time," he said. "I am excited to see him. Don't tie yourself in knots thinking this is all about you. There may even be a few teachers from my day still around. And I know the family that runs the campus bar."

Si pulled an apple out of his coat pocket.

"Niloc gave me this." He took a large bite from the apple and a little juice hit me in the face.

He did it on purpose, I was sure of it.

"Nice." I wiped the juice off my cheek. Most Vampires couldn't eat solid food, but Si could eat apples. He'd made some kind of deal with a low-level god, or something . . . I didn't know much more than that.

"Would you like to hunt before we get there?" he asked.

"Sure," I said, picking dirt out from under my fingernails.

"I hate it when you do that while I'm eating." He scrunched his nose.

"Oh, the crosses we must bear," I said, glaring at his apple. It looked so good and so unappetizing at the same time. I'd decided that it was nostalgia that made me jealous, not actual desire. "So, this guy, Niloc. You visit him a lot?"

"Whenever I'm in the Old World," Sahrias said, and we started to run.

"Isn't Europe 'the Old World?' " I asked through the rushing wind.

"Only to the young."

We hunted and drank sparingly from several musk deer. When we'd first started traveling, I was excited for the flavor possibilities of new wildlife. But alas, that excitement was in vain. The deer in western Europe tasted identical to those of the Canadian Rockies. The Himalayan deer were no different.

With only a few hours of night left, we sped through the dense forest toward the Luman school. The ground sloped up under our feet, and I felt something tug in my chest. I tried to pinpoint what it was.

Something is missing. I looked around the montane forest. Something is not here.

The trees were so familiar yet so different. I looked at them and reached for my necklace. The faint buzz of the stone was comforting.

I'd had this feeling, like I was missing something, for a while. Maybe since Paris, although that was almost seven years ago, but maybe I had been feeling it since we'd left the Rockies.

"It's just over here," Si said, slowing.

I pushed the feeling out of my mind and looked up to where he pointed. The trees broke as we crested the top of the hill. The land dipped down into a large valley. I saw a small hut in the center, barely visible.

"What is it—a school for ants?" I asked.

He squinted at me.

"Never mind." I waved away his confusion. Pop culture references were always lost on him. Except for *Star Wars*. "I mean, it's pretty small for a school."

He didn't answer. Instead, he extended a hand to me and I took it, feeling like the child I was in comparison to his centuries of life.

If we'd been Human, it might have been awkward to walk hand-in-hand down the hill. But our feet moved smoothly over the uneven ground. We walked down the hill and stopped at the edge of a clearing. Through the last few trees, I could see the small hut. Sahrias released my hand and walked forward without comment.

I followed him.

A slight breeze tingled over my scalp. When I looked at where the hut had been, my mouth fell open.

"Magic is so cool," I breathed.

We were no longer in a small clearing. Moonlight bounced off white turrets and onion-domed tops of an enormous structure in the center of a wide valley. A vaulted rooftop stretched between the four towers, all of differing heights and widths, green vines growing up one side.

"Holy," I breathed.

"In a manner of speaking, yes, but that is quite complex," Sahrias said. He looked at the structure like he was seeing an old friend. "It has been a while."

"This is incredible." I stepped forward.

"Welcome to Erroin Peritia." He raised an arm in the direction of the school.

"Wait a second." I went back into the trees.

The breeze gave my scalp that tingly feeling again. I turned and saw the hut. Walking out into the clearing for the second time, I paid special attention to the Magical illusion.

"I felt something there," I said when I was standing next to Si again. "A veil?"

"Well done." He smiled. "Few can feel it, even if they know it's there. It shows power, awareness. Come along."

As we crossed the sweeping lawn, and my eyes paused on a glass turret that was taller and wider than the others. A young man walked down the spiral staircase within. When he saw us, he paused, his large eyebrows knitting together.

"Is that him? That's Niloc?" He looked younger than I'd imagined. "Did he know we were coming?"

"Yes," Sahrias sounded stiff. "That's him. And yes, he knew."

"Then why was he looking at you like that?"

The man in the turret started walking again and Si raised an eyebrow in my direction.

"He wasn't looking at me."

Me? Why would he look at me like that? I opened my mouth to ask, but Si's stony expressions stopped my words.

We continued across the starlit lawn to the grand front doors. At first, I thought they were made of stone but the closer we got, the more I could see it was expertly painted wood matching perfectly to the lines and grooves running along the exterior of the building.

The doors swung open.

"Sahrias Gillrana. It has been a lifetime," said a tall strongly built man. The black hair, broad shoulders, and muscled arms were not exactly what I'd envisioned when Si had talked about Niloc.

"Or two, but who's counting," Si said. The man took one of Sahrias's hands in both of his and shook.

Si smirked, looking the man up and down. "You look younger."

"Do I?" He seemed confused. "Gods of the Far World, I forgot I put this on."

A strong breeze swirled around us, and the young man began to age.

His hair grew past his shoulders and its jet-black coloring streaked white and grey. Thin lines of laughter and time crept across his face. His height decreased and his back bowed slightly.

"I like to do my own yard work," he said to my slack-jawed expression. "But it gets uncomfortable to hold an unnatural form for too long. Better?" he said, opening his arms to Sahrias.

"Niloc!" Si threw his arms around his old friend.

A small "ouf" escaped Niloc as Si hugged a little too tightly.

"Easy, my boy—but it has been too long."

"Indeed." Si released him.

I enjoyed the ease that seemed to settle on Sahrias. Though he had seemed calmer when we'd left the mountains, and calmer still as my control grew, there was something about him that always made me feel like he was waiting for the other shoe to drop.

For a moment, that was gone.

"Let me introduce you to my progeny." Si held his arm up in my direction. I stepped forward.

"Yes," Niloc snapped his fingers and a walking stick materialized out of thin air. He used the cane to step forward. "I thought I felt you have a daughter a few years ago." He reached his hand forward. "Niloc Erroin."

"Dyson Blake." His handshake was firm, but gentle. "You can feel me?"

He smiled and nodded.

"Her Spark is bright," he said to Sahrias. "Just like Rayyan. Gods of World Far, it feels like yesterday you two were here and . . ." Niloc trailed off when Sahrias stiffened. The burden of waiting for the other shoe to drop seemed to fall back onto my maker's shoulders.

"Oh, Sahrias, my boy," Niloc said with an apologetic look. "I misspoke. I am sorry. Well, come in, come in. Never mind me."

I looked from Si to Niloc, and back. Sahrias's reaction to Rayyan's name made me simultaneously hungry to learn more about her, and reluctant to ask. Any questions I had were driven out of my mind when I stepped through the front doors of the school.

"Oh my god," I said.

"Gods," Niloc corrected, "and thank you."

The massive entry had two archways branching off to the right and left, and a stairway in the center that was twice as wide as my first apartment. Everything was whites, and blues, and warm, warm browns. It felt bright, and open, and welcoming. Halls and doorways lined either side of the staircase.

So much exploring to do. And it's so quiet here. Though, I guess—I looked down at my watch—it is only 5 a.m. I thought there would be others like me and Si. Those who preferred the night. But maybe students don't live here in the summer.

"Are you here alone?" I asked.

"Oh, sometimes. The summer is quiet," Niloc said. We paused in the front hall. "But even then, there are usually a few students who stay, who don't have anywhere else to go. At the moment, most of them are on a trip. But one student will be by shortly, I'm sure."

"It's so late," I said. "Or early, I guess."

"Yes." Niloc started down the hall to the right. We followed him. "This is only a little earlier than normal for him. And he is excited to meet you."

"Your first friend," Si whispered.

I elbowed him in the ribs.

"I asked him to show you around a little," Niloc said with a knowing smile. "I thought that might be better than Si or myself— ahh, and here he is."

A lanky boy with alabaster skin walked down the wide hall toward us. He looked young, maybe seventeen, but the closer the boy got, the more he seemed to hum with power. It was quiet and subtle and I reached a hand to my necklace.

They felt the same. Him, and the necklace. Then I blinked and he was just a boy. No power at all.

Had I imagined it?

"Your timing is as impeccable as ever," Niloc said to him.

The boy seemed pleased at the praise and smiled, pushing thick black-rimmed glasses up his nose.

"Dyson Blake, Sahrias Gillrana," Niloc said. "This is Lochlan Ellyll. He's been a student with us for the last four years."

"Hello," I said with a little wave.

"Hi," he said, looking at me with the brightest green eyes I'd ever seen. Sahrias extended his hand and the boy shook it.

"Well, I'll leave you to it, Lochlan," Niloc said, then turned to Si. "We'll go off for a drink, hmmm?"

"Is your apartment in the same place?" Sahrias asked.

"Ahh, no," Niloc said. "We'd not put the addition on when you were here last. That's where one of the paintings you acquired for that family hangs now. They gave one back as a thank-you, some years ago. My, it has been a long time."

"I would love to see it," Si said.

Niloc patted Sahrias on the shoulder, then to Lochlan he said, "Would you meet us back here in an hour or so?"

Lochlan responded.

I blinked, took a breath, and ran over the boy's words.

I'd spent time in Ireland, both in my Human life and as a Vampire, and I'd rarely had trouble understanding what was said.

"Yes," Niloc said, seeming to understand the boy perfectly. "Around 6:15."

Lochlan spoke again, and I began to make a mental shift. It sounded like an Irish accent . . . but different. Lochlan turned to look at me and said something, a question. I thought it was a question.

I closed my eyes and swore that this was the only time I was going to make him repeat himself. My ineptitudes were not his responsibility.

"I am so sorry," I said, ready to focus. "Can you repeat that?"

"I said—" He smiled a little and I could tell he worked to enunciate his words. "Where would you like to start?"

"Oh," I nodded.

"I know I'm a little hard to understand sometimes." He ran his hand through his jet-black hair.

"No," I insisted. "No, you aren't. I wasn't listening properly, and that was my fault."

He smiled and inclined his head. "Do you know where you'd like to start?"

"No idea," I told him. "We just arrived. How about you show me your favorite spot? And take me there the long way."

He nodded and led me down the wide hall. I reached a hand to my necklace—and stretched my senses out towards him. I'd felt something when he first arrived, but whatever it was, it was gone now.

Lochlan and I walked in awkward silence. I inwardly wondered why Niloc thought a kid, barely eighteen, would be a good first friend. What could we possibly have in common?

"Woah," I said, when we turned down a hallway lined with paintings. I walked over to one I recognized. "This is pretty cool."

I pointed to a reimagined version of *The Raft of the Medusa*. The original painting had been controversial in the Paris Salons in 1819, in part for its depiction of a Black man saving the crew of a wrecked French ship.

This painting, a fraction of the size of the original, showed a crowd of protesters carrying a raft of . . .

"Is that Ilhan Omar?" I said, pointing at one of the people on the raft. I don't know why I asked him. I doubted this kid even knew who Ilhan Omar was.

"It is," he said, surprising me. "And here we have a few students from May 1968. See there, he's holding a cobblestone, and so is she." He pointed at the painting. "Mohamad Bouazizi to show the start of the Arab Spring, and here is John Boyega." He pointed to one of the people holding up the raft, megaphone in hand. "Every face in this painting is based on someone the artist saw in a history book, or newspaper clipping, online somewhere . . ."

He trailed off, catching my look. He huffed out a laugh, reading my expression.

"I'm an old soul," he shrugged.

"Hmmm." My eyes moved from Lochlan back to the painting, and its title. "This is pretty cool." I nodded to *The Raft of a Movement*, then gestured to the artwork filling the walls of the wide hallway. "These are all amazing."

"And all done by students," he said. "A few were donated by families who had their art stolen and returned at one time or another, some were found."

"And prints," I pointed to a Gustav Klimt. "Or amazing reproductions." I stepped close to a beautiful painting I'd never seen before. "Acquired by R. Hode"? I read.

I mentally pulled on the history and literature electives I'd made it through before dropping out of school.

R Hode? R Hode. Hood. No way. I looked at Lochlan.

"Not Robin Hood? The Robin Hood."

"Hmmm," Lochlan smirked and kept walking.

"Wow," I whispered, as I followed.

We turned down a hallway where the artwork was replaced by evenly spaced doors of varying colors, though all in the same pale shade. Lochlan slowed when we reached a light green door.

"One of our lecture halls." He opened the door to reveal a room full of chairs and desks arranged in a large semi-circle.

"Small class size," I noted.

"Yes, Niloc doesn't like the ratio to get much higher than fifteen or sixteen to one. It happens from time to time. We have a few classes of over a hundred. But they all have breakout groupings."

"Oh," I pulled my head out of the doorway and we started walking again.

"The school is also a shelter," Lochlan said. "They call that part the Shine House. Niloc said you are finishing a psychology degree? Maybe going into social work after?"

I'd been two years into a psych degree with a double minor in history and English when my father had died and I'd left school to work. I was looking forward to finishing it.

"Luman who don't understand their gifts come here," Lochlan continued, when I didn't speak. "Or those who have nowhere else to go. Those are the ones who stay here in the summer."

"Like you?" I asked before realizing how rude that was. "I'm sorry."

"S'all right." He adjusted a chain under his shirt. "My family has long left the land of the living."

An orphan like me. More in common than I'd thought.

"I found this place four years ago," he said. "Been here ever since."

"You never travel at all?" I asked.

"A bit in the summer, but not for the whole three months off."

"And you came here when you were what." I tilted my head. "Thirteen?"

"Fourteen." He met my eyes and I saw something in that green gaze. Something much older than his claimed eighteen years. "I was fourteen when I got here," he said. "But the school takes all ages. We have a class of five- and six-year-olds. That's rare. Gifts don't usually show so early. I'll be starting in the university program this semester."

"Me too," I nodded. I'd liked university when I'd gone before. I was ready to do it again. "What will you take?"

"Computer sciences," Lochlan said, then added as an afterthought, "and maybe Serbian."

I'd expected him to say something like spell work or alchemy. Defense against the dark arts at the very least but—

"Computer Sciences?" I asked. "That's so—"

"Normal?" He smiled. "Aye. Most subjects here are. There are a couple combat classes and power control, but other than that, it's just a school. The students are what's different."

Lochlan led us through a door in an exterior wall that blended in so perfectly I wouldn't have known it was there. Outside, the sky was dark, but I could smell the sunrise coming.

"This is my favorite spot on the grounds," Lochlan said as we walked around the back of the school to the small lake.

"It's glowing," I said.

"Aye." Lochlan smiled.

An iridescent light came off the clear water. I could see right to the bottom for several meters before it got too deep and all I saw was black.

"I mostly only swim in the day," he told me. "But sometimes I come out here when it's really dark to see it like this."

"It's beautiful," I said. "Almost bright enough for Human eyes to read by."

"'Tis," he told me. "I read out here some nights." He pushed his glasses up his nose.

Surely, there was a being here who could fix his eyes. Or laser eye surgery, at the very least. I turned my gaze from Lochlan to the water, and saw something move almost too fast to track.

"It's Humanoid," I stated.

"There are Mers in this lake," he said casually, turning to head back to the school. I tried to see another one, but the water was still. "Or mayhap it was a Yacuruna. They weren't keen on sharing a lake. Niloc sat them down to work it out. But anyway," he said. "Daylight's coming. We should head back."

We met Niloc and Sahrias in the entrance hall. I thanked Lochlan for the tour, and he left to go for a swim.

"This is one of the apartment sections of the building," Niloc explained after leading us through the weaving halls. He pushed open a door labeled Gillrana-Blake, snapped his fingers, and the lights turned on. "This is where you'll stay."

He walked in after us, snapped his fingers again, and the door closed. "Until school starts, that is."

"Nice," I said looking around at the open concept kitchen, dining room, and living room. Small, but manageable. Especially with an entire school to explore.

"Well, it will have to do," Sahrias said, looking around.

"Si, stop it. It's nice," I chided. "What happens after school starts?"

"I dare say, you may want to have your own dorm room," Niloc smiled.

"Oh?" I felt the smile slide off my face. It had been so long since I'd lived alone.

"Probably for the best," Sahrias said. "It will be an adjustment, but you'll want your own space. I assure you."

I nodded, not really agreeing.

I settled onto one of the grey-blue couches in the small living room as Sahrias and Niloc exchanged a few words before Niloc said goodnight and left.

"How was the tour?" Si asked. "Do you have a new friend?"

I shrugged.

"Oh, stop pouting," Si waved his hand through the air. "It's not as if we'll never see each other. We will technically be living in the same building."

"Yeah," I said, even though that wasn't at all the same.

"How was the tour?" Sahrias repeated.

"It was good," I said. "Lochlan is cool. Definitely potential friend material. He's kind of weird, though."

"Elaborate," Sahrias said, before sitting on the couch opposite me.

"I don't know," I said. "Just different, I guess. He's young but . . . not."

"I got to know Lochlan over the next couple weeks. When I asked him why he hadn't gone on the school trip he was . . . very Lochlan about it."

Dyson remembered him hunching his shoulders and pushing his glasses up his nose. When she smiled at the memory, a scab on her upper lip broke. Her expression fell.

" 'I like it here when it's quiet,' he'd told me. 'And I, well . . . just not my thing.' "

Dyson licked her lip, hoping her saliva might help heal the opened wound. "I wandered the grounds a lot. Sometimes with Si or Lochlan, sometimes alone. Niloc lent me a few books, and Si showed me where I could watch some old TV shows. I made him watch a bit of *Remington Steele*. I used to watch that show with my brothers. Si hated it. There is just no accounting for taste."

Dyson brought a hand up to her lip and dabbed at the cut with her sleeve. Though losing this tiny amount of blood wasn't going to make or break her, it punctuated the fact that her body was so weak that it couldn't even heal the smallest of wounds.

"You know it's a myth, the whole technology and Magic thing. They work perfectly well together. There still wasn't much tech on campus, though. At least not like a normal university would have. No. Niloc wanted us to think of other ways to solve our problems.

"Those years were the quiet before the storm, I think. The time just before my life changed all over again."

Dyson remembered the peace of that time.

No, that's not right, she thought. Not quite peace. Something else.

True peace would not have had that nagging feeling in the back of her mind. That space inside her where something was missing. Something that made her life at Erroin just shy of peaceful.

"Simple," she said. "I long for that simplicity again."

But she knew she'd long for nothing soon enough.

CHAPTER THIRTEEN
2038

A group of giggling teenagers bumped into me as I moved with the rhythm of the crowd.

Had it been just yesterday that Lochlan and I walked unencumbered through these halls?

It was midafternoon. I was nervous about moving through a building with such large windows in daylight. Lochlan told me I'd be fine, but I didn't believe him right away.

"It's Niloc," he'd said. "I swear. He fixes it that way. You think you're the only being that prefers darkness?"

"I wouldn't call it a preference," I'd grumbled.

"You're not so special." He'd shoved me and I'd grinned.

He was right.

All the windows in the school were Magically protected. I wasn't convinced they were windows at all. Sure, if you looked out, you'd see the tree line, and if you looked in, you'd see a hallway full of students, but that wasn't sunlight shining through.

It couldn't be. It didn't feel the same. Not the same as I remembered anyway.

I looked away from the window showing a cloud-covered sky outside to the hallways Lochlan had helped me learn. Or I thought I'd learned them. The cream walls and pale-colored doors all looked the same when the halls were swarmed with students.

I swear Lochlan changed his whole sleeping pattern for me. I was grateful. But now I was lost and continually distracted by the other students.

There were students with wings, and others who hovered inches off the ground. Some had skin that was as blue as a clear sky, and others let off a faint glow. I walked past a boy who was over seven feet tall. He creaked a little when he walked. There was a girl so small and fast that she flitted through the legs of the other students.

And everyone seemed to know each other.

All around me there were hugs, and handshakes, and shrieks of recognition as friends saw one another for the first time since the summer break. Some recapped trips, others listened with a mix of interest and jealousy. And I walked through them, not knowing a soul.

"Hey, Curly," I heard from behind me. I turned. My long brown curls were up in a high ponytail today. "You lost?"

The speaker was a woman who looked to be in her early twenties. She had rich brown skin and short tight black curls. Her blue collared shirt was tucked into dark-washed jeans. The thin belt that snaked around her waist was the same shade of brown as her oxfords.

I liked her immediately.

"Yes," I said. "I'm trying to find Professor Medina, Ancient Egyptian History."

"Medina on your first day, huh?"

The young woman's face held a look of pity that worried me.

"He's bad?" My eyes went wide. "It's an elective. I thought it would be fun."

"Lots of homework." She leaned forward to read my schedule.

I caught her scent when she moved. It was familiar, but I couldn't place it.

"You're in second-year sciences?" she observed. "I'm doing my Specialty. You're in your Primary right?"

"Yes," I said. "Finishing a degree I started a long time ago. I actually have to redo most of it."

"Walk with me." She tilted her head down the hall. "We're going the same way and we have some time. You're Dyson, right?"

"Right." My brows knit together. I couldn't be the only new person in a school this size. "Not many new faces here?"

"Not a lot of new Vampires," she said.

I knew the Vampire population in the world was small. It wouldn't be any different here. Still, I wasn't sure how she'd picked me out on sight. Most people couldn't tell a Vampire from a Human, not unless they were baking in the sun.

"And Lochlan told me about you." She looked me up and down. "Tall mixed girl with big curly hair."

"You know Lochlan." I smiled.

"Yeah," she said. "I've known him for a while but we only became friends about a year ago. He kinda keeps to himself."

"It doesn't surprise me to hear you say that." I ducked a little when someone with sky blue wings whooshed over our heads. It wafted the woman's scent towards me.

"Sanatorum," I snapped my fingers. "Yes, you smell like Tarin, but a little different."

"What?" she halted abruptly. "Who do I smell like?"

"Oh, no one." I'd stopped moving when she did. The students around us bumped and bullied their way past. "A friend of my maker's."

"Tarin—you don't mean Tarinsalus Day?"

"Yes." I looked at her sideways.

"Tarinsalus Day?" she repeated, starting to move again. The traffic we'd created eased.

"Yeah, you know him?"

"Do I know—" she scoffed. "Tarinsalus Day is only the greatest Sanatorum to roam the halls of Erroin Peritia. He is the one who comes to do our final testing and clears us for work in healing."

She was walking a little faster in her excitement. I lengthened my stride.

"Oh." I looked at the woman, then thought of Tarin's small frame and cedar-brown skin.

Sanatorum was a Specialty, I remembered. Not a species. Tarin said he was a kind of Wood Nymph. I wondered why they'd smell similar. It must have something to do with the Magic they learned.

"He comes in once a year to give a lecture and test the potentials," she went on. "The potential Healers." We turned right down a hall that looked identical to the one we'd just left. "You said your maker knows him?"

"Speak of the devil, there he is. Si!" I called down the hall. Sahrias paused, turned, and started walking toward us.

"Hello, Dyson. What class are you off to?" he spoke softly. Too softly for unenhanced ears. He did this sometimes to force me to practice. I picked the words out in the melee with ease, but I was sure my new companion had not.

"Si," I admonished, my eyes flicking to my side and back.

"Indeed, apologies." He waited until he was within Human earshot and repeated the question.

"My first class is Ancient Egyptian History. Sahrias Gillrana, this is— I don't actually know who this is," I said.

"Agatha Roberts," Sahrias extended his hand. "Charmed."

"Likewise." Agatha narrowed her eyes as she shook. "How do you know my name? You aren't a Reader too, are you?"

She released his hand.

"It's rare for a Vampire to have extra abilities," Sahrias said. "Only happens when a Gifter is turned, or a Vampire is cursed, or perhaps when something is gifted by a powerful being."

I thought of his affinity for apples.

"And I, alas," he continued, "was born Human, not Luman."

"So how—" Agatha started to ask, but Si cut her off.

"I have been sent as a spy." Sahrias leaned in conspiratorially. "I am to keep an eye on all the Sanatorums and report back to a friend of mine."

"Oh," Agatha whispered, her dark skin turning chalky.

"I didn't know Tarin was such a big deal around here," I said.

"Yes," Si nodded. "He is quite popular within the Sanatorum Specialty. They get to know him as he lectures here every year, and that particular Specialty is four years long."

"Five, if you plan to apprentice," Agatha said, her voice a little higher-pitched than before. "Which I do," she said in her normal register. "Dr. Vaidya plans to retire from Erroin in a few years. I want to take over. I have already started volunteering in the hospital and she told me if I volunteer and am on the List of Excellence for three years, she'll take me as an apprentice in my fifth."

"That's generous of her," Sahrias said knowingly. "She usually only accepts applications from students who've been on the List for all four years."

Agatha scuffed the ground with her shoe. "I had a bad start."

"But more than made up for it, I've heard," Sahrias said encouragingly. "At any rate, I must be off and I dare say you both have somewhere to be."

"Yes," I nodded.

"It was nice to meet you, Agatha," Sahrias said. He nodded to me and walked away.

"That's your maker?" Agatha asked as we continued down the hall.

"Yeah," I said.

"He's hot."

"He's my dad," I said flatly.

"Oh." Color rushed to her cheeks. "I thought—never mind. Here's your class." She gestured to the door in front of us.

"Thanks." I hadn't been paying attention to where we were going. I looked at the number above the door, then back down to my schedule.

"Can I take you somewhere after class? Introduce you to a few people?"

"Yeah," I said. "I'd like that."

With pale caramel skin and disheveled black hair, Professor Medina's warm tone disguised keen senses. His kind almond-shaped eyes were so ready to pick out the one student who wasn't paying attention and call on them. The first half of the class was a lecture, the second half a discussion.

The small professor paced back and forth in front of us, listening and nodding along when students spoke. I was grateful I'd done the extra reading on social hierarchies of Ancient Egypt when he pointed at me.

By the end of the class, my brain was fried. The discussion was draining but interesting. I'd always loved and romanticized Ancient Egypt. My brothers and I had planned to go. That was part of the reason I'd gotten an ankh tattoo in my Human life.

We never did make the trip.

A wave of sadness swept over me as I walked out into the crowded hallway. I hadn't thought about my brothers in a long time. I tried not to most days.

"Dyson!" I turned to see Agatha jogging up to me. "I thought we were going to meet at your class." She hooked her thumb over her shoulder. "Good thing you're tall or I might've lost you in the crowd."

I raised my eyebrows as a student some seven and a half feet tall walked by. I smelt the faintest hint of cigar smoke as he past.

"Well," Agatha shrugged. "No one is as tall as the Kapre."

"That's a Kapre?" My eyes went wide. "I've never seen one before. I didn't know they were so . . ."

"Sweet-looking?"

"Yeah." I nodded. The boy's eyes were so kind.

"Well," she walked down the hall and I followed her. "They all communicate with nature, and that type are always gentler than others. They can hide their gifts pretty well when they want to."

I nodded.

"You okay?" she asked.

"Sorry I didn't wait," I said. "I was a little distracted."

"No problem." Agatha waved away my apology. "Medina can do that to the best of us. This one year I had him for a class on the Ottoman Empire. I don't even know why I took it. It was an elective."

Agatha told me about a harrowing semester she'd spent as Medina's favorite student to question. "I learned so much that semester because I was terrified of not knowing the answer when he called on me."

"I've decided that I will hide in the back of his class," I said.

"Good luck," she snorted.

"This one guy went on and on about how important Ankhians were to the Ancient Egyptians. Medina kept saying this was a Human history class, not a Luman one. A few other students got into it too. The most I know about Ankhians is the ankh I have." I held up my right wrist. "I don't know how deeply they're connected."

"I didn't think Vampires could get tattoos," Agatha mused.

"I was Human when I got it," I said. I didn't want to spiral back into thinking about my family so I changed the subject. "You had class?"

"I was volunteering in the hospital. We're headed to the library. It's just here," she said, pointing down a long hallway.

"Woah," I stared at a girl whose skin was glowing.

"You get over it," Agatha shrugged. "All the different beings. She's an angel—or part angel, I guess. 'Seraph' is the classification."

"Angels exist?" I raised my eyebrows.

Agatha nodded.

"Not in the way they're written, but they're real."

"Cool," I said.

"If you say so." She shrugged again.

We were at a large set of doors that read "Aatmyaagan Library." Agatha reached forward for the huge bronze handle, but she paused when I asked my next question.

"Why do I feel like you don't like Seraphs? Am I to assume that not all angels are good and not all Demons are bad?"

"At the end of the day," Agatha smiled and pulled open the doors, "we're all just people."

CHAPTER FOURTEEN
2038

I'd gone to university when I was Human. There was a campus bar where people gathered and a library where students studied—but nothing quite like this.

I felt a slight breeze lift my hair as we walked through the doors, and sound exploded around me.

"Welcome to the Fifth Floor," Agatha said with her arms out, walking backwards a few steps into the enormous room. "Its actual name is the Aatmyaagan Library, but no one calls it that."

Worn brown leather armchairs and couches lined the walls. Two long rows of tables took up the empty space that wasn't occupied by a circular café bar in the middle of the "library."

It was more like a colosseum, though only three levels. I glanced up at the floor above. I could only imagine there were more couches, tables, meeting rooms and study spaces, just like on this level. My eyes moved up further, past the third level to the glass ceiling showing a dark night sky.

If that's real glass, I'll have to avoid this place in daylight.

And the noise. How could anyone focus? Wait a minute, Fifth Floor? I looked around again. Why is it called the Fifth Floor when—

"There are only three floors in here," I said. "We're on the ground floor of the school. The building only has four floors."

"We're not on the ground floor, and don't think about it too hard," Agatha said, leading me around a row of tables and away from the bar in the middle of the space. Shiny espresso makers gleamed behind the baristas.

We walked passed the café, and on my left I saw an old-school library index-card cabinet, with a lineup of waiting students.

"No one knows why this place is nicknamed the Fifth Floor," Agatha said. "I heard a theory once that it was because there's a secret fifth floor of the school, and the entrance is in the library somewhere. I don't know anyone who's found it."

My eyes, still roving around the space, stopping again at the card-index as my brain caught up to what I was seeing.

A card-index? It's 2038 and this place has got a card-index?

"It's Magic," Agatha said, following my eyes. "The index absorbs energy from the sun, and the excess Magic in the air. You search the catalogue by asking it for what you want."

"Woah," I said. If it absorbed energy from the sun, the windows above were real, and that meant no library in daylight for me.

My eyes lifted and saw a piece of paper and a pen fly from one side of the second level to the other. "Asante," was shouted from one side, and "karibu," from the other.

The place hummed with power. It was different than the rest of the school.

Students weren't allowed to use their abilities in the halls, and only in class when given express permission. Technology had similar rules.

Not here. Maybe part of the reason was to power the index. Spark was thick in the air. I inhaled deeply, taking in the scent of Magic flowing around me. Computers were open, and watches were projecting screens and keyboards all over the library as students worked, and talked, and—

Oh. Get a room!

I looked away from a couple not quite hidden in a corner, before I followed Agatha through tables and couches to a small nook in the back. The student population thinned out the further we got from the center hub. Sound quieted as she led me back behind a few bookshelves to a small opening. Pockets of "study areas" lined the edges of the space. Some of the gatherings were surrounded by a shimmering bubble. I eyed them, confused.

"Silence," Agatha said, following my eyes. "Inside the bubble, it's quiet."

"Huh." We walked to a small group sitting in an unbubbled study area.

"Hey, guys," Agatha said. They all looked up.

"Dyson." Lochlan raised a hand. He was sitting on a pile of cushions that only slightly resembled a chair. "You found where all the cool kids hang out."

"Cool kids?" Agatha said.

"I was led here." I nodded to Agatha, who had settled herself on an empty loveseat beside Lochlan's cushion pile.

"Who here do you think is cool, Loch?" Agatha asked.

His eyes flicked across the circle and to the ground.

"Let's pretend I didn't ask," she muttered so quietly I don't think anyone else heard her.

Lochlan adjusted the chain around his neck and the stone around my own neck seemed to buzz in response. I reached for it, but the feeling was gone as soon as it had come.

"This is Nemo Alkevic," Lochlan said, introducing me to the two people in the group I didn't know. "And his sister Zemila."

Zemila removed the large book from her lap and stood. Her long wavy hair cascaded in a dark curtain over her shoulders. She extended a hand.

"Hello," she said. "I am Zemila."

She was stunning. Olive-toned skin, full lips, and bright eyes. She was tall, lean, and carried what little extra weight she had in all the right places. I shook her hand, and tried to place her thick East European accent.

"Dyson Blake," I said. "Nice to meet you."

Strong handshake, I noted before mentally chiding myself for expecting otherwise.

"Nemo," Zemila said to her brother. "Nemo."

He was leaning over the arm of his chair staring at a girl in the adjacent study area. No, not staring.

"He looks preoccupied," I observed.

His hand was moving like he was drawing, though he had no pen and paper. Across the room a girl giggled and tucked a piece of midnight-blue hair behind her ear. She was looking down at her own pen and paper as the pen moved by itself.

Huh… he's Telekinetic.

I focused on the paper across the library. I was able to see the sketch of her he was drawing in the top right-hand corner of her notebook.

He's Telekinetic, and a flirt.

"Bože," Zemila said under her breath and rolled her eyes.

She lifted her palm up and I saw a small pebble rise off the ground. She flicked her fingers and the pebble flew toward Nemo, hitting him in the back of the head.

"Aoww," Nemo said. The pen in front of the girl across the room dropped. She looked over at him to see why he'd stopped.

"Zemi, what the hell—oh. Hello," he said, noticing me for the first time and standing.

Hello to you too, gorgeous.

He had the same dark hair and ever-tanned looking skin as his sister. And he was tall. Really tall.

"Nemo Alkevic, pleasure to meet you," he said smoothly.

Weird. No accent at all.

"Hi." I shook his hand. "I'm Dyson."

"Hi," he said in what I assumed was his seductive voice. Then he winked at me.

"Did you just wink?" I asked and pointed at my own chest. "At me?"

"I, ahhh." He deflated and Zemila turned a laugh into a cough at a sharp look from her brother.

"No, no," I said. "Do you, baby. If that's your thing, you wink all you want."

I turned my head slightly and gave him an over exaggerated open-mouthed wink. Nemo laughed a little and seemed to relax.

"He is not used to women who do not like his winking," Zemila said, though "winking" came out more like "vinking."

"Oh, and you just love it when guys don't fall all over you," he retorted in unaccented English.

Zemila pouted, crossed her arms over her considerable chest and sat back down in her chair. It was adorable. I was sure men fell at her feet.

"Yeah, that's what I thought," her brother said.

"Always bickering." Lochlan closed his book and smiled at Zemila.

"Loch's right," Agatha waved for me to sit beside her.

"We do not." Nemo flopped down and picked up his cross-library flirting.

"Yes," Zemila said. "We do."

Nemo scoffed. Agatha and Lochlan both gave me a significant look. I smiled at them before letting my eyes roam over this part of the library. We were under an overhang of the floor above, where the walls were lined with alternating bookshelves and study spaces.

"Where does that hall lead?" I asked, looking over Lochlan's shoulder to an archway between two book cases.

"It's the student tunnel. Plastered with photos," Lochlan said. "It's all right. Nothing special."

"Don't lie," Agatha said.

"Truth." Lochlan nodded once. "It doesn't interest me."

Over the weeks before classes started, I'd noticed that Lochlan was a bit of a stickler for the things he liked. He knew what they were and spent little time on anything else. Like it was all old hat. Like the world bored him.

"Okay, but what is it?" I asked.

"Come on," Agatha said. "I'll show you,"

"I am coming also." Zemila jumped up from her armchair. "I need a study pause. Break," she corrected with a look at Lochlan. He nodded at her.

"Study break," he confirmed and returned his eyes to his work.

"Study break," Zemila repeated. Lochlan snuck another glance at her, then seemed to refocus on his book.

Agatha waited at the mouth of the Student Tunnel for me and Zemila to catch up. Zemila skipped through the archway and down the hall. The overhead lighting turned on as she went. It bounced off her long dark hair.

Motion-sensor pot lights? Seems pretty pedestrian for a Magic school.

Zemila waved an arm ahead of her, more lights came on, and she started to search the wall of photos. Hundreds and hundreds of photos.

"Wow," I said, overwhelmed with the images covering every inch of the walls and rounded ceilings, leaving only the pot lights free.

Three young girls playing double Dutch. A boy surrounded by books in a high-backed chair with his friend standing behind him. Two men, holding hands and walking through the front doors of the school.

"It is gone," I heard Zemila say from down the hall. "My favorite one. It is gone."

She put her hands on her hips and her perfect eyebrows knit together.

"Which one?" Agatha asked, walking over to see the gap in the photos.

I followed and saw a clear rectangle where a picture had been. The faded images around had odd bits still bright where the missing photo had protected them.

"It was a man and woman. He had dark hair to here." She put her hand to her jaw. "It had waves and he had dark skin, like—" She paused.

"Like me?" Agatha asked.

"No, more like Niloc," she said.

"Indian?" I thought aloud. Like Si.

"Da, he was Indian, and I think the woman was from Egipat?"

"Egypt?" I asked.

"Da," Zemila said again. "Egypt. The woman is laughing, looking down, I do not know at what. The man, he is smiling and looking at her like, like . . ."

She trailed off and sighed with a dreamy look in her eyes.

"Pull it together, Mila," Agatha laughed.

"Oh, ne, you stop." Zemila shoved Agatha lightly. "It is a beautiful picture and all I want is to be looked at like that."

"Please, Mila!" Agatha chided. "Every boy in here looks at you like that. I wouldn't mind a quarter of the attention you get."

Zemila scoffed.

"My favorite's over here." Overhead lights turned on as Agatha led us deeper down the tunnel. "See this one? I think she looks like me. I don't know much about my history, but I like to think maybe these people were my distant family."

I pulled on my knowledge of American history and tried to place the photo in time. Over a span of more than fifty years, some six million Black Americans migrated up and out of the Jim Crow South. They left their southern rural homes with the dream of better economic prospects, and equality in the North. Some found it. Some didn't.

Many still fought for the right to not have their skin seen as a weapon.

The photo of a large family looked like it could have been taken in that period. They stood together, hats on their heads and coats over their shoulders. There were three children and a few suitcases in front of the group.

Early 1920s, maybe?

"The Great Migration," Agatha said, confirming my thought. "I think."

"I think so too. This woman," I pointed to someone in the back row of the photo. "Your eyes."

"Yes . . ." Her smile was broad. "I was adopted. I love my parents; my mama is a Healer too. But I don't look like them."

"Have you tried to find out who these people are?" I lightly touched the photo to see how it was adhered to the wall. "Maybe there is some information on the back."

"I didn't want to ruin it, trying to take it down, so I got Jose, he can see through things, to look for me. He said it's blank."

"Too bad." My eyes moved over the other photos.

I noticed another spot where a picture had been newly removed. Like Zemila, I'm sure every student has their favorite. And I'm sure some of those favorites go missing.

"The past is a simple place to live," Dyson said from her seated position on the floor. She leaned back against the wall beside a fully intact desk drawer.

Reaching her hand into a pocket of her dress, she pulled out a laminated photo. Dyson knew exactly why Zemila had loved it.

"Zemila said she wanted what the couple in the picture had. She didn't know what she was asking for. But I'm getting ahead of myself again," she said, gazing at the people in the photo. "They do look happy, don't they?"

Dyson looked up.

"But you know exactly how much they love each other, don't you?" She waited for a response, but received only silence. "After I understood the scope of what she'd done—not just to him, but to the world—after I'd learned how ruthless she'd been, how many lives she'd destroyed, I'd look at this picture and I'd see love in her eyes.

"Anyway." She tucked the old photograph back into a small pocket. "Sahrias was right. University was a great place to make friends.

"I assumed the first day I met them, that Nemo and Zemila were both Telekinetic." Dyson picked through the drawer as she spoke. "Zemila was something a little different. I didn't learn the extent until years later. Neither did she. But Nemo—"

She sighed and shook her head.

Poor guy, she thought. Hurt people hurt people and his father was a real son of a bitch.

"I knew someone who was similarly Gifted," Dyson said. "To Zemila, I mean. You knew him too. Or at least one of your followers did. Gideon."

It hadn't been so long ago that she'd been fighting side by side with him. She missed those days. The small team of rebels she'd had then. She missed Nemo, and Agatha, and the rest of them too.

"The past is a simple place to live," she said again. "You already know what's going to happen."

CHAPTER FIFTEEN
2038

"I will not miss catching you and Dean on our—" Si put extra stress on the word "our," "couch every time I come into the apartment."

I scoffed and put a box of books on my desk at the back of my new dorm room.

"You'll miss me, though, right?" I asked. He raised an eyebrow. "And it was one time!"

"It was at least three times." Sahrias moved the box from the desk to the floor in front of my bookshelf. "I don't know why you insist on not putting things away." He started moving the books from the box to my shelf.

"Sue me." I flopped down on my new bed. "And I'm not seeing Dean anymore. He broke up with me two weeks ago. Thanks for noticing."

"You sure go through them quickly, don't you?" he asked.

"Excuse you!" I lifted myself up onto my elbows and glared at him.

"Isn't that five in as many months?" he asked, keeping his eyes on the book shelf.

"What?" I sat up all the way. "First, who are you? The Patriarchy Patrol? Chairman of Chastity? If I was a guy—"

"Dyson, you know very well I didn't—"

"Second, I have had exactly one boyfriend since I got here, and I'd barely call him that. Dean and I were seeing each other for two months."

"Well, if you don't call it that, what would you call it?" Sahrias muttered.

I ignored him. "And third, how the hell did you get to five? Who are the other four?"

"You know the one," he said, pausing with a copy of *Rafe: A Buff Male Nanny* halfway to a spot on the shelf. He squinted at it, read the title, then looked at me.

"It was actually pretty good," I said.

"The one with the hair."

"The book with the hair?" I asked.

"No, the boy you were seeing." He put the romance novel on the shelf. "With the hair."

"Wow," I said, sarcasm dripping off the word. "Your descriptive vocabulary is immeasurable."

"The one with the long silver hair."

"Tobin," I said. "We went on one date. We hung out one time. He was kind of boring."

"And Lochlan," Si said. "I thought when you got here you started, ahh . . . seeing him."

I narrowed my eyes.

"I thought people got wiser with age."

He smirked and flung a book at me. I caught it easily, as he'd meant me to.

"Lochlan is so stupidly infatuated with Zemila, he wouldn't notice another girl if she was naked in his bed."

Si looked at me with obvious skepticism.

"Really," I said, my tone flat. "And even with," I put the next part in air quotes. " 'The one with the hair' and Lochlan. That makes three. Who are four and five?"

He turned away from me and continued to shelve books.

"Perhaps it was only three. And Dean."

"One," I corrected. "Dean was the only one that counted."

"Well, you know if you ever bothered to introduce me to your friends, I wouldn't have to make these assumptions."

Oh, that's what this is really about.

Sahrias rose from his squatting position and piled the now empty box with the others by the door.

"Was there anything else that had to come over?" he asked.

"Nothing I can't get later," I said.

Si looked from me to the fully packed suitcase at the foot of my bed.

"I was gonna do it laterrrr," I whined, dragging out the "r" just to annoy him. He rolled his eyes and I grinned.

"Why don't we do it now?" he asked. "Then, 'laterrrr,' when you get back from Roswell's, you won't be scrambling to find pajamas."

Roswell's. The campus bar. It wasn't actually on campus, you had to take a portal to get there, but it was the closest Luman bar to the school.

"Let's go," Si said.

I huffed out a breath, got off my bed, and started unpacking. "You just want to come and see who I'm dating."

"So, you are dating someone." He gave me a wicked grin.

I wanted to ask who he was "dating," but I knew that was a non-starter. It always was. The few times I had tried to get any information out of him in Paris, or Istanbul, he'd clammed up. I figured he was still hung up on this Rayyan person. But it must have been years and years since they'd seen each other.

I'd asked Niloc about it.

"I'm sorry, Dyson," Niloc had said. "But that is not my story to tell. He'll tell you when he is ready. She broke his heart, and they were together for a very long time."

A long time. But how long? Did they meet here at Erroin? Before?

I knew Sahrias had been here for at least sixty-five years, and at some point, they had been here together.

"Who were you just thinking about?" Si said, interrupting my thought process. "Can I meet him?"

I scoffed.

"You really don't want to," I said.

His eyes went wide.

"There is someone new?" he asked.

"What has gotten into you?" I laughed and fit a hanger into the crew neck of a dark green sweater. "Am I your favorite soap opera or something?"

"You have no idea," he muttered. I took the sweater off the hanger and threw it in his direction. It hit him, but only because he let it.

"What if you just come to Roswell's and meet my friends?"

Sahrias opened his mouth to answer, but was interrupted by a knock on the door.

"Hello," said a thick Irish accent. "May I—"

"Come on in, Loch," I said. "I'm just trying to convince Si to come with us tonight."

"Excellent idea," Lochlan said. "We can play Pyramid Pong with even teams."

"Play what?" Si asked.

"It's easier to explain while you're playing," I told him.

"That is a horrible lie," Lochlan said.

"He deserves it," I muttered. "He didn't know that Dean broke up with me, and he thought we," I motioned between me and Lochlan, "were sleeping together."

Lochlan's eyes went wide, then he burst out laughing and collapsed on my bed.

"Ho, ho," Sahrias said. "Very funny."

"You're great and all, Dyson," Lochlan said. "But—"

"Don't even finish that sentence," I ordered. Lochlan nodded and wisely changed the subject.

"This is a pretty nice room." He stood from the bed and looked around. "Why did it take so long for you to get it?"

"I was dragging my feet." I looked at Sahrias. "I wasn't sure I was ready to live alone."

"Dyson," Lochlan said. "You live in a school of over two thousand students."

"This is what I have been telling her," Si agreed. "She still doesn't live alone."

"Well!" I protested. "Whatever."

Lochlan slow clapped at me. "Amazing comeback. Very dignified."

I stuck my tongue out. What I wasn't saying was that I hated change, and I hated being alone. But I knew I had to get over that. I had gotten over a lot, and living on my own again wouldn't be that big of a deal. It would be better . . . or at least that's what I kept telling myself.

"You two ready to go?" Lochlan asked. "The others are already through the portal."

I stood next to Sahrias and Lochlan in front of a circle of flowing blue and black space. The portal. The doorway that led directly into the campus bar in a small city some two hundred kilometers away.

The first time I'd used it, I almost puked. It gave you kind of a flipping whooshing sensation. The trick was to breathe at the right moment. Sahrias took in a deep breath and stepped through. Lochlan went next, then it was my turn. I breathed in, walked forwards, and exhaled as I stepped through the portal. I felt the slight flip of my stomach.

"I cannot believe you're just meeting everyone now," I heard Lochlan say to Si when I exited the portal. The sounds of the busy bar drifted down the hallway in front of us.

"I met Agatha once," he said as the three of us walked towards the light and sound of Roswell's. "I think there are only a couple more in your group, no?"

"My roommate and his sister," Lochlan nodded just as a pair of sprites zipped around us as we entered the main bar.

"There." Lochlan pointed over the sea of students to Agatha and Zemila before peeling off to find Nemo. Booths and some old arcade games lined one wall. We made our way around a few pool tables and over to the bar.

"Hey, girl," Agatha said. She hugged me and whispered in my ear. "Oh my god, you brought your maker, he is so h—"

"He can hear you! He can hear you!" I squeaked.

"Hello, Agatha," Sahrias said smoothly. She flushed with embarrassment. "Nice to see you again. And you must be Zemila." He extended a hand. "The Earth Driver I've heard so much about."

"Hi." Zemila sounded surprised. She stood from her barstool and shook his hand.

"We've heard about you too," Zemila said. "But Dyson never wanted to share."

I snorted.

"Si is too busy for me these days," I said.

"Please," he smirked. "Other way around. Since she's met all of you, I have barely seen her. And now that she has her own room—"

"Finally," Agatha said, throwing up her hands. "She can stop hooking up with Dean on my couch."

"You too, huh?" Si muttered at the same time as I said, "I have done no such thing! And he broke up with me. Is he here? I hope he's not here."

"He's here," Zemila said. "But you don't have to talk to him."

"True." I turned to say something to Lochlan, before remembering he'd gone off to join Nemo. I spotted him across the room chatting with a small group. Dean was there. He was tall with warm ivory skin, classic good looks, and a killer smile.

He was gorgeous. Painfully my type. I wanted to want him.

My pride was hurt more than anything. He said he broke up with me because I didn't really seem into it. He was right.

"Nemo is over there with Lochlan," I said to Sahrias. Nemo had an arm wrapped around the waist of his on-and-off girlfriend, Nianca, and

Lochlan was following his regular protocol of avoiding Zemila as much as possible in public settings.

So weird. I have to ask him about that sometime.

"Let's get a drink and play Pyramid Pong," Agatha suggested.

"I don't want to talk to—" I started.

"You didn't even like Dean that much," Agatha said. "Why do you care?"

"We wouldn't have even numbers if he played anyway." I shrugged. I saw Si scan the bar. "Looking for someone?"

"An old friend," he said. "I just wondered if he still worked here. His family owns the bar. I'm sure I'll see him around."

"Yes!" I pumped my fist in the air as Si sunk the last ping pong ball. It was a beautiful shot. Off the table, narrowly missed by Nemo's lax defense and into the last red cup on the table. Nianca had sidled up to Nemo at exactly the right moment for us.

"Killer shot," Zemila said, putting up her hand for a high five.

Sahrias smiled and obliged.

"I hardly think it's fair to have two Vampires on the same team," Nemo protested.

"You're Telekinetic," Lochlan said, smiling even though his team had just lost.

"Yeah," Agatha glared, her eyes moving to Nianca. "You just need better focus."

"Another round?" Nemo asked.

"I think I'd better leave you," Sahrias smiled. "Perhaps your companion can take my place."

"No!" Zemila said, before she could stop herself. "I mean, sure . . ."

We all knew Nianca was as bad at Pyramid Pong as Zemila was competitive. Zemila swallowed hard, then said, "Nianca, would you like to play on our team?"

If looks could kill.

Nianca shot daggers at Zemila, then she said to Nemo, "Babe, let's go get a drink."

His face fell. He was competitive too.

"Let's re-convene in a few minutes," I said, then I turned to Si. "I'll walk you to the portal."

I smiled at Lochlan who knew exactly why I was taking this opportunity to get away. Zemila was about to get into it with Nemo, Nianca, or both.

"Good luck," I mouthed to Lochlan as I walked past him. He scowled at me.

"I like your friends," Sahrias said as we walked away. "They are good for you. You seem happier. More present."

"I am happier," I said. "I feel like I have purpose again. School is good for that. But I'm—" I broke off, both not knowing how to articulate my feelings and not knowing if I should.

"What is it?" he asked.

It was quieter once we got into the hall leading to the portal. We walked slowly, shoulder to shoulder.

"I'm happy," I said. "Really happy. I just feel a little . . . disconnected? Does that make sense?"

"You've only known these people for four months, Dyson. Rome wasn't built in a day. A lasting friendship is no different."

I nodded. He was right, of course. But I didn't think that was it. I was getting more and more homesick in a way I couldn't explain. I was happier than I'd been in decades but for some reason, I felt pulled away. I wasn't even sure to where.

I didn't understand it.

"Dyson," he said, snapping me out of my reverie. We stood in front of the portal. "Give this all some time. We will be here for a little while. Enjoy the friends you have. Enjoy this," he waved back to the bar. "There are few places in this world where we can truly be ourselves."

"I'm starting to get that," I said, knowing part of the reason I'd been so happy was that I didn't have to lie to the people around me.

"Shall we hunt tomorrow?" he asked.

"Sure," I said. "But I'll come by your place. You don't have to come wake me up."

"I wouldn't dream of it," he grinned. "I've walked in on your escapades enough as it is."

"Shut it." I shoved him.

He pulled me to his side, kissed my temple, and walked through the portal.

I stood there for a moment, looking into the portal's swirling depths. Then I turned and walked slowly down the hall, thinking about my new friends and what Sahrias had said. I knew he was right. I knew I needed time. Being away from the world for so long, then being thrown into a highly social interactive environment would give anyone whiplash.

"Marty's shift just started," Agatha said as soon as I slid into the booth beside her. "He was asking about you."

"He was not," I said, rolling my eyes. I looked over to the bar. To say that Marty was lanky would be an understatement. I watched as he elongated his arm to deliver a pint to a girl five feet away from him. "Marty flirts with everybody."

"That may be true, but he was asking about you," Agatha said.

The last thing I wanted was to start something with someone who worked at a place I frequented. Then a thought occurred to me.

Maybe his family knew Sahrias? If that was the case, I would definitely be keeping Marty on my platonic list. Si was nosy enough as it was.

"What are we talking about?" I asked, trying to direct the conversation away from Marty.

"Zemila wants to go to Ireland," Lochlan said, eyes bright.

"One of the many places I wish to go when I am finished school," she clarified.

"But you're not done for a while." Nemo plopped down next to Lochlan.

"Where's Nianca?" Zemila sneered. I hid a smile and intentionally did not make eye contact with Agatha or Lochlan. Zemila and Nianca's distaste for each other was hilarious and made absolutely no sense. Zemila's frustration at how funny we found it was equally hilarious, but I thought she'd been tested enough for one night. I schooled my features.

"You two need to work out whatever your problem is with each other," Nemo said. "I'm not getting into it."

Zemila squinted at him.

"Sahrias seems cool," Nemo said to me, ignoring his sister. "He didn't want to stay, huh?"

"No," I said. "He had fun, though. He likes you guys."

"He's probably like, fifteen hundred years old, Nemo," Agatha said. "I don't know that he finds Pyramid Pong as interesting as we do."

"Older than that, I think," I said, and Agatha's mouth fell open.

"Mayhap he loves it," Lochlan said. "Just because you're old doesn't mean you don't like new things."

"Not like you, huh?" Nemo shoved him, and laughed. "You hate new things. You might as well be fifteen hundred years old."

Lochlan rolled his eyes and sipped his beer. Zemila poured me a glass and slid it across the table. It didn't taste the same as it used to, but I was ecstatic that I could participate in this part of social interaction.

"Remember that picture that used to be in the Students Tunnel?" Zemila said. "The one of that couple and the guy is—"

"Yes," Agatha said. "We all know you're obsessed with that picture and will murder whoever stole it."

"I think it was Sahrias," Zemila looked at me. "In the picture, I mean."

I blinked at her.

"I think it was him," she repeated.

"What?" I said.

Agatha closed her eyes, and Zemila looked from Lochlan to Nemo.

"Don't look at me," Nemo said. "I only saw it once. I don't remember."

"I don't know that I ever saw it," Lochlan said. "Just heard you talk about it . . ."

"Ad nauseum." Nemo finished Lochlan's sentence.

"Aye," Lochlan laughed and met Zemila's eyes. "Ad nauseum."

Sparks basically flew through the air between them. Then Lochlan blinked and looked away and, as per usual, we all pretended we didn't notice.

"Maybe," Agatha said, eyes still closed. "Yeah, it totally could have been him."

"It was a while ago, and maybe I'm remembering the picture differently now, but—" Zemila turned to me. "How long ago was he here? The picture looked like it was from the nineteen twenties, maybe earlier."

"I don't know," I said. "But he was here for a long time."

"I wonder who the woman was," Zemila asked. "She obviously isn't in his life anymore, right?"

"I haven't met too many of his friends," I said.

"Who could she be?" Agatha wondered aloud.

Rayyan. It must have been Rayyan.

"Rayyan," Dyson said, looking at her wrist. Her gaze moved from the small ankh tattoo to her finger tips. She closed her eyes and tried to focus. Nothing happened. "I don't even know what I'm trying to do."

She knew she didn't have the energy for much other than survival right now. She let her hand fall to the floor and her eyes went back to the ruined desk.

Nothing there.

"I really can't describe the next three years of my life in any other way but . . . normal. It was so normal. Pedestrian. I went to my classes, I went to Roswell's, I hung out with my friends. I worked with some of the kids in the Shine House. I traveled a bit in the summers. It was so simple."

I loved it, she thought. I miss it.

"I never went home, though. No matter how much I missed Toronto. The first summer, I took some make-up classes. The next, Si took me to Russia. One year we just stayed at the school and toured around the country side. Lochlan always stayed. He barely left the grounds.

"It wasn't until my last year, my last eighteen months at Erroin that things started to get—"

She cut off and adrenaline filled her body. Her eyes snapped to a large mirror frame, glass now broken, revealing the wood and stone backing.

She'd heard something from behind it. A small sound. Just an intake of breath.

Dyson squinted at the edges of the frame and noticed a pair of well-hidden hinges. The frame started to open.

"Interesting."

CHAPTER SIXTEEN
2041

"Ethics," I said to the students. "If you aren't supposed to be in Primary Ethics, year one, then you're in the wrong room."

My hands felt clammy as I set my bag on the desk at the front of my very first class. Looking up at the three-tiered seating, I saw a couple people quickly pick up their books and hurry to the door.

"Okay," I breathed. There were sixteen students. I knew a few of them from working in the Shine House. Most were new faces.

"I assume you are all in the right spot. My name is Dyson Blake. We are going to start with a simple exercise and end with a discussion." I walked in front of the podium, forgoing a physical soapbox. "Can someone tell me what ethics is, what it means?" I looked over the group. "And please give your name when you answer."

A couple hands went up.

"Ethics is the philosophy of right and wrong," said a sixteen-year-old boy.

"And your name, Haiden?" I smiled. Haiden moved into the Shine House when he was twelve. His parents thought he was going to grow out of his talking-to-animals phase.

He didn't.

Haiden was lucky. There was a Luman living in his neighbourhood. A Telepath. Once she realized what was going on, she spoke to his parents and connected them with Niloc.

Most kids like him weren't lucky.

"Haiden." He rolled his eyes at me.

"Does anyone disagree?" I waited for a beat. "No? Good. Neither do I. What is right and wrong?" When no one raised their hand to answer, I added, "Just take a guess—what's right and wrong? Yes?"

I pointed at a girl around Haiden's age in the front. Another one I knew from the Shine House. Luci looked like a chestnut-colored doll, right down to the sparkly pink heels that perfectly matched her freshly painted nails. I could smell the polish.

"It depends," said the girl. I blinked slowly at her, waiting, until she said, "And I'm Luci."

"Okay," I nodded. "Does anyone disagree with Luci? Yes?"

"Saad," said a boy with a green tint to his skin and hair the color of damp earth. "It depends for some things, but not for all things."

"Can you give me an example, Saad?" I asked. "An example of a universal truth? Meaning that something is always true no matter the circumstances."

There was the scratching of pen to paper at my definition.

Human universities might be filled with Intelliglass desks or watch-projected keyboards, but not here. Though technology had taken over the

Human world, and the Luman world too, I could understand why Niloc insisted students took notes with pen and paper.

"It is wrong to kill people," Saad said.

Immediately, four hands shot into the air. I smiled.

An hour and twenty minutes later, I put away the chalk and packed up the textbook and papers I'd used throughout the class. The second half of the class was an open discussion. It had gotten pretty heated.

"Of course, it was the two Seraphs that were having it out," I muttered to myself thinking of how close Ezekiel and Luci had come to throwing spells at each other. I was all too familiar with the damage Luci could do when she wanted to. The common room of the Shine House had been put back together many a time after Luci had gotten upset.

"Excuse me," said a deep southern drawl from behind me. "Ma'am?"

"Come on in," I said without looking up.

I hope this kid didn't hear me talking to myself. Man, I corrected when I turned to look at his broad shoulders and tall frame. Enormous man.

"What can I do for you?" I asked.

"Are you Dyson Blake?"

"I am," I said. "And you are?"

"Duke, umm, D-Duncan James, Ms. Blake."

"Hi, Duke. 'Dyson' is fine." His huge, well-muscled shoulders relaxed when I used his nickname.

"Professor Medina said you were the person to see if I needed a tutor for a history class?" he asked running a big hand through his blond hair.

"Did he say anything else? Maybe that I was his favorite student?"

Duke gave me a closed mouth smile, but didn't answer.

Wow, lady killer.

"What year? And you're new, I guess?"

"Yeah" he said again, shuffling his feet. "I'm twenty-six, but I just heard about this place, so I'm in my first year Primary. The class is History of the British Empire."

He held the straps of his backpack and hunched over.

For a big man he sure manages to make himself seem small. I wonder what happened to him. I wonder when he lost his confidence.

"So, what do I get out of it?" I put my books in my bag, stood, and swung my navy-blue backpack over my shoulders.

"Excuse me?" A bit of color left his face and he sunk in on himself even more.

"I'll tutor you, sure." I led the way out of the empty classroom and into the bustling hall. All the 7:30 to 9 p.m. classes were letting out and the hall way was full of students. "But if you're learning from me, then I want to learn something from you too."

"Oh, Ms. Blake, I'm not that good at anything. Not good enough to teach it."

"I'm sure you'll think of something," I said, then waved to Agatha who was weaving through the students toward me. She looked a little dazed. "Call me Dyson," I said. "We can meet tomorrow around eight?"

"Yes ma'am." Duke looked down at the books in his huge hands. "Ms. Bl—"

"Dyson," I corrected.

"Dyson," he repeated. "I'm not very good at anything. Not here anyway, I used to be but, things changed and, well . . ."

He trailed off.

"We'll meet here," I said, laying a hand on his arm. I waited for him to meet my eyes. "Okay?"

"Thank you, Dyson. See you tomorrow." He turned and walked away.

Agatha came up beside me. "Do you know who that is?"

"Yeah, he wants some help with a history class. His name is Dun—"

"I know what his name is," Agatha hissed.

I squinted at her. She was staring dreamily down the hall at the broad shoulders cutting a path through the melee of students.

"Duncan James," she sighed.

"Should I leave? Are you having a moment?" I smiled.

Agatha blinked.

"Huh? No." She turned to me. "I gave him directions to a class. We started talking. I saw him again a few days later and tried to ask him out. I don't think he noticed." She finished on a sigh and we started walking. "He used to be really into MMA before his Gift mani—"

"Wait." I pulled her to a stop. "He's a fighter?"

"That's what I—"

I took off, weaving in and out of the students, hearing a couple woahs and heys as I blew by almost faster than they could see.

"Mary, mother of God!" Duke jumped when I—to him—materialized at his side. "You startled me."

"You're a fighter." I said it more as an accusation than a question.

"Umm, a while ago . . . I used to be." The slouch was back in his shoulders. "Before I changed—or whatever it's called here."

"I want to learn," I said.

He didn't need to know that the want had manifested about twenty seconds ago. Sahrias had taught me the very basics. I'd never really had a desire to fight, nor, thankfully, had I ever had the need. With Si it was more about control. Learning to not rip people's arms off when I shook their hand, and the like.

But I'd seen this look before, this attitude. The one Duke wore like a coat. The feeling of shame, of worthlessness, of being adrift with no anchor.

I used to feel that way too.

"What?" Duke looked confused.

"I want to learn," I repeated. He squinted at me. "I refuse to tutor you unless you teach me how to fight."

His eyes lit up.

There it is.

"Really?" he said, standing a little taller.

"Oh yeah!" I said excitedly. "I'm a Vampire, though, so I don't know if—"

"I'm a Shifter," he interrupted. "We should be pretty evenly matched, strength-wise."

"We can talk about it more tomorrow," I said.

"Sounds great," he smiled and seemed to grow in energy if not size. "Thanks."

"All right, get out of here." I gave his shoulder a little shove. "I'll see you tomorrow."

He walked away standing taller than he'd been before.

Faster than Dyson thought she could move, she was on her feet and across the room. She pressed herself up against the wall behind the shattered mirror frame as it opened another few inches. She would have cursed herself for not finding and barricading this door too, but then she wouldn't have a meal walking into the room.

Dyson strained her ears to hear how many there were.

One heartbeat, she thought. It's slow. It's too slow. She felt her fangs push free of her gums.

The barrel of a gun peaked around the mirror. A man's face followed it. There was another sharp intake of breath as he no doubt took in the blood and destruction of the room.

Just as the man started to turn, a second before he would have seen her, she slammed her foot into the back of his knees. A shot rang out as he collapsed. His gun skittered across the floor and before he had time to regain his feet, Dyson was behind him. One hand under his chin, pulling up, the other on his shoulder pressing down. She sunk her teeth into the exposed flesh of his neck.

As soon as the hot blood touch her tongue, she spat it out.

It tasted sour, and sharp, and wrong.

"They dosed you," Dyson said, pushing the man, rolling away from him, and getting quickly to her feet. "I should have known."

I should have snapped his neck as soon as he walked in, she thought. And I won't be able to compel any information out of him.

She looked him over. His uniform told her he was a soldier. The color of his jacket told her what side.

"How did you get in here?" the soldier asked, never taking his eyes off her.

"I walked in." Dyson bared her teeth. "Did they not tell you I could do that?"

"Impossible." He moved slowly, stepping over the splintered wood and smashed china on the floor. She did the same. They kept equal distance from each other as they circled. "The barrier is still up, no one can get through."

"The barrier here is weak," Dyson said. "The 'person', " she put extra emphasis on the word, "your barrier is sucking dry to stay up, isn't high enough in their line. And even if they were, I could still get through."

But she was the only one who could. And that's why it had to be her.

God, this would have been so much easier if you weren't dosed, she thought.

She could have fed, healed, and compelled the information about the barrier she needed out of this man. Then she could have called in her own reinforcements. But no.

Nothing can ever be easy, she thought.

"It's not a person," the soldier said. "You're not a person either, and you will die this day." He drew a knife from his belt.

"Am I not already dead?" Dyson asked as they surveyed each other. "Am I not Death itself? Is that not what you all call me?"

If Dyson hadn't been a Vampire, she wouldn't have seen the small shudder that ran over the soldier's body. She scared him. That was good. He would be easier to kill if he was scared.

Easier, she thought. Not easy. Nothing can ever be easy.

He lunged.

CHAPTER SEVENTEEN
2041

"Well, that was exceptionally rude," Agatha said when I reappeared at her side in the busy hall way.

"I caught up to him," I told her.

"You caught up to who?" Agatha started walking with the flow of traffic. Most students were ending their day—some, like me, were in the middle.

"Duke. For lessons. Wanna join?" I smirked.

"I thought you were going to tutor him—Zemila might want to learn—and is there anyone you can't catch up to?" Agatha asked.

"I'm sure there is some speedster Gifter who would leave me in their dust, maybe a Shifter. I used to watch this show about—"

"I'm going to stop you right there." Agatha held up a hand and stopped, causing a bit of traffic in the process. "You're dating yourself, baby. I know exactly what show you're talking about because my parents watched it too."

She smiled but when I looked more closely, she seemed stressed.

"Hey." I pulled her off to the side of the hall and we stood in the doorway of an empty class. "What's going on with you?"

"It's starting." Her eyes were wide.

"This week is your last Trial," I remembered. "I'm sure you'll do fine."

"Fine!" Agatha nearly shouted and started walking again. "I doubt very much that I will be fine. I heard that he got here today," she said over her shoulder to me.

We were headed to Fifth. That was good. Agatha needed a distraction.

"Who's here?" I asked, catching up after getting caught behind a group of teenaged boys walking painfully slowly.

"Tarinsalus Day," she said in an awed voice. "Nemo said he saw him come in last night."

"Tarin is here?" I smiled. "Si didn't tell me."

"Right," Agatha said bitterly. She turned down the hall that led us to the student commons area. "I forgot you two were besties."

"We know each other," I shrugged "That's all. He's Si's friend."

"You said you marathoned *Star Wars* together," Agatha shot back. "How much closer can two people get?"

"Who's dating themselves now?" I mumbled.

"I was born in 2021, Grandma."

"Yeah, yeah, COVID kid," I rolled my eyes. Agatha shoved me, and I saw the beginnings of a real smile push away her worry.

We walked the rest of the way down the busy hall in single file. In a few minutes, we were in our regular corner where Zemila, Nemo, and Lochlan sat studying.

I peered over at Nemo's notebook. He wasn't doing homework. He was sketching. It was a landscape and it was pretty good. Nemo usually drew faces. He usually drew Nianca, but they were on one of their many breaks. I'd seen her at Roswell's with Dean the last time I was there.

Lochlan looked up at us and said, "Aga, here."

He stood up from the couch and moved into one of the chairs.

"Thanks, Loch." Agatha flopped into her favorite spot with a sigh of relief. "You're the best."

I looked at Lochlan, always so considerate, and noticed the bags under his eyes.

"What do you need?" Lochlan asked Agatha.

"More time," she said.

"Ahh, don't we all," he said sagely. "Alas, Time is a fickle mistress not to be toyed with. Not that I even could, come to think of it."

Agatha smiled, sat up and punched him lightly on the arm.

"She's a witch, really," he continued, "Time is. With a capital B, if you're picking up what I'm putting down."

"You're such a goof." Agatha laughed.

I smiled at the running joke, even though it wasn't funny.

All of us at one point or another had wished for more time, less time, enough time, and every time Lochlan said the exact same thing. Time was a fickle mistress, a witch with a capital B.

Though he was a very talented Caster, few had the gift of working time.

"I am amazed—" Zemila didn't look up from her book of English grammar, "—that your brain hasn't turned to mush yet."

Determined to live and work in the United States, Zemila was trying to speak English like an American. I knew Lochlan was helping her, though I had no idea how. Whatever he was doing, it must have been working because his accent was thicker than hers now.

I thought the whole thing was hilarious.

"Seconded," Nemo said, keeping his eyes on his work. "Mush."

"And what is that supposed to mean?" Agatha raised her eyebrows.

I knew exactly what it meant and hid a laugh behind my hand.

"What!" Agatha whirled on me too.

"I just think," Lochlan said in a soothing voice, "we have all watched this show before."

"What show?" Agatha looked from Lochlan to each of us in turn. "What show?"

Zemila looked up and Nemo had a small coughing fit that sounded suspiciously like laughter. Lochlan pressed his lips together, obviously not trusting himself to speak.

"Oh, no, team," I said in my best woe-is-me-Agatha impression. "I'm so behind—I'm not prepared." Nemo stopped trying to hide his laugh. "I only studied seventy-five hours for this interactive."

Lochlan grinned and Agatha's face went stony.

"I'm going to fail. I'm never going to apprentice. My life is ov—Oh!" I said in surprise. I reached out as an imaginary teacher handed back an imaginary test. I took the invisible paper and gasped.

"What's that?" I exclaimed.

Zemila was laughing too. Agatha couldn't help but smile.

"I got the top mark in the class?" I said.

"Oh, shut up." Agatha tried to keep her expression angry.

"No? Not the class?" I continued. "The entire year?"

"That has never happened!" Agatha protested.

"Second year Primary," Nemo said through his laughter. "The Theory of Casting for Healers."

"That's one time!"

"Not the entire year? The entire school!" I went on.

"First year Secondary." It was Zemila this time. "You got such a good mark in your interactive in Modern Medicine for Human and Luman, the Examiner didn't know how to score you."

"The Highest Mark of All-Time Ever Award?" I pretended to accept a trophy and started to fake cry. "Thank you, thank you. I have no words. But I do have this thirty-five-page paper."

"I get it," Agatha rolled her eyes. "I know I'll be fine. I'm just worried."

"Of course, you are," Lochlan said. "We all understand that you too are a fickle mistress."

He barely got the words out before he succumbed to laughter again. Agatha finally broke her resolve and laughed too.

I felt a familiar presence come into the library and heard the small shriek of a girl near the door.

"Feeling better?" I asked. The presence grew closer and I couldn't help but smile wider. "Ready to face anything?"

"Ready to face the world!" Agatha said triumphantly.

"Good," I said, at the same time Nemo said, "Holy . . ." and Zemila dropped the book she was holding.

"What?" Agatha asked. Lochlan stared wide-eyed over her shoulder. Agatha slowly turned. "No. Freaking. Way."

"Dyson," squeaked a voice. "Deary, you don't call, you don't write! What do I have to do to get a letter from you?"

"Oh, just save my life," I said, standing from the couch and kneeling down to say hello to Tarin.

"I never did that," he scoffed. "And don't just kneel there!" His small arms were open for the hug he knew I was about to give him.

"Hi," I said. "I've missed you."

"Quite!" he squeaked and pulled away. His pale green eyebrows always seemed bushier than in my memory, even though I saw him once a year.

"Of course, you missed me," he said. "Si is much more fun when I'm around."

"That's painfully true," I nodded. "Come, I'll introduce you to my friends."

Though Tarin came to the school once a year, no one had met him. Agatha was always too scared, Nemo and Zemila were too, and Lochlan . . . was very Lochlan about it. I had no idea why.

Agatha stuttered and her dark cheeks turned pink when Tarin said her reputation preceded her. She was so flustered she made a half-squeak, half-cough sound, then muttered something about studying and ran out of the library.

Nemo and Zemila were calmer, but neither of them knew if they should stand to shake Tarin's hand as a sign of respect or stay seated so they weren't towering over him.

Lochlan took a knee before Tarin and lowered his head. He spoke in a language I didn't recognize. Tarin answered in kind.

I reached for the stone around my neck as I watched.

"A formal greeting from the Old Court," Tarin said excitedly. "Where ever did you learn that?"

"My family was . . ." Lochlan trailed off.

"Yes," Tarin said, thinking. "Quite, Lochlan Ellyll. Hmm."

Lochlan's eyes stayed down. Tarin placed a small fist gently under his chin and pushed it up. They made eye contact. "We must not take on the sins of our forefathers, but try to right them if we can."

Lochlan gave him a stiff nod.

"Well, dearie," Tarin said, ignoring the confused looks of everyone around us. "I have come to collect you. Let's go."

The halls were quieter now, most students were in class, heading to bed, or maybe to Roswell's. Tarin and I walked silently side by side for a few minutes before curiosity got the better of me.

"I have known Lochlan for three years and he has never, never spoken about his family." Tarin remained silent. "You aren't going to tell me about him," I stated.

"It's his family to speak of," Tarin squeaked, "not mine. And, Gods High, slow down, girl."

"Sorry." I slowed, noticing Tarin taking four steps for every one of mine. "So, that's a no."

"Quite! That's a no."

"Will you answer my next question?" I asked. Tarin was guiding me to a nearby stairwell that I knew led to my favorite part of Erroin, from an architectural point of view. The glass turret. Niloc's study was at the top.

"Well that very much depends on the question, doesn't it?" he said. We walked in silence up a flight of stairs and across a short hall.

"We're going to see Niloc?" I asked. "That's not the question, I'm just warming you up with one I know you'll answer."

"He has invited us all for tea and cake," Tarin said magnanimously. We entered the glass turret and started to climb the two flights to the top.

I smiled. "I can't eat cake."

"Blood pudding?"

"Ha, ha, very funny."

"What was your real question? I will answer if I am indeed the one you should be asking." Tarin stopped a few stairs ahead of me and turned. We were nearly the same height this way. "Let's have it."

I paused and stress creased my brow. I took a steadying breath and looked out over the grounds. The moon was fully hidden behind a cloudy sky. The wide lawn and surrounding forest were dark. Far to the right, I saw the dim glow coming from the iridescent lake Lochlan loved so much.

"Were," I paused, sure he wouldn't answer. Sure that he wouldn't understand why I felt I needed to know. Needed to help in some way if I could.

Despite my misgivings, I asked anyway.

"Were Sahrias and Rayyan together here?" I looked to him. "At Erroin?"

Tarin didn't answer right away.

"He told you about her," he muttered. "But if you are asking me, he didn't tell you much."

"Just that they were together, and then they weren't." I tried to keep my body relaxed, my mind calm. "He is tight-lipped about her. He hasn't been with anyone since, as far as I'm aware."

"You're worried about him." Tarin's smile was sad.

"A little," I admitted, because I was, but my curiosity was selfish too. "Before he told me, I would notice this look he would get. This way he would be sometimes. Maybe he would receive a letter, or maybe nothing would happen at all, and he would be different for a while. He would look at me different. Like he was broken. Like I had done it."

"Oh, Dyson," Tarin whispered. "It was not you."

"When he told me about Yamini, and how Rayyan was the reason he was able to leave her, he had that same look. Or maybe a shadow of it." I turned to meet Tarin's pearl blue eyes. "I know it wasn't me. How could it have been? But when he looks at me like that," I put a hand on my chest. On where I felt an echo of the emptiness he held.

"Yamini was long before I knew him," Tarin sighed as though he knew exactly what I was feeling. "And Rayyan had a long life before that. A legacy, I dare say."

"Did you know her?" I asked. "Rayyan, I mean."

"I did," he said. "And, in all honesty, most of this is not my story to tell."

"What can you tell me?" I asked, and started moving again. We were almost at the top of the stairs. "If I could just understand more, maybe I'd be able to . . . I don't know if I could help, but I could try."

"That she hurt him. Badly. She chose power, not him. He broke and is still putting himself back together. You help with that." He smiled at me. "He has been so much happier since you came into his life."

My chest warmed a little. It was nice to know that I had helped him as much as he had helped me. That I was still helping.

"That is why he was so rough with you, all those years ago," Tarin explained, and his eyes downcast. "Why he handled that situation so poorly."

I remembered all too well.

"He was so afraid that he was going to lose you," Tarin went on. "You are his anchor. You are helping him put himself back together. And you should be patient with him about it."

"Patient?" I joked. "Have we met? Hi, I'm Dyson."

Tarin tutted and waved his hands in the air, shooing away my attempt at easing the seriousness of our conversation.

"Few of us are lucky to love as they loved," Tarin went on. "And they did love each other, they still do I think. No matter what he might think now."

"But I guess that wasn't enough, was it?" I asked.

"Well, they are both immortal." A mischievous glint replaced the sadness in Tarin's bright eyes. "Their story is far from over."

CHAPTER EIGHTEEN
2041

"Be careful," Haiden muttered when I walked into the Shine House for my evening shift. He was sitting in his regular spot by the door with a book in his hand. His chair was tipped onto its back legs, leaning against the wall. I was surprised it didn't slide out from under him, but if it did, he would learn.

"Why?" I asked. "What's going on?"

A loud shriek cut through the air, and I knew exactly what was going on.

"Luci is in one of her moods," Haiden said, unnecessarily and not quietly enough.

"I fucking heard that, Haiden!" said the bright ball of light that flew through the kitchen doors and into the common space. "I fucking—"

"Hey!" I said sharply. "Language, Luci. Now sit your ass down, take a breath, and turn off the light show."

The ball of light didn't move from her place between the kitchen door, and the small grouping of chairs and sofas around the fire place. I glared into the ball of light, ignoring the pain in my eyes. Then I pointed to a loveseat by the fireplace and said with only a hint of compulsion, "now."

The ball of light seemed to rotate, then stomp towards the sofa.

I never really compelled the kids to do anything. I never wanted to take their choice away, but I had learned early on that a small push, rather than forcing their decisions, would break through whatever hormone-filled rage they were in, and morph them back into the semi-rational hormone-filled teenagers they usually were.

They were much easier to communicate with that way.

I turned to Haiden.

"What did you do?" I asked.

"Wasn't me, Dys," he said, moving a finger over his chest. "Cross my heart. She stormed in like that about ten minutes ago and no one has been able to calm her down."

I turned to look at the pulsing ball of light sitting on the sofa.

"Okay," I said and walked towards Luci.

"Better you than me," Haiden whispered behind me.

I smirked and crossed the wide room, then sat down next to Luci. It was uncomfortable for me to sit so close to her when she was like this, but I did it anyway. We sat in silence for a full sixty seconds before Luci spoke.

"Why do you get to say 'ass' but I don't get to say fu—"

"Because life isn't fair," I told her. "Because you're sixteen and a student, and because Haiden isn't who you should really be swearing at."

"Why are you sitting next to me?" she demanded, the ball of light still pulsing around her.

"Because you need someone to sit next to you," I said. I took in a shaky breath.

"It hurts you," she said.

"Yeah, it does." My exhale was harsh. "A slight manipulation on my part. But I also think it's more important for me to support you and be uncomfortable, then to leave you alone right now."

She took in a slow steady breath, and the bright light surrounding her began to dim. In a few moments, Luci sat next to me with nothing more than the usual glow of a Seraph.

"You could have just sat over there," Luci pointed to the couch across from us. "And not been in pain."

I looked over at the three-seater on the other side of the fireplace, then back to her dark chocolate eyes, brimming with tears.

"Would you have calmed down as fast if I'd sat over there?" I asked.

She smirked, then sniffed as the tears started to fall.

"You know what, Dyson? You can be a real jerk sometimes."

"Yeah, I know," I said, wrapping an arm around her shoulders and pulling her close. "You're not so bad yourself."

She squeezed me tight and took in another deep breath.

"Luce?"

Luci and I looked up. Haiden had slid his chair over to the table and was shuffling a deck of cards.

"Wanna play?"

Luci exhaled sharply, wiped her eyes, and nodded.

"You too, Dyson," Haiden said. "But none of that listening to our heartbeats cheating stuff."

"Who, me?" I placed a hand dramatically on my chest. "I wouldn't dream of it."

"So, she tells me that one of the other Seraphs in her physics class called her a half-breed cast off, and said that she's such a stuck-up bitch because her parents didn't love her, and nobody else ever will either."

"Ouch," Sahrias said.

"Yeah," I nodded and slowed my run to a walk. We'd gotten to the top of a hill near where we hunted. I looked around the small clearing and tried to focus on my senses. I stretched them wide in search of prey, but I was too distracted by the Luci incident.

"And then one of Seraphs and a Telekinetic kid exploded a few sharpies on her face and clothes, a bunch of kids started laughing at her, and that's when she lit up."

"Poor girl," Si said, his eyes closed, no doubt also scanning the surrounding area for wildlife. "It's tough when the mean kids say something you think is true."

"Right. I spent the next two hours of my shift playing cards and talking her out of leaving the school. This kid is so smart. So smart! She just judges herself on this impossible scale of Seraph lineage and purity. But she is so powerful. She just doesn't see it."

"Haiden was there?" Si asked, opening his eyes. In the moonlight, his eyes and hair were so dark, they almost looked blue.

"Haiden was there. He is great with her," I said.

"He's a good kid," Sahrias nodded. "So is Luci."

Si had spent some time in Shine House with me early on and popped in every so often. Haiden decided I was his favourite person in the world as soon as we met. At twelve years old, and a fan of the 2036 hit kid's film, *Hotel Dracula*, his meeting a real-life Vampire was a dream come true. He would follow me around for most of my shift, until I told him to go to bed. As a result, Sahrias got to know him too.

"They're good kids most of the time." I said.

"You sat inside her sphere?" Sahrias asked, and for the first time since we had started our run, I felt his full attention on me.

"Umm, kind of half in, half out, I guess," I shrugged. "Why? Is that bad? Like bad for us?"

"Oh no, Seraph light is nothing like daylight," he said. "Well, it is. It's just . . . not."

"Wow," I said dryly. "I totally understand."

"It's Magic, Dyson. Not everything has an easy answer. Besides, Vampires are one of the few Luman that are unaffected by Seraph lure, the other exception, of course, being Demons. It comes down to some kind of defense mechanism evolved over time, or so the theory goes," he said, closing his eyes again. He turned a little on the spot, facing back the way we came. "You should have asked Tarin when he was here."

"I didn't know to ask Tarin when he was here." My eyes scanned the tree line for nothing in particular.

"Shall we run to the old tree?" Sahrias asked, starting toward the small path on the other side of the clearing.

The old tree was only a few minutes away from there, deeper into the woods. The tree Sahrias was referring to wasn't that old, compared to some of the other giants in this forest, but it bowed in a way that made it look like it was.

"Will you tell me about this Seraph thing first?"

He sighed. Resigned.

"Always hungry for information," he smirked.

"Always," I smiled.

"Both Demons and Vampires can feed off Seraphs in different ways," he explained, taking a few steps back toward me. "For Demons, it gives them certain Seraph abilities."

For a moment, I thought of Rayyan. Since Si seemed to be in a chatty mood, maybe he would talk about her today. I knew I was just being nosy at this point, but I was curious to know who she was, and who she really was to him.

"And for Vampires," Si continued. "It allows us to walk in the sun."

"What?" I said, the mystery of Rayyan being pushed aside by this new information. "How?"

"Don't get your hopes up." He waved away my shocked expression. "You would have to kill and drain a full-blooded Seraph to get that particular benefit."

"Oh," I said, my hopes dashed. Then I thought about the social implications of that. "That tracks. Luci and a few of my other students were really wary of me when we first got here."

"We are the boogie men for Seraph children. We are the villains in their bedtime stories."

"There aren't many full-blooded Seraphs left," I said.

"You can thank our ancestors for that," he said wryly. "We're in those stories with reason. The Starlit Shield put a rather brutal stop to that. It is part of the reason it took so long for a Vampire to sit on the council."

"Oh," I said, thinking about what "brutal stop" could mean. "Is there any non-lethal way for a Vampire to walk in daylight?"

Sahrias shrugged. "The only other way I've heard of is by the willing blood of a Sun God."

"A sun go—"

"Sh-sh," Si said softly as his gaze snapped to the side with the changing wind. I could smell it too. A black bear. It wasn't far. Sahrias's eyes glinted in the moonlight as they met mine.

A smile curled the corner of my mouth, as I let hunger and the hunt take over my thoughts.

The soldier was good with a blade. His strikes were fluid, and his footwork was smooth. Dyson could see the frustration in his eyes as she parried his attacks. There was little space free of debris, little space to move, but the man maintained enough distance to keep his blade effective.

The adrenaline that had run through her was waning, and she tired of this show. She didn't need to perform; her point was made. She just needed to end this now. Stepping left as he attempted another strike, Dyson realized her mistake a moment too late. She'd slowed down more than she'd realized and given the man time to switch hands. He buried the dagger in her back.

Dyson cried out in pain, turning back to him, leading with an elbow to his jaw. The man stumbled. She kicked him in the chest, helping him down.

He groaned from his prone position on the floor, and before he had time to recover, Dyson had her boot on his throat.

"It doesn't matter who comes," she croaked, twisting her foot and pressing down. A deep snap echoed through the room. "They will all be too late."

What a waste, she thought, spitting blood onto the fresh corpse. She tried to breathe—and had a coughing fit instead.

The man's blade had gotten in between her ribs and punctured her lung.

"Lucky, hit," she gasped, spitting up more blood and falling to her knees.

CHAPTER NINETEEN
2041

I shook my head to clear the haze, pushed myself back to my feet, and looked across the blue padded floors. It was almost 9 p.m., I was at the end of my session, and Duke was kicking my ass.

"He hits like a hammer," I said, wiping my face with my t-shirt. It was more habit than anything else as I rarely sweated.

Si leaned up against the wall, grinning.

"His shift is . . . big. Have you seen it?" Sahrias said.

I turned to face Duke who, for the last month or so, had decided I was ready to go harder than usual. I'd been taking lessons for almost a year now, but I'd stalled out.

Si had suggested I needed more motivation, and if I was actually getting hit, my reflexes might start to improve. He'd also suggested I not use my vampiric speed because that would be "cheating."

I was still working out how that was cheating but Duke—who shifted into the biggest hybrid animal I'd ever seen—using his strength wasn't.

"I've seen it," I said, remembering the white and gold mixed fur, the mane, the thick powerful body. Duncan James was a chimera, part polar bear, part lion, and I was pretty sure he was one of a kind. "I think the problem is compounded by his superior skill."

"Yeah, yeah." Duke drawled lazily and waved away my words with a red-and-black-gloved hand. The gloves matched his shorts and their minimal padding did little to lessen his blows. "How are you countering that? How are you beating it? And how have you been alive for so long and never learned this?"

"How am I beating your superior skill?" I moved forward, but stayed out of his reach. "I don't know—running away?"

We'd been training once or twice a week pretty consistently for the past year. At this point, he was training me more than I was tutoring him. Our study sessions were more about focus than understanding the text. He was smart, just had a little trouble with application. When we had our combat sessions . . . well, let's just say I wasn't as quick of a study. Duke had promised it would all get easier.

It hadn't.

"God, Lochy would have a field day with this," Duke muttered. "Aside from running away. In the real world, maybe you wouldn't be able to run."

"He wanted to wake up early for a swim." I moved back and let my arms fall.

Lochlan had made a habit of watching us spar over the past month. He and Sahrias cracked jokes in the corner while I got my ass kicked.

"And excuse me," I said, "but I'm only fifty-two. Twenty-seven, if we're just counting the Vampire years."

"I'm twenty-six," he drawled. "I'm a Scorpio and like long walks on the beach. What's your point?"

"No one in the world is as big as you," I continued, ignoring him. "I think I'm preparing for something I'll never face. Plus!" I exclaimed turning to Sahrias. "You aren't letting me use all my spe—"

I broke off, dropping to the floor as a huge fist attached to a huge arm came whizzing through the air at me. Kicking out a leg and whirling in a circle, I caught Duke off guard. Though he tried to jump, my leg connected and brought him down.

"Dirty cheater." I smiled. He rolled away and hopped to his feet. "You didn't let me finish speaking."

"I guess that makes me rude too—and whoever said fighting dirty was cheating has never been in a fight for their life," Duke said.

"I've been in a fight for my life," I told him. We circled each other, both in a half-crouched defensive posture, waiting to see who'd make the first move.

"Oh, yeah?" Duke raised an eyebrow.

"Yeah," I said. "I lost, and lucky for you I did or you wouldn't have a history tutor."

I heard Si snort at the same time as Duke advanced.

"It's English now." He moved like he was going to kick me.

I fell for it.

A moment too late, I saw the hit coming and tried to move away. Duke connected and the contact sent me flying.

The combat room was quartered into sections. A small set of weights, a pull-up bar, and an open space for strength training in one corner, and beside that, a row of lockers and storage. Across from the lockers, was a line of heavy bags, a few speed bags, and my maker leaning against the wall, looking smug. And in the padded sparring corner, me, face down on the mat after hitting the equally padded wall.

"Your reflexes are still off for fighting," Duke said.

I slowly picked myself up for what felt like the twentieth time in the last hour. Sparring at Erroin wasn't quite like sparring anywhere else. After I'd began taking lessons, Duke had had a few requests from other students, all with strength or speed levels that precluded them from learning in other situations. Duke loved it.

Not only was he able to re-engage in a sport he adored, but he was coming to accept and appreciate his Shifter abilities.

"Not only are you fast enough to land on your feet on the wall, let alone the floor," he said, exasperated, "but you gotta lean in to a punch. When you see it coming at you, you have to take it." He leaned forward in demonstration.

I pointed at Sahrias. "He told me I wasn't allowed to use my full speed. That it would defeat the purpose of practicing."

"It would," Si shrugged.

"I'm just happy you're also freakishly strong, so I don't have to hold back there too," I said.

"There is a difference between using your speed to fight and using your speed to see. To take in your surroundings. You're too focused on one thing, instead of everything," Duke said.

"Yeah, yeah." My tone was bitter. "I got it."

Before I knew it, I was staring at the ceiling near where Si leaned against the wall. He and Duke both looked down at me.

"It doesn't appear that she gets it," Si mocked, "or she wouldn't attack in anger."

A roar of frustration ripped from my throat and I threw myself at Duke, totally ignoring Sahrias's words.

Block, jab, jab, cross, DUCK!

"Aoooww," I groaned, on the floor again. I'd seen that hit coming. I didn't move out of the way. But I didn't take it either. The absolute worst response.

Duke walked over to me. I rolled away with Vampiric speed and jumped to my feet.

"Hey, now," Duke said, a smile in his voice. "We're working on reflexes, not outright speed."

"Yeah, yeah," I repeated with only a hint of my earlier bitterness. "I got it."

I was on the attack. Block, block, jab, cross . . . there it was.

I saw his fist coming at me in slow motion. A quick flare of pride bloomed in my chest as I recognized what to do in time to actually do it. I leaned in to take the hit. He connected.

BANG!

The explosion of sound was followed by the crack of bone, and for a moment, I was weightless.

I felt light.

Light as air, hot and bright as the sun, heat building in my chest.

Total silence filled my mind.

Clarity. Strength. Awareness. And a space, an odd empty space inside me. A space that was suddenly full of light.

I didn't gasp for air this time. I didn't scream. As strange as this was, it was familiar. Like I'd done it in a dream. I was connected to everything. To my body. To this power. To the world.

And the space, that forgotten thing, the one that longed to be filled. It was smooth as silk as my thoughts ran over it.

A second wave of energy coursed through me and the light pouring out of me grew brighter. I threw my head back as a current of bliss and lust ran over my skin.

It sped into my soul.

Then a memory surfaced, a phrase.

"Dear God," Sahrias had said. "How do I protect her now?"

I landed on the ground. Hard.

I caught myself in a crouch, one hand and knee on the padded combat room floor. I hadn't realized I'd actually been floating. I stayed there, crouched on the ground, trying to process what had just happened. Trying to hold on to that feeling of bliss.

Someone groaned. My head snapped up.

Duke was lying on the ground, cradling his hand. Sahrias was on the ground too. It looked like he'd been thrown backward. They both had.

"I think she gets it," Duke said, through gritted teeth. "Christ, this hurts."

"Indeed," Sahrias said from behind me. I heard darkness in the word and turned to him. He smoothly pushed himself off the floor, graceful as ever.

The look he gave me was chilling, but familiar.

"Sahrias," I breathed. "What . . ." The question died on my lips.

He stared at me. I knew that look. I'd seen it before. I waited for him to speak, to give me an explanation, a reason for what happened, for what I felt. I waited for him to not make the same mistake as the last time I'd done something really wrong.

But just like with the girl at the lake, and everything that happened after, he gave me nothing. He just looked at me the way he sometimes did. Like I'd done something more than I had. Maybe this time I deserved it, but I didn't know why.

And if he'd been looking at me like that all this time, he did.

"Don't," I said as he turned. Sahrias paused for a moment. "Please,"

I begged, but he left anyway.

I wanted to follow him through the glass door slowly closing behind him, but I couldn't leave Duke alone. He groaned and I rushed over to him.

"Are you okay?" I asked, kneeling on the blue mats.

He rolled onto his side and started to get to his feet.

"I think you broke my hand," he said.

I gripped him under the arm and hauled him up. "God, I'm so sorry."

"I'm okay, I'm okay," Duke insisted as he found his feet. "I heal quick. I'll just go to the hospital to make sure the bones will set right."

"Is everything okay?" I heard from behind me. I turned to see Agatha and Zemila walk in. Agatha must have come from apprenticing, because she was wearing a v-neck t-shirt in the pale purple of the hospital staff.

Surprising no one, she'd aced her Final Trial and had been apprenticing in the hospital for the last eight months.

"We saw Sahrias in the hallway." Agatha continued, her sunshine yellow headband a stark contrast to my current emotions. "He said Duncan was hurt, then ran off."

"You were training without me?" Zemila said, oblivious to Duke's pain. Agatha, on the other hand, walked over to him immediately.

"Are you okay?" Agatha asked, carefully pulling Duke's injured hand away from his body and examining it. "What happened?"

"Oh," Duke said. Color flooded his cheeks. "Ahhh, hi, Aga, Agath— Doc. H-hi."

I squinted at him and almost smiled, despite the situation.

"How are you?" he said, trying to hide his pain and she slowly turned his hand over.

"We'll have to cut the glove off," Agatha said. "What happened?"

"I broke Duke's hand." I looked between them. "Can you help him?"

"You what?" Zemila said, eyes going wide. "I didn't even know you could do that." She looked at Duke. "I didn't know your bones could break."

"Of course they can bre—OW!—break," he said.

"Sorry," Agatha whispered, still examining his hand and arm.

"They just never have before," Duke finished on a whine.

"I'm really sorry, Duke," I said.

"Don't worry about it." He tried to shrug his shoulders, but stopped mid-way through the motion.

"This makes me think twice about my last request." Zemila leaned over Agatha to see the damage.

A few months ago, I'd started teaching Zemila the basics of what I'd learned. Sometimes she'd come and watch my lessons with Duke. On even rarer occasions, she'd join in. When we started sparring, she asked how soon she'd be able to do the same.

"No, no, Mila. You should start whenever you feel ready. I'm fine," Duke said, cheeks flushed. He pulled his hand away from Agatha. "I am really fine, and Dyson would be more careful with you. So would I."

"We need to get you to the hospital," Agatha looked up at Duke. "I can set and heal the bones here, but I think going to the hospital would be best."

"Yes, umm, right, hospital, healer, bye." Duke pushed past us and sprinted for the door, still cradling his broken hand.

"But . . . I am a healer," Agatha said, staring after him. Then she asked, "What just happened?"

"He likes you," Zemila said. "So, he is weird with you, and you are weird around him. That is what happened."

Zemila's w's still sounded a bit more like v's, but her accent was fading.

"What?" Agatha looked back and forth between me and Zemila. "I'm not—"

"Oh, please!" Zemila cut her off. "You two dance around each other with your eyes all filled with love."

"I do not!"

"Goo-goo eyes," I nodded. "All the time."

"And it makes me so happy and jealous and angry all at once," Zemila said.

"Oh, yeah?" Agatha's dark eyebrow rose. "You don't seem to mind those looks when you're getting them from Lochlan. Even though you're sleeping with Driss."

Zemila looked sharply at Agatha.

"It's true, Zemila," I said, laughing despite my mood. "I don't know how you haven't noticed."

"She notices," Agatha muttered. "We all notice."

"He isn't—he doesn't, he is, no," she said, her eyebrows pinching together. "He is Nemo's best friend. He helps me improve my English so I can get a job in America. He is my friend. That's all."

"Uh huh." Agatha seemed unconvinced.

"He doesn't think of me that way," Zemila said.

I was amazed at her obliviousness.

"Besides," she went on. "I can just be when I am around Lochlan. I don't have to pretend anything like the others."

I blinked at her.

"And that's," Agatha gave her a questioning look, "bad?"

"The others never last," Zemila waved her hand through the air like she was shooing away a fly. "Lochlan has to last."

We stared at her.

"And he's . . . Lochlan!" she said, exasperated. "He does not see me that way. I am not right for him."

"Okay, psycho." Agatha looked confused, then shook her head. "That's not what I meant anyway." She turned to me. "I meant what happened here? How did you break Duncan's hand?"

"I—" The concern that had momentarily left me came rushing back. I thought of the feeling of light and lust and bliss. The connection to what felt like everything in the whole world, and that one spot inside. That one spot where something was missing.

But what?

I squeezed my eyes shut, trying to figure it all out. I remembered the bright white-gold light, so similar to that weird dream I'd had all those years ago.

"Dyson?" Agatha's voice was soft. "What happened?"

"I have no idea." I opened my eyes. "But I have to find Si."

I turned to leave the combat room. Agatha and Zemila called after me, but I kept moving. I needed to talk to Si. I shouldn't have waited. I should have followed him the second Agatha arrived, but the panic I'd felt when Si left the room had been pushed out of my mind by Duke's injury.

Why didn't Si wait?

I ran through the halls, thankful they were empty.

I went to Sahrias's apartment first. Our previously shared apartment. I still had a key, and slept there from time to time. Holidays mostly, when the rest of the school was quiet.

"Si," I called as soon as I pushed open the door. "Si, can we talk? Si?" I walked into his room. He was shoving clothing into a bag and didn't look up. "Si."

"I have to go," he told me. "I have to go check on something. I need to talk to someone. I will try and be back quickly, but I must go."

"What?" I was confused. "No. Wait, can we talk first?"

"I have to go," he repeated, and started to move towards his bedroom door.

"Wait, no," I blocked his way. "What—what is happening? You need to tell me what's happening."

"I don't know what's going on, Dyson," he said, and I could hear the lie.

"Why aren't you telling me the truth?"

"Dyson, please," he begged. "I have a flight to catch—"

"A flight?" My eyebrows went up. "We came here on a private plane—I don't think it's going to leave without you."

He took a step back into the room and I followed.

"I am going with a friend," he explained. "And she is on a schedule."

"Can we please talk first?" I asked again. "Can you not leave me in the dark about something that is happening to me?"

"Christ." He hissed out a breath. "I am cursed."

"You're cursed?" What the hell was he talking about? "This is happening to me."

He took a heavy breath and looked at me.

"Dyson." His eyes held unguarded fear. "I am so sorry. I—"

"What's got you so scared?" I asked, my concern shifting from myself to him. "Si," I stepped towards him and reached out an arm. "Si, whatever it is, we can figure it out."

He squeezed his eyes shut and shook his head.

"I don't think we can," he told me.

I pulled him into a tight hug and he wrapped his arms around me.

"Of course we can," I said. "Just tell me what's going on."

He pulled away.

"I love you." He cupped my cheek in his palm. "You have made my life so much better. But I fear what is coming. I fear what I must do. This power you have manifested—"

"What power?"

"—it's a curse that I can't explain right now."

"A curse?" I said, dumbfounded. "Like, a real curse?"

"Our blood line," he started, then he caught my wrist in his hand and swore in a language I didn't understand. "There is so much I should have told you, but if you'd known—how could I have protected you if you'd known?"

I'd never seen Sahrias so frantic. So nonsensical. The man I knew was gone, and he was replaced with an anxious doppelgänger who couldn't string a coherent sentence together.

"Gods, I hope you forgive me for this. For not telling you then, and not having time to tell you now. I will be back as soon as I can."

He kissed my forehead—and was gone.

It took several tries before Dyson was able to remove the blade from her back. It took several minutes before she worked up the strength to start looking for the oushifa again.

Would've been easier if you hadn't been dosed, she thought.

Her eyes moved from the dead soldier on the ground, to the dead eyes that held a mix of horror and repulsion, to a small hutch against the wall.

Of course, she thought, and crawled across the room.

There was a bullet hole where the top hinge used to be. The door swung open awkwardly. She pushed bottles aside for only a moment before her eyes fell onto a small tincture of deep blue liquid.

She could have cried with relief. She could have cursed herself for not starting there.

Taking the small bottle out of the cabinet, she twisted open the top. The thick scent of lavender, iris, and Magic hit her nose. She brought the small half-filled bottle to her lips and allowed three drops to fall on her tongue.

She felt the Magic immediately. Noticing that the piano bench had somehow survived unscathed, she righted it and slowly sat.

As Magic moved through her body, healing as it went, she thought of Sahrias. She thought of that moment where everything had changed.

When everything started to change, she mentally corrected.

Bending low to reach the broken keys of the piano, she ran her fingers along the ivory. Some keys played the notes they were made for, others made a more haunting sound. Some made no sound at all.

If she could point to a moment, to one thing, it would be that conversation—or the lack of one. Dyson thought back to how things could have been, how they should have been. But a part of her knew now that it was always going to be that way. Every version of them was . . . cursed.

"Duke was a great teacher," she said when she was able to breathe without the gurgling sound of blood in her lungs. "I actually made money as a cage fighter for a while. But I didn't have the fight in me then. I wasn't desperate. I'd never fought for my life . . . except for the time I'd died."

She reached down to the piano again and tried to play something. It came out all wrong. She knew it would.

"I once read a biography of a fighter from the sixties. The 1960s," she clarified, then looked over her shoulder. "You are a couple generations too young; he was long before your time. He said 'you have to want to see the light go out in your opponent's eyes. You have to need it.'

"When Sahrias left that day, it fractured something between us. It threw me backward in time. I felt all the things I'd felt when I'd lost my family one by one. The fight wasn't in me then. Not when my parents died, not when Si . . . well, not then either. There was just a craving, a desire to know what was happening and why."

Dyson looked over at the man she'd just killed. He was one of thousands. One of the thousands of lives she had ended.

She'd lost count a long time ago.

" 'You have to want to see the light go out in your opponent's eyes,' " she said, then looked up. "I didn't then. I do now."

CHAPTER TWENTY
2042

By the time I thought of forcing him to take me along, he was already gone. I was sitting on the edge of the bed, staring stunned at the floor.

"Si," I whispered and rubbed tears of frustration from my eyes. Fear and loneliness were building in my chest. Though I knew Sahrias wasn't gone forever, in that moment, it felt like he was. It felt exactly the same as when my father went to the hospital for a check-up and never left. The same loneliness pushed in around me. The same anxiety, the same fear. At least I'd had my brothers then. Now I had nothing.

"I need you," I said into my hands. "I need my father!" I screamed. I was scared. I'd never felt so alone in my life. Not even when my Human life had ended.

Unbidden, my first memory of Si came back to me.

I'd been choking on my own blood, determined to keep fighting those men off, no matter how painful it was.

But I couldn't feel much. I couldn't feel anything but their hot rank breath on my cheek.

"Not so tough now," the voice had rasped. "Looks like you turned out to be a different kind of fun."

Fuck you, I'd thought. I knew I'd hurt him a little. I tasted his blood in my mouth from where I'd bit him.

I gathered every last ounce of strength I had and spat that blood right in his face.

"You bitch!" I'd heard from above.

I'd felt another kick to my stomach. I'd heard another snap ripple through me. I couldn't breathe anymore. There was a grunt above me. I'd waited for the last hit. The last kick. The one that would kill me.

But it never came. The blackness had pushed in. The pain had seemed to ebb away. I felt nothing.

At least I'll see my parents.

A figure loomed over me.

See there, that's my father now. Come to collect me. Come to take me to the other side.

Then I remembered something, maybe for the first time.

"Oh no, I am so sorry, child," my father had said. There was a soft touch to my wrist. A sharp intake of breath. "How odd."

I'd thought it was my father. I'd coughed . . . I'd tried to cough. I'd tasted blood.

Sitting on the edge of Si's bed, I looked down at my wrist. At where he'd touched me. I'd remembered the touch, but not the words.

"How odd," I said, running my thumb over the ankh tattoo, just as Si had. "Our blood line," he'd said, some thirty minutes ago, before he'd abandoned me here. "Cursed."

Why would he have said that?

"How odd," I said, again.

I don't know how long I sat on the edge of my maker's bed, thinking over everything. I thought of every strange look, every strained conversation. I thought of that light in the combat room, and the dream I'd had two and a half decades ago. They'd felt the same. Was that first one a dream?

The more I thought, the more I wanted answers. I needed to know where I fit in, where this uncontrollable burst of light fit in. I was confused, and scared, and worried, and pissed.

I was really, really pissed at Si. I ran my thumb over the hieroglyph on my wrist again. I stood up and walked over to the book shelf against the wall by the door.

"I don't even know what I'm looking for," I told the books as I shifted them around.

I moved to his dresser next. This was an invasion of privacy. I knew it was. I knew looking through his stuff was a shit thing to do. Especially since I didn't know what I hoped to find. A file labeled Cursed Vampiric Bloodlines wasn't likely to be lying around.

I looked under the bed, then moved to the closet.

The one other time Sahrias had acted even remotely like this was with the girl at the lake. Did this have something to do with that? But how could it?

The look he'd given me then, flashed before my eyes. I thought of how he'd looked at me today in the training room. The same worry, the same helplessness. I searched through the trunk at the foot of his bed. And that dream. Was it a dream? I wasn't sure any more.

"Dear God," Sahrias had said. "How do I protect her now?"

Protect me from what? This curse? If that wasn't a dream, if it was some curse, he was doing a shit job of protecting me.

It couldn't have been real. There was no way Si would've seen me floating over my bed and not talked to me about it.

Right?

I wasn't sure anymore. We'd started making plans to leave the country that next night.

Another coincidence? I pulled open the drawer of his bedside table. Add to that the fact that if he'd wanted to give me answers, to help me, he would have. He'd left instead. And I wasn't going to wait for him to get back. I would find answers on my own.

But not here. I flopped back down onto Si's bed. He would smell I'd been all over his room, all over his things.

He'd be upset.

Well, he'll be upset for nothing, as I didn't find anything.

My eyes traveled over the trunk at the foot of the bed, and the shelf across from it. I'd tried to put the books back as they were but had done a poor job. Walking over to right a few fallen books I saw a thin leather folder I hadn't noticed before. It was large and flat and was a similar color to the dark wood of the shelf.

I took it and unwrapped the leather cord holding it shut. It fell open in my hands. If I'd still had a heartbeat, I think it would have picked up.

"Yamini." I ran my finger lightly over the name at the bottom of an old painting.

Her expression was one of distain, but her beauty shone through. The portrait was from her shoulders up and had little to no detail of her clothing. The painter had put all their energy into her face. Just a sweep of the brush over her shoulder to show a sari. That was all.

I gently moved the painting to the other side of the folder. Underneath it, I was surprised to see photos of me. There were a few. Mostly I was alone. In some of them I was with Si.

I have this one too. I smiled and touched a photo of the two of us in Paris.

Si and I had danced salsa on the banks of the Seine. One of the organizers had snapped a picture for the website. Si was smiling, I looked focused but we had just met each other's eyes, and I could see the grin starting in the corners of my mouth.

He'd moved so gracefully. I'd had to work hard to keep up.

Usually Si was more careful, especially as the world had grown digital. I didn't know why he'd let this photo happen. It was one of my favorite pictures, so I was happy he had.

Next was a picture of a woman on a beach. It looked like it had been taken in the 1920s. She had tattoos that I could see peeking out under her swim suit. They were huge and barely darker than her dark skin. There was one just above her knee, and another that seemed to curve over her left breast. I could see the top of it just above her bathing suit.

"Huh," I said aloud, and flipped to the next picture. The same beach. The same woman. Si was in this one. The woman was looking at him and he was looking at the camera.

There were photos spanning the next few decades. Some I recognized to be at Erroin, some were places I didn't know. One was a drawing that looked almost as old as the painting of Yamini. It must have been Si, and the woman beside him wore a red . . . no, maybe an orange dress. She had on a long black cloak and her hood was up. The colors reminded me of a robin.

I carefully turned over the ancient looking paper. Tarin was in the next one and I smiled, then . . .

"Ha," I breathed.

There it was. The corners worn and the edges frayed like someone had peeled it off a wall.

Zemila was right. You could see how much he loved her.

"So this is Rayyan," I whispered. Or a completely different woman—but somehow, I didn't think so.

Why did he take the photo off the wall in the library? What was happening in his life when the photo went up?

I looked back through the others, seeing if I could find her again.

The woman on the beach. That was her. Looking at her expression in the one with Si, I thought she loved him. It looked like she loved him. Something stirred inside me. A feeling of shame—and loneliness.

What am I doing? Why am I prying into his personal life like this? I looked at the photo. Would I ever have what they had? Do I even want it?

Now that I'd found something, even if it wasn't what I'd been looking for, I'd lost some of my conviction.

Then my brain caught up to what I was seeing, and I flipped back to the photo of Sahrias and the woman, Rayyan, on a beach. In daylight.

I ran my fingers over the woman in the picture.

"The willing blood of a Sun God," I whispered to her. "What are you?"

My head was spinning as I closed the folder and replaced it on the shelf. I looked at the clock on the wall. 2:30 a.m.

I needed to cool off, to think, to reconcile what I had just seen in that picture. Sahrias in daylight. A Vampire, on a beach. In the daytime.

"The willing blood of a Sun God," I said again.

He'd never told me about her, and now I wanted to know. Was he protecting her? From me? What am I compared to a literal god? If that's even what she was. But, if there was one thing I'd learned over the past three decades, it was that the word "god" was thrown around pretty loosely.

I left the apartment and walked to Lochlan's favorite spot on the grounds.

The iridescent glow of the small lake was soothing. It lulled the ache in my chest that made me feel like I was alone in the world. The ache that had doubled after seeing the pictures of Rayyan and Si and understanding the depths of his lies.

I laid my hand on my chest. On the spot that the light had come from, or so it had felt. The spot that felt like there was a space. An empty space that could never be filled.

All these years, Sahrias had been my number one. My priority. My father, brother, and friend. I needed him now. And he was gone.

Sadness and solitude turned to frustration and anger. Something was happening to me, and he was gone. He'd left. Spouting off about a curse and leaving me with only questions. I needed help, needed him, and I was alone.

Staring at the dancing light of the lake, I knew the only thing I needed now was answers.

The library was empty but for a few night dwellers like me. Normally, I would have appreciated the quiet. Today it seemed sinister.

I walked over to an old card-index cabinet. Made of dark-stained teak and with antique brass finishings, it was full of Magic.

Hopefully enough to help me find what I was looking for. Even though I barely knew what that was.

The library index was four feet tall and half as wide. It didn't have nearly enough space for all the books the library held. But it didn't need to. I ran my finger across the top of the cabinet, stopping at a drawer labelled "Va-Vl."

"Vampiric curses," I said and there was a soft whooshing sound as the cards inside the drawer changed. I opened it and started searching.

After pulling the cards of books I thought might hold some answers, I moved over to the drawer labelled "S." I looked through what came up under "Sun Spells." Next, I searched "Vampire, Sun," and felt pretty stupid with the results.

Vampiric Mythology. Of course.

"Okay," I said through a yawn. I had to get more specific. The cabinet was good, but it was still a cabinet. I looked through the cards I had pulled and a book titled *Vampires, Magic, and Ancient Curses* gave me direction.

I tried "Curses, Ancient," and grinned when I saw a card for a book called *Ancient Druidic Curses*. I knew I wouldn't find anything useful there, but it made me think of Lochlan. He got so grumpy when people called him a Druid.

Could I find a curse in this book to use on him? Not that it would work. Vampires had no direct connection to Magic and couldn't cast spells.

I looked down at the ankh tattoo and remembered the light and heat that levitated me off the ground.

Maybe I shouldn't. I put that particular card back. Maybe I do have that connection after all. But I should talk to Lochlan about all this. I could trust him with this, and he was . . .

"How odd," Sahrias had said when he'd first seen my tattoo. And today, again, he'd touched my wrist and spoke of curses.

The Egyptian hieroglyph symbolized life—and light. The key to the Nile. I thought of Rayyan again, and a shiver went down my spine.

Rayyan. Ray. Ra.

"And I think the woman was from Egipat?" Zemila had said when she first described the photo of Sahrias and Rayyan.

"Life and light . . . and Magic?" I thought of that first day in Professor Medina's Ancient Egyptian history class.

"Please tell me my maker wasn't dating Ra," I muttered to the cabinet.

I'll have to talk to Medina about this too, but I'll deal with how to start that conversation later. I slid my finger over to the drawer labeled "Aj-Ap" and said, "Ankhian."

The sun rose. I'd already found a dark corner of the library, so I ignored it. The dust on the shelves in this part of the library told me that no one would find me unless they were looking, and who had reason to look?

After speed-reading three books on curses—with barely a mention of Vampires— I'd finally found something useful. The short description of Ankhian Magic was the closest thing I'd found to what I'd experienced.

Ankhians were an extinct race of Luman, or their lines had been diluted to the point of near extinction. Powerful Ankhians could harness the light of the sun.

That is for sure not what I'm doing. I'd be burned to a crisp if it was.

I picked up *Forgotten Gods: A Collection of Essays on the Egyptian Pantheon.* I skimmed through the essays on the many theories of who should have been included in the Egyptian Pantheon, and why they were left out. I was starting to lose hope that I'd find a connection between Vampires and Ankhian Magic.

I turned a page and gasped.

Daughter of Isis? the chapter heading read. *Who was Rayyan of Ortis and what were her crimes?*

A rush of adrenaline pushed away the pull to sleep now that the sun was up.

This can't be the same woman.

The essay compared her to the potential brothers and sisters of Jesus, left out of the Bible for their own protection. But Rayyan of Ortis didn't like being left out of the Pantheon. She craved power and recognition. The essay went on to discuss her place in the "Nahal Conflict."

I had no idea what that was.

My eyes felt heavy, but I wanted to know. I had to know. I was determined to find out if this Rayyan was the same Rayyan. If this Nahal Conflict was the reason she'd left Si, if that was the power she'd chosen over him. If that had to do with this new Magic I had. Or whatever it was.

I had to go back to the card index. There must be books on the Nahal Conflict. I just needed to close my eyes for a minute. Just one minute and I'd—

My eyes snapped open. It took me a moment to remember where I was and why I'd slept on a pile of books in a dark back corner of the library.

Duke. Sahrias. Curses. Ankhians. Rayyan.

Rayyan. I frantically scrabbled around for the book I'd fallen asleep reading. I re-read the essay, then went to the card index.

The sun had set. The library was sparsely populated.

All I could find from the index was an old magazine.

I pulled it carefully off the shelf, sliding the dusty magazine from between its fellows. I flipped through the thin pages of the 1998 issue of *Luman Mysteries* until I found what I was looking for. *The Nahal Conflict: Fact or fiction? How did it start, and did it ever end?*

It was short, and gave me a brief overview of an ongoing Ankhian civil war. One side wishing to remain hidden and the other wanting to regain their lost control over Human and Luman alike.

"Ankhians," I whispered, running my hand over the word. "What are you? And how do you have anything to do with me?"

The article gave no mention of Rayyan, but it did mention the role of Nefertem, son of Sekhmet. He had been mentioned in the *Daughter of Isis* chapter too.

The magazine looked like more of a rumor report than anything. It wasn't particularly well-written or well-researched. I flipped to the back where there was a short "About" section.

"*Luman Mysteries* is the first crowd-funded zine for those who crave to know more about the secret world within our secret world," I read. "You can donate to our cause of uncovering the hidden histories and ancient mysteries of our kind by credit card or cheque."

There was a phone number and a PO box listed.

I rolled my eyes, questioning the legitimacy of the article. Looking up at the shelf where I'd found *Luman Mysteries,* I saw there were only five issues. I skimmed all of them for any mention of Rayyan, Ankhians, or Vampiric curses. The more I read, the more ludicrous the stories got.

I choked in surprise at the sheer stupidity of one article titled *Is the President a Succubus?* and laughed out loud reading the article *France's World Cup Win: Talent or Telekinesis?*

Soon, I returned to more legitimate sources. Jumping from book to book, skimming for Rayyan's name or any connection linking Ankhians to Vampires. I tried to find a connection to me. I was retaining little to nothing of what I read, forgetting it as fast as I deemed it irrelevant.

Was there any connection between me and Ankhians? Between me and Rayyan? Between blood, kin, and curses? If so, what? And why?

I had no answers. All I could do was keep searching.

So I did.

CHAPTER TWENTY-ONE
2042

"Dyson?"

I felt a hand on my shoulder.

"Dyson, are you okay?"

Arms underneath me. A chest under my cheek.

"Nartha," the accented voice said. "Féath fíadha dorcha ditiun."

Lochlan?

"Yes," he said.

Had I said that out loud?

"Yes," he repeated. "I'm taking you back to your room."

"But—" I said, fighting the sun's pull to sleep.

"Worry not," he said. "Féath fíadha dorcha ditiun. I will protect you."

I woke up, and for the second time in as many nights, had to remember where I was.

The library.

But, no, that wasn't right. I was in a bed. I was in my bed. I rolled over.

Lochlan was asleep on my floor. He'd carried me through the sunlit library. The memory made me wince, but it was confirmation of his power level and gave me another piece in the puzzle that was Lochlan Ellyll.

Run-of-the-mill Casters couldn't protect Vampires in daylight.

"Dyson?" Lochlan squinted at me through square rims.

Geez, this guy even sleeps with his glasses on.

"Get up here," I said. "I'm gonna go out for a bit. I want to find Professor Medina. You can sleep in my bed if you don't want to go back to your room. Does Nemo have someone over or something? Nianca?"

"No," he shook his head. "They're still 'on a break.' "

I laughed. Nemo and Nianca were together as much as they were "on a break."

"I was worried," Lochlan continued. "I wasn't really sleeping. I just wanted to be here when you woke up and I—"

"Fell asleep?" I said.

"Aye." He pushed himself up to a seated position. "I guess I did. What's going on with you? Are you okay? I haven't found you asleep in the library since your second year."

"That's why you were concerned enough to sleep on my floor?" I looked at him skeptically. "Because I was studying all night?"

"Two nights and two days, Dyson," he scooted back on the floor to lean against the bookshelf on the far wall. "I didn't know where you were."

He pushed his glasses up his nose before his hand fell to the chain around his neck.

"Okay," I said. "I guess that's fair."

"Two nights ago, Zemila told me that something weird had happened," he said. "And that you and Sahrias left together."

"Two nights ago?" What time had I seen her? It was after ten. "What were you and Zemila doing at that time of night?"

I raised an eyebrow.

He ignored me.

"She said you broke Duke's hand."

I sat up, pulled my covers around me, and leaned against the wall.

"Not on purpose," I said. "Wait a minute, left with Sahrias? She knows where he went?"

"What? No," Lochlan shook his head. "She didn't know where you were. She went to ask Sahrias and he was gone. She assumed you two left together." He shrugged. "I knew you hadn't."

"How?" My eyes flicked to the gold chain peeking out from under his shirt.

"I had a feeling," he shrugged.

"So, you found me and decided to sleep on my floor?" I asked. "Not that I don't appreciate your concern."

And I really did. Lochlan had been one of the best friends I'd ever had. But I was starting to think this reaction had more to do with him than it did with me.

He sighed, confirming my thought.

"I have been . . . I needed—" He paused and ran a hand through his hair. "You have more Magic in you than any Vampire I've ever met."

I blinked at him. Lochlan was twenty-two years old. The Vampire population was small. How many Vampires could he have met?

"Aye, I know what you're thinking," he said. "You're just going to have to trust me on this one, all right?"

I nodded. Placing another piece in the puzzle.

"You have this energy, this presence. Sahrias has it too, but it isn't as strong. It's . . ." He trailed off and seemed to look at something I couldn't see. A memory maybe? "It is very calming," he finished. "And I've been having a tough time with a few things. Being around you helps."

"Okay," I nodded again. "I'm assuming, by your wording, that I'm not going to learn what these tough things are?"

His sad smile concerned me. "Mayhap another time."

"So . . . you were hiding here?" I asked.

"Seeking refuge here," he said.

"You can do that any time. And you don't have to sleep on the floor." I patted the bed.

He pushed off the ground, walked across the room, and sat down beside me. We leaned back against the wall. His feet hung off the side of the bed. Mine were still tucked under the covers.

"I was actually worried about you," he said.

"I'm sorry I made you worry," I whispered, leaning my head on his shoulder.

"Aga said she saw Duke today to check on his hand, and it's healing, but slower than usual for one of his kind. What did you do?"

I told him everything. Everything I could think of. What happened with Duke, and the empty space in my chest. I told him about the dream I'd had so many years ago and about Rayyan. I told him about my ankh tattoo, and how mad I was at Si. How hurt.

When I was done talking, when I had told him everything, I felt better. Still confused, but better. Like I had someone to share the load with.

"You're going to ask Medina about it," Lochlan said. "That's a good idea. 'Ankhian' sounds familiar, but I'm having trouble placing it. I know I've heard it before."

"What did you mean when you said I have Magic?" I asked. "More

Magic than other Vampires."

"I don't know how to explain it," Lochlan said. "It's more of a feeling to me. You remind me of my brother a little. Maybe that's why it's calming."

"The one who died?" I asked.

Lochlan barely spoke about his family. I knew he had two brothers, and one had died when he'd been a kid—but beyond that, nothing.

"No," he said. "The other one. He is very empathic, calming."

"I've never been called calming before." I cracked a smile.

"Don't let it go to your head." He smiled too. "I don't feel so adrift when I'm around you. You feel safe."

"Are you sure you don't want to talk about what's going on with you?" I asked.

"Later," he said.

"Duke!" I moved through the busy halls. "Duke!"

It was dark outside, and the day students were filing out of their last classes. I hadn't seen Duke for a few days. After talking to Lochlan the night before, I'd gone to make my apologies for missing my meetings at the Shine House, then to Niloc for missing a class.

My students didn't mind, of course. Niloc was more understanding than he should have been, and told me Sahrias would be back soon. His lack of answers was infuriating, but not surprising.

"Duke," I called again, catching up to him. I was on my way to meet with Professor Medina, but I hadn't seen Duke since the night everything happened. I needed to apologize and I wanted to check in.

"Dyson," Duke wore the same easy smile as always. "Come to break my other hand?"

"I'm really sorry." My brows drew together. "I don't know what happened. I just felt this weird calm and then—"

"I'm just playing with you, Dys. Don't sweat it." He smiled. "Besides, Sahrias warned me that this might happen."

"What?" I adjusted my backpack higher onto my shoulders. "He told you I'd break your hand?"

"Yes, well, no. He told me I'd get hurt. Maybe I'd break a few bones." Duke raised his injured arm, wrapped and splinted. "He was right. Hurt more than I thought it would, though."

Si knew. The thought made my blood boil. I tried to push that to the back of my mind.

"And you still agreed to train me?" I asked.

"I really don't like history."

"Why did you run away from Agatha?" I asked, and Duke's eyes immediately went to the ground.

"Well, ahh . . ." He scratched the back of his head with his uninjured arm. "I didn't want to bother her, you know."

"Uh huh," I said. "Have you asked her out yet?"

"Agatha? Nah, I couldn't," he said, color rising in his cheeks. "She's too . . ."

A dreamy look fell over him. I snapped my fingers in front of his nose to get his attention.

"Too what?" I asked. "Nothing? She's great, you're great, let's go do it now."

I started to turned away and Duke gripped my upper arm.

"No no no no no." He let it out in a little whine. It was adorable.

"Okay, okay," I smiled, turning back. "But you should definitely do it.

She'll say yes. We can talk about it over a few drinks at Roswell's. On me. I owe you for the broken arm."

"You can drink? I mean, your kind?"

"Sure we can." I brightened. "It's a bit of a new addition for me. Just in the past few years. It doesn't taste as strong as I remember, and it takes a lot for me to feel it, but we can."

"Yeah, that's what they all say." Duke shook his head. "Everyone acts like they're such heavyweight drinkers, and I end up putting them to bed at the end of the night."

"Care to put your money where your mouth is?" My smile widened.

"All right. You're on, little lady. What are your terms?" the big man asked.

"Little lady?" My eyebrows rose. "You're going to eat those words soon enough."

"Sure, sure." Duke smiled wide and waved off my words with a massive hand.

"Roswell's," I said. "You let me know when you're free."

"Shot for shot," Duke stated. "If I win, you have to write my next three English papers."

"I will do no such thing. I am a teacher here," I said.

"You will lend serious aid," he put a strong emphasis on the last two words, "to my next three English papers."

"Agreed," I nodded. "But if I win, you ask Agatha out."

"Deal," he said.

We shook.

I walked up to Professor Medina's office still smiling at Duke's bravado.

Poor guy. He doesn't know what's coming to him.

I knocked on the door a few minutes before Medina's office hours ended.

"Go away, you insufferable child," Medina said when I poked my head in. "I was just about to lock my door."

"Hey, Professor," I said with a smile. "You know I'm older than you, right?"

Gerry Medina, a Psychometry Gifter, had started teaching at Erroin in 2023 at the age of thirty. Originally slated to join a shipwreck exhibition in the Egyptian Red Sea, Niloc had easily coaxed him away with mention of the vast collection of historical artifacts within the school's possession. With his gift of reading the histories of the objects he touched, the offer was too good to pass up.

"I do not care how old you are." He waved me in. "Do you know how many lives I've lived through the artifacts I've held? Close the door behind you."

"Only because you bring it up every time I see you." I grinned.

"It's been a while. No more ancient history classes?" he asked. "I also notice you skip staff events."

"I go sometimes," I protested. After I finished my Primary, I did a Secondary in social work and started spending a lot of time at the Shine House.

"The full-time Shine House people need a break," I said. "I work nights and they go to the staff events."

"Yes, yes, aren't you a saint." He smiled. "One of my current favorites speaks very highly of you. He knows you from Shine."

"You're not supposed to have favorites, Gerry," I said.

"Neither are you." He pointed at me. "Yet, despite that spot of trouble last year with the Seraph girl, I am sure Haiden is on your list."

"Guilty," I shrugged. "And her name is Luci."

"I know what her name is! God, I was trying to sound annoyed." He grimaced. "What can I help you with today, Professor Blake?"

"I have been doing some research into the Egyptian Pantheon and I've run up against a few dead ends."

"Oh?" He gestured to the chair on the other side of the desk. "For a course?"

"Personal interest," I said.

He leaned back in his chair, his brown almond-shaped eyes curious.

"What are Ankhians," I asked, "and how are they connected to Vampires?"

"Two sides of the same coin. That's what Medina said. Where they thrive in sunlight, we depend on darkness. They're rarer than we are, though once their numbers were larger. They interact with time the same way we do. Sometimes moving smoothly through years of routine, sometimes sleeping for decades on end. Both our kinds are immortal. They have a stronger connection to Magic than we do. A more direct link. They are Gods, and we are . . . not."

Fully healed, but still hungry, Dyson turned back to the hutch and properly examined its contents.

"But you know that already, don't you? Did they tell you, or did you learn it on your own?" She pulled out a bottle and a glass. Dyson removed the lid to smell it. "Strong. You don't mind, do you?"

Cold silence answered her.

"There is a legend, a myth . . . whatever you want to call it." Dyson poured herself a glass and sat back down. "Did they tell you this part?"

She didn't wait for an answer this time.

"There were seven, and they ruled with one mind. One day, one of the seven thought to rule differently. The seven were divided. They fought. They fought so long and hard that they destroyed all life but their own. By the time that fight was over, they each had their own piece of land to rule."

She took a sip, her lips avoiding the chip on one side of the crystal tumbler. Her eyebrows went up. It was good.

"Some of the allied seven stayed closer together, others drifted away. The world populated. The next time they fought, one pulled a stone from the sky and the world was swept clean.

"Time passed. The Seven remained. Some slept. Some walked their lands. Some created life, animals, insects. But eventually, they became lonely, left their lands, and gathered in one place. Together, they created a new kind of life. One that was like them. These children of the Seven called themselves the First Line."

Dyson lifted her eyes from the dark liquid. "Medina said the rumor was the First Line made children of their own. Their children were powerful. Almost as powerful as they were."

"The Seven left the world to the First Line and slept. There was peace as the world grew and matured. Then they created new life, the Children of the Earth." Dyson met the stony gaze across the room from her and clarified. "Humans, or some early version."

She looked away before continuing.

"But just as with their ancestors, a millennia ago, peace didn't last. Desire for total control overwhelmed the descendants of the First Line. The desire for power. To be worshipped. The war was devastating. The world was again, but for a few, wiped clean."

"This time the First Line kept a closer watch on their children. They all stayed in the same place. They were named and worshiped by Humans. Their symbol was an ankh and they were named Ankhians.

"Many slept and were forgotten. Few craved power, and for the most part, those few were controlled.

"Three descendants of the First Line rebelled and tried to recreate the old ways. They killed many. They enslaved more. They were stopped, disciplined, but not killed. They vowed to try again, one day, when the time was right. And now they have." Dyson shook her head.

"God," she sighed the word. "After that conversation, I needed a drink."

CHAPTER TWENTY-TWO
2042

"You sink, I mean think . . ." Duke slurred slightly as he searched for his words. "You think I go down that easy?"

"Actually," I raised a finger quickly and swayed. "For th-sake of my very dear friend Agatha, I hope you do."

I snorted a laugh at my own joke.

"Hey!" Duke's eyebrows knit together. "Wait, what?"

He started laughing too.

"I'll have you know," he said, listing to the side and knocked over a beer bottle and an empty bottle of Rossy's Moon.

It was moonshine, homemade by the owner Roswell, herself.

The elongated arm of a server three tables away stretched out and grabbed one of the bottles Duke tried to catch. Rossy's Moon squirted out of my nose as I laughed at the enormous man scrambling to grab the last falling bottle.

"Yes!" Duke proclaimed. He raised the bottle above his head in triumph. "I'll have you know," he said, as though he hadn't been interrupted, "that I am a very generous lover."

"Well, Duke," the lanky bartender said as he came over, "that's a little more than I needed to know about you."

"Hi, Marty," he said. "Howrr you?"

"Ready to call it a night, beautiful?" Marty asked.

His olive toned skin seemed to glow when he smiled at me. I knew that was just his bartender charm. Nothing magical about it.

"Lord, no!" Duke cried, "She spat out her last one! That puts her . . ." He counted on his fingers. ". . . only five ahead of me now."

"Eight," I said under my breath.

"Whaaa?" Duke asked, swaying more heavily.

"Marty," I said. "If you could jussstand here for a minute."

"He doesnneeda stannerrr." Duke's eyes were working to focus on Marty but he couldn't quite do it.

"Waait for it," I said. "Four, free, two—"

Duke's head hit the table with a loud thunk. I straightened to my usual posture and lost the fake slur.

"One," I said. "Poor guy. Didn't know what he was up against."

"Dyson, you lied to him!" Marty said. "You devious temptress. You told him you could get drunk."

"I did no such thing," I protested. "And, for your information, I can get drunk. I haven't been this buzzed since I was Human."

Marty shook his head and laughed. "How much did he actually have?"

"After the second shot, I thought it best for Duke to slow down."

"Evil," Marty said.

"You will take that secret with you to your grave." I smiled and pointed a finger at him.

He nodded, clearing the table.

"I pay for the beers, right?" I knew the bar had a running contest when it came to Rossy's Moon. My eyes flicked up to read the sign and remind myself of the rules. "Second shot is on the house," I read aloud.

"Keep reading," Marty said from behind the bar.

"Third shot and you drink for free . . . well." I looked back at him. "That doesn't sound very fiscally responsible."

"It's the most expensive shot we have. We also have an arrangement with the inn next door. Students usually stay away from the stuff, but we have a bit of a reputation in the summers."

"Right," I nodded.

In the summer, the student portal closed, and portals from all around the world opened.

"I guess you don't get many Vampires in here?" I asked.

"Until recently, the last time was maybe some hundred years ago," he said. "He would come in here with my cousin Ray when I was a kid. This used to be my father's place." He waved a hand around the bar.

"You were a kid 'some hundred years ago?' " I asked, looking into the young man's slate grey eyes.

"I'm one hundred and thirty-eight years old, Dyson," he said, knowing what I was asking. "It's better this way. We can be together forever."

"Sure," I laughed.

"My great-great-grandfather was Anhkian," he said.

I could have slapped myself in the face for not thinking of this sooner. I should have come straight here, to Marty. Sahrias knew the family that owned the campus bar. Medina had mentioned this school was the place to meet an Ankhian descendent. I guess he wasn't wrong.

"We age differently," Marty explained. "Do you know much about Anhkians?"

"A little," I lied. I'd gotten a full history from Medina, but no connection to Vampires. "Just that they have some connection to the sun."

I went over to sit on a barstool across from where Marty washed glasses.

"Yes, that's right. You know," he said, looking at me in a way he hadn't before. "You kind of remind me of her—my cousin, I mean. I don't know why."

"Oh?" I said, trying to keep my face neutral as my mind raced. This must be the same person, it must be.

"You don't look like her at all. I never really noticed before." He shrugged. "Your presence, maybe. Your aura."

I turned around in the stool, put my elbows on the bar, and looked at my fingernails. "I don't suppose Ray isn't, in fact, your cousin's full name."

"No, actually it isn't," Marty said. I looked over my shoulder at him. "Her name is—"

"Rayyan," I supplied.

"Oh, Gods," he said, catching my wrist over the bar and turning me around. "You're Si's kid, aren't you? I've heard about you two."

He pushed my sleeve up where the small ankh tattoo peeked out.

"Guilty as charged." I gently took my hand back. "You've heard about us."

"Does Si have one as well?" He nodded at my ankh. "I didn't know Vampires could get tattoos."

"I got this when I was Human." I squinted at him. "What do you mean you've heard of us?"

"Family gossip," Marty shrugged. "Si had a progeny who was a daughter not a lover. Si and Ray were . . . anyway. If you got that tattoo before you became a Vampire, it's a funny twist of fate." He rolled up his left pant leg to reveal a very small, very faint ankh symbol on his outer calf.

"How odd," Sahrias had said. And now I knew why. That's when he would have seen my tattoo. "It was one coincidence too many," he'd told me that first night. "And I was suddenly so hungry. It was like a gift, a sign. There you were, and there I was. And I needed a reason to . . ."

"All Ankhians have the mark of the ankh," Marty said, pulling my attention back to him. "We are born with it. It's small on most of us, but on the old ones, the Ancients, well—" He shook his head. "Just hope you never run into one."

Oh god, the picture of Rayyan and Sahrias on the beach. It wasn't multiple tattoos on her side, it was just one. And it wasn't a tattoo. It was her birthmark. And it was enormous.

"Are they dangerous?" I asked.

"They're powerful. Unpredictable. They're very old, and sometimes they go a little mad."

I thought of the Nahal Conflict and wondered it was worth asking Marty about it. Medina said it has gone by many names. The Anhkian War, Battle of the Lines, the Children's War. And many other titles lost to time. So many that it was hard to track.

"Is your great-great-grandfather still alive?" I asked.

"I don't know," Marty said. "I never met him. I don't think my dad did either."

"Rayyan was a full Ankhian?"

"High in the Line too," he nodded. "Si was good for her. He made her more . . . Human, I guess." He got lost in thought for a few seconds.

This was big. Sahrias dated the daughter of Isis. Isis! And she fucked him up. Does that mean Isis was one of the Seven? Or maybe one of the First Line?

"That happens sometimes," Marty continued. "When we, Ankhians, get old. We forget what the world is—we see it for something else. I remember Ray being happy then. And Sahrias was too."

There was a quiet beep and Marty turned around to open and empty a small dishwasher. I took the moment to debate whether or not I should tell Marty what had happened to me. Was he someone I could trust?

"Did Rayyan do anything to him?" I asked instead.

"Other than break his heart?" Marty said over his shoulder.

"I've heard that."

"Whatever you've heard," he said as he pulled small bowls and pint glasses out of the dishwasher, "you haven't heard it all. I don't even know what really happened. All I know is—well, there are some things we aren't supposed to say—she hurt him. Bad."

That piqued my interest. I had to stop myself from asking the stupid question "What aren't you supposed to say?" and settled for, "Is there anything you can tell me? Anything that might pertain to me?"

"What are you asking, Dyson?" He paused in his cleaning. "Why would what happened decades before you were born, let alone changed, have anything to do with you?"

"I just mean, does being with someone like that change you? Physiologically?"

He looked at me like I had eight eyeballs.

"If a Caster falls in love with a Shifter, do they start changing shape?" he asked.

"Okay," I said. "Okay, you don't need to make me feel stupid. But I mean my maker dated a sun god . . . he drank her blood, he walked in daylight because of her. You don't learn that every day."

"Damn!" Marty threw a towel on the bar. "Is that what it would have taken to snag you? I don't have enough Ankhian in me for that, but I would be willing to test it out." He lifted his chin, offering his neck.

"You're too much," I said, shaking my head at him. "Save your flirting for better tippers."

"Go home, Dyson," he smiled. "Ask Sahrias about Rayyan."

"You think I haven't?"

"The sun is coming up soon," he said. "You'll be too tired to carry that mountain of a man if it does and you're still here."

I pushed away from the bar, sure I wasn't going to get any more information.

"What is it with this Rayyan?" I asked.

"There are," he paused. "There are things we are not supposed to say."

In that moment, he seemed as old as his years.

"Well, that's cryptic and stupid," I told him.

"I'm sorry," he said. "I wish I could be more help. If it makes you feel better, I don't even know all of it."

I shrugged, walked over to Duke and pulled him up over my shoulder in a fireman's carry.

"It doesn't," I said—and left.

Dyson looked across the room at the heavily curtained balcony doors. She needed to feed. The feeling was getting desperate, but the sun was still up. She could smell it. She had to distract herself. She had to keep talking.

"Duke had never been so hung over," Dyson said, ignoring the dryness of her throat. "Marty was true to his word. Duke never learned I drank for him or that I was faking. And, of course," Dyson smiled in earnest, "Agatha went out with him. They got married, had kids.

"I met one of their grandsons later on. I met their kids too, but it was their grandson that I really got to know. Duncan James III. He was big like Duke, a Shifter like Duke. You wouldn't know him, but you almost ruined his life," she said her eyes flicking up then away.

"Maybe you did. I never learned how that whole poison thing turned out." She shook her head. "That's a completely different story."

Dyson stood quickly, and without thinking about it, she was across the room with her fingers circled around the balcony doors' cold metal handles. Strong fingers that could kill a man without a second thought. Fingers that had killed many times over.

She let her hands drop and she moved back to the piano bench.

Not yet, she thought.

CHAPTER TWENTY-THREE
2042

I walked slowly from Duke's room back to Sahrias's apartment. I'd been sleeping there since he'd left two weeks ago. Sometimes in his room. Sometimes in mine. I didn't know why, but it gave me comfort, even though I was still upset.

I thought about what Marty said, about what he wasn't allowed to say. I thought about the history lesson from Medina and how Rayyan fit into it. How I fit into it. I thought about everything Sahrias should have told me a long time ago.

I unlocked the apartment door and walked in. Had I left the lights on?

"Dyson?"

My head snapped up as Sahrias's door opened.

"Dyson," he said again, stepping into the living space.

"You're back." I was shocked to see him. I'd started to think he'd left me forever. "When did you get back?"

"About an hour ago." He took a cautious step forward. "How . . . how are you doing?"

I raised my eyebrows and pointed to my chest. "Me? No. No, you don't get to disappear without an explanation, muttering about curses, then come back two weeks later and expect me to answer questions."

His brows drew together and his eyes turned down. "I suppose that's fair."

"Where were you?" I asked.

"I went to see someone," he said.

"Who?" He was testing my patience by making me ask. "And why?"

"A being who sees," he said. "Aurraya. She sees things, sometimes. Sees how things will turn out."

"Why?" I pushed the word out through gritted teeth.

"I needed to know if the Starlit Shield would come for you, for me. I didn't mean to be gone for so long. Time moves differently in Aurraya's realm . . . when she wants it to."

I blinked. That was not the answer I was expecting.

The Starlit Shield. I remembered Si telling me about them. The group of Luman who created and enforced certain laws.

But I haven't done anything wrong. Have I?

"Why would they come after me?" I asked.

"Can we sit?" Sahrias gesturing to the couches.

I obliged him, and asked again, "Why me?"

"I was not supposed to sire," he explained. "I was told not to."

"What?" I said.

"The Starlit Shield forbade the continuance of our line. Yamini did horrible things. Things she shouldn't have been able to do. The Shield thought her power came from our line. Our blood. God, I should have told you all this before." He shook his head. "But it was my burden to bear. I didn't want to give it to you. And you were so strong. You are so strong. I will never regret bringing you into my life."

He looked at me. He looked at me in the way that made me feel as though he was seeing my soul. "You have made my life so much better, Dyson. I will never regret going against the Shield."

I didn't speak. I didn't know what to say. He opened his mouth to continue, but I raised a hand. I needed a moment. He waited.

Sahrias's maker, Yamini, had done something. The Starlit Shield had attributed it to her bloodline. It must have scared them if they wanted the line to end. And if Si had listened, I wouldn't exist. I would have died forever that day on the cold tile of the subway platform.

I wasn't sure how to feel. How would I have reacted to learning this before now? When would have been the right time to tell me that I shouldn't have been turned? That there was a shadow organization of law enforcement that outlawed my existence?

I'd spent years feeling like there was something off, something missing. Years feeling like there was this secret happening just outside my reach and, somehow, I was in the middle of it. I was right, and Sahrias had lied to me. For decades.

I wasn't even sure I disagreed with his decision.

Fear crept into the corners of my mind. Were they going to come after me now? I looked back up at Si.

"But they haven't found me," I said. "Why haven't they found me?"

"The stone," Sahrias gestured to the pendant hanging around my neck. "Niloc cast a protection spell on it when he gave it to me."

That just confused me more.

"So, all this time, you haven't been protected from them?" I said, anger tainting my words.

"They are not what they once were," he said, shaking his head. "As the Luman world has calmed, so have they."

"And now?" I asked.

"I don't know what this ability you have is," Sahrias said, dropping his eyes to the table between us. "We have a complicated lineage, you and I. There is great power in our blood. Power that, for some, is uncontrollable."

"What did she do?" I asked. "And what does that have to do with me?"

"Whatever madness I thought she had," Sahrias explained, "it was nothing to what happened once I'd left. I was holding something together for her, keeping her darkest monsters at bay. In the decade after I left, she sired some thirty new Vampires, and together they decimated everything in their path."

"What does this have to do with me?" I asked again.

"Our line carries something unique," he said. "It doesn't manifest in all of us, and it shows itself in different ways. Creating a new Vampire is hard. It takes time and power to care for a young one."

The memory of being surrounded by blood bags with a sandpaper dry throat came to mind. The cool press of composure washing over me when I was overwhelmed. Time and time again. For months.

Yes. That would take power.

"It is very draining," Sahrias said. "A Vampire should not be able to sire so many, especially at the same time. The Shield thought this power, this level of control over the minds of her get, was a manifestation of our line's curse."

"And they killed her?"

"She's dead," he said, only partially answering my question.

"And why aren't you?" I asked. "Dead, I mean. If the Shield wanted to end the line, why didn't they kill you too?"

"After a very extensive and painful process, they decided I have no special talents. No extra abilities. I think that is the only reason they allowed me to live . . . one of the only reasons." He muttered that last part so quietly, I wondered if he meant to say it at all.

"This thing," he gestured to me. "This thing happening to you. It is a manifestation of this power, this curse. I don't know." He shook his head. "I'm doing this wrong. I want to be better. To say the right things. But I just don't know."

He took a deep breath. I let the silence stretch.

"I needed to know if Aurraya saw the Shield coming for us," he said. "I know Erroin has special protection spells that likely kept you from their gaze, but I was frantic. Panicked. I had half a mind to take you and run, but I know how much you love it here. Your friends. I didn't want to make you leave if you didn't have to. And if this place is the only reason— I didn't . . ."

He squeezed his eyes shut. Tears fell down his face. He didn't wipe them away.

"I fear what's coming," he said. "I fear the Shield. I acted out of that fear when I left as I did. We all have our triggers, Dyson. I am still getting over mine."

"Is the Shield coming?" I asked. "Do we have to leave?"

"Not yet," he said. "Thank the Gods, no one has noticed you yet."

I stayed in Sahrias's apartment. I laid in my old bed. I didn't want to be alone. Maybe I should have left. Maybe I would have actually been able to sleep in my own space. I wasn't strong enough to fully throw off the sun's call to sleep, but I wasn't so young that I had to submit. It was torturous.

My head was spinning with everything I'd learned, and I wanted it to stop. I wanted a respite from the madness. From the complexity.

As soon as the sun set and I got up, I decided I'd try to get back to normal, and that meant sleeping in my own bed. I left my room in hopes of seeing Sahrias. In hopes of speaking to him—but his door was open, and he wasn't there.

My heart sank. I needed something from him, but I couldn't articulate what. I stood in the doorway, looking into his empty room.

My father, I decided. That's what I needed right now. I needed my father, and I wasn't going to get that. Not my Human father, and not Si.

Not right now, anyway.

I went to the bookcase in Sahrias's room and took the leather folder off the shelf. I flipped to the picture of Rayyan and Si on the beach. The ankh was barely visible under Rayyan's bathing suit, but I could tell what it was.

"Si was good for her," Marty had said. "He made her more ... Human, I guess."

I flipped to the next photo, the one Zemila loved so much.

"They're powerful. Unpredictable," Marty had told me. "They're very old, and sometimes they go a little mad."

"Were you the real reason the Shield didn't kill Si?" I asked the picture.

It was what I'd been thinking all night. How was this connected to the Ankhians? Sahrias had said he was only able to leave Yamini because of Rayyan. Then the way Marty had reacted to my tattoo. Were Ankhians connected to this curse? If not, was my Magic like theirs?

"Did you protect him from the Shield?" I asked the woman in the photo. "If you did, why did you leave?"

I took the photo before replacing the folder on the shelf. I don't know why I took it. I wondered if he would even notice. But I felt less alone, taking it with me.

When I got back to my room, I dug through an old box until I found a thin plastic folder. I cut it to the size of the picture and put the photo inside, then placed it into my father's copy of *Carmilla*. I left the small book on my bedside table and I went to the library.

"The Starlit Shield," I said to the index.

CHAPTER TWENTY-FOUR
2042

My ethics class was a welcome reprieve from reading about the most powerful Gifters, Vampires, Witches, Sirens, Beast Lords, and Dragons—yes, Dragons, I had to read that twice—that formed the Starlit Shield.

Lochlan walked into my class just before we started and sat in the back. He was an entirely different distraction. He wasn't doing well, and I didn't know how to help. Just being around him didn't really feel like I was doing anything.

After my class, I worked a shift at Shine House. Lochlan came with me. He brought Nemo. The kids loved them. Nemo loved it too.

"This place would have changed my life," Nemo said, "if I'd known about it earlier."

Nemo had been sixteen when he arrived at Erroin. He had the option of living in the Shine House for a year, maybe two, and being one of the oldest kids, or living in a dorm room. He'd picked the dorm.

Nemo and Lochlan had been roommates ever since.

"Aye," Lochlan clapped him on the shoulder. "But then we wouldn't have lived together and you'd surely be lost without me."

"I'd be failing everything but math," Nemo said.

Lochlan smirked.

"I'll be right back," Nemo spotted Marines, one of the Shine House administrators. She was walking into a back office after shooing the remaining students upstairs to their rooms.

"It's getting late," I said, tidying a large table where the kids ate and occasionally did homework. "You guys should go."

"Aye," Lochlan nodded and I saw stress around his eyes.

The kids were getting ready for lights out, and most of the other teachers and caretakers were leaving. I was the overnight person for obvious reasons.

"I can work with some of the artists," Nemo bounded back to us with a bright smile. "Marines says I can start a weekly class."

Once the kids were in bed, and Lochlan and Nemo had left, I had nothing to distract me from thinking myself in circles. I thought about Sahrias, and Rayyan, and this curse, this power. How would it manifest in me? Would it continue to just unexpectedly explode out of me? And would I ever be able to control it?

Eventually, I pulled a book off one of the shelves that surrounded the fireplace. It was one of my all-time favorites and I had started reading it on my last shift. I sat down on one of the couches and hoped it would distract me.

With an hour left to my shift, I heard familiar footsteps outside the front door. I was confused. It was 3:30 a.m. Maybe I'd misheard.

"Lochlan?" I said, when he opened the door. I put my bookmark in place and set my copy of *Moon Called* by Patricia Briggs down on the coffee table. "Are you okay?"

"Aye." He shut the door quietly, walked around the large table, and sat beside me on the couch. "I just couldn't sleep and . . ."

"Okay," I said, not needing him to explain.

Lochlan slid off the couch and knelt beside the empty fireplace. He started casting under his breath and an aura of power seemed to rush into him. I'd seen this before. He usually did a better job of hiding it.

When he was done and a low fire crackled in the grate, he sat beside me again.

"Do you want—" I started.

"No," he cut me off. "I just . . ."

"Okay." I nodded and picked up my book. I took out the bookmark and flipped to the beginning. "You're lucky this is the first in the series," I said, before I started to read aloud.

I wasn't sure if it was the right thing to do, but as soon as I started reading, he sighed, leaned back, and seemed to relax.

Four chapters later, Tamira and Salem—the early morning shift—arrived. Once we were out of the Shine House, I linked my arm through Lochlan and we ambled slowly through the empty halls.

"I liked that book," he said.

"It's one of my favorites," I told him. "Easy escapism."

"Even though you know all the monsters are real?"

"Even though I know all the monsters are real," I repeated.

When we got to my room, I showed him the picture of Sahrias and Rayyan. I told him everything.

His face darkened when I mentioned the Starlit Shield.

"Do you know who they are?" I asked.

"No," he said, "No more than you."

I knew he was lying, but I didn't push.

I was in my bed when I felt the sun rise. Lochlan was sitting on the floor.

"Just until you fall asleep," he said. "Then I'll go for a swim."

"All right," I agreed. I didn't want to be alone. "All right."

"Hello," Agatha waved a hand in front of my face some ten minutes after she'd flopped down in her favorite spot in the library. "Earth to Dyson?"

Lochlan, Agatha, Nemo, and Zemila had been chatting and I'd added a few "ohs" and "uh huhs" in the appropriate pauses, but I hadn't been following the conversation.

"I'm sorry. My mind is just somewhere else today," I said, trying to cover how out of it I was.

"Share?" Agatha asked. The word was soft and kind.

"I learned some interesting stuff from Marty when I was at Roswell's," I said. "And me and Si had a really intense conversation a few nights ago. I've just had a lot on my mind."

"He's back?" Nemo asked.

"Yeah," I nodded. "He's back."

"You had a conversation with Marty?" Agatha asked. "Duncan said you were both smashed."

I was pretty sure he hadn't asked her out yet, and I made a mental note to bug him about it.

"Duke was smashed," I said, a smile reluctantly pulling at corners of my mouth. "I was okay."

"I don't know which to ask about first," Zemila said. "Marty or Sahrias."

"You want to hear what Marty had to say." I pointed at Zemila. "You were right. It was Sahrias in that photo."

"You saw it?" Zemila's eyes lit up, and I nodded.

"I found it in his room, but I haven't worked up the courage to ask him about it yet, not with everything else."

I didn't tell them that I stole the photo, and I didn't tell them that I was cursed.

Zemila's eyes narrowed. She knew I was hiding something, and she knew I didn't want to talk about it.

"What did you learn about the woman in the picture?" she asked, and I breathed out a sigh of relief. "Do you know her name?"

Zemila had a way of getting information out of people. Thankfully, she also knew when not to push.

"Rayyan," I said. "I did some research but didn't come up with too much."

"Rayyan who?" Nemo asked.

"Ortis, I think," I said. "I can't be sure. I didn't find much. Just one article."

"Loch, you remember that project you helped me with a while back?" he said, sending another bit of paper flying at Lochlan's head.

"Brother, you'll have to be more specific," Lochlan said, trying to catch the paper out of the air with his teeth. He missed and the paper hit him lightly in the cheek. "I'm a ghost writer for many of your projects."

"Shut up." Nemo smirked. "I think it was a few months ago, for my essay on Luman Ancestry and the Shaping of the Modern World?"

"Yes," Lochlan said. "I liked that one."

"I forget most of it," Nemo went on. "But what was that one bit about the Originals? Or the Rulers, or something? The one group that wanted to rule the world and there was a huge war?"

"The Dominion War?" Zemila offered. "Angels and Demons?"

"No, no, before that." Nemo waved her off. "Lochy, come on, you remember. The Eternal Life race or something like that."

"Ankhians," I said.

"Yes!" Nemo snapped and pointed at me. "And that name, Rayyan. That name stuck in my head for some reason. I doubt it was the same one, but there was an Ankhian with that name. Rayyan of Ortus."

"Gods Below." Lochlan looked at me. "I should have remembered. I'm sorry, I've been . . ." He trailed off, his eyes shifting to Zemila, then the floor.

"You wrote about her in your paper?" I asked, eager to take my mind of the Starlit Shield and my maybe cursed blood.

"No, not at all," Nemo answered. Disappointment ran through me. "But she was mentioned in an article. It was comparing the little we know about the Anhkian Civil War and the Ascendancy War. I should be able to find it."

How had I missed it? I thought I'd found all the books pertaining to Rayyan.

Nemo put down his sketch pad and went over to the library index. He returned a few minutes later with an old softcover textbook called *How We Came to Be: The Intersection of Physiology and History.*

"Shall I read it, then?" Lochlan asked, after taking the book from Nemo and flipping through.

"Yes," Nemo started sketching again. "Page eighty-four. I hate reading aloud."

"I'll try and skip over the boring bits," Lochlan said. "Okay, introduction, blaa blaa, boring boring, blaa blaa—ohh, I like this bit," he said. "It talks about the Ascendancy War or War of Dominion; the conflict was between Seraphs and Demons. Both sides took huge losses and then this guy cites a brutal article on the issues with the reproduction of Demons."

Lochlan looked up in disgust. We all looked back.

"Right, sorry." He nodded. "Less commentary, more relevant information."

"No, that is interesting," Zemila said. "Why is it harder for Demons to reproduce?"

"Ask Loch's mom," Nemo muttered.

"Piss off." Lochlan turned the page without looking up. "Ahh, here we go. So, basically, it says that Ankhians all lived in one spot, near Egypt, some eight thousand years ago—though the race has been around much longer. It says that there were the Originals, or the Ancients, who were like the leaders. Over the next couple thousand years—"

"Jesus, they live a long time," Nemo said.

"—they all spread out," Lochlan finished.

"Why?" Agatha asked.

"I think because they all wanted to rule, or something. Yes—" Lochlan skimmed a little more before continuing. "They separated and ruled their corners of the world, then a group who called themselves—" He squinted at the paper. "It's written in a hieroglyph or something predating that, I have no idea, but there is a note saying the translation is 'Ortus,' and perhaps 'Occulta Ortus' or 'Cucullatus Ortus.' But those last two are written in by hand. Someone added them."

Interesting. This article had the Originals separating, each taking a continent. Medina's version was a creation myth. The separation of Pangea.

"Rayyan of Ortis?" Nemo said.

"Aye," Lochlan nodded. "But this is spelt with a 'u' not an 'i.'"

"'Ortus' is Latin." Lochlan continued. "It means rising. Occulta or cucullatus, is hidden or hooded. Hidden rising?"

"Ortus can also mean birth or origin," Nemo said. "Hidden origins, or . . ." He trailed off as we all stared at him.

There was a beat of silence.

"What?" he said. "I know things! You guys think Lochlan is the only one who can know things?"

"Yes," Zemila nodded. "And Aga."

Everyone but Nemo laughed.

"I remembered that Rayyan name, didn't I?" he said.

"But, Latin?" Agatha asked, shocked. "You can speak Latin?"

"You can't?" Nemo said bitterly. "I know lots of things," he muttered.

"Okay," Lochlan said, bringing our attention back to the actual article. " 'The Ortus War was an attempt by three very old and very powerful Ankhians who were the rallying point for those who believed the old ways of rule were best. They were Rakal, Rayyan, and Rahor.'"

The three children of the First Line who'd tried to bring back the old ways . . . she was one of them. Rayyan was one of them. Peace didn't last. That's what Medina had said. She was one of the three who'd rebelled against the First Line.

"They killed many," I remember Medina saying. "They enslaved more. They were stopped, but vowed to try again."

" 'Whether these names were chosen or given,' " Lochlan read, " 'the three took on the surname of' . . . there is that symbol again . . . 'but essentially of Ortus. All three could also link themselves back to the rulers of old by as little as one generation.' Gods, I guess that means at least one of them is the daughter or son of an old ruler."

"Wow," Zemila said. "And she went to school here?"

"You have to remember that this war was thousands of years ago, Mila," her brother said. "She probably got over it."

If she left Si for this cause, I doubt she got over it.

"Can you imagine living that long?" Agatha said. "Wow. You would have to watch everyone you know die, if you even had friends that weren't immortal. And one lifetime would seem like nothing. I'd go crazy. How could you stay—"

"Human?" I finished her sentence.

Lochlan shifted in his seat.

"Oh, I'm sorry, Dyson. I didn't mean it like that," Agatha tried to backtrack.

"I know, Aga, but I think about it too. Si was born in the twelfth century."

"Woah," Zemila said. "He's so . . . normal."

Lochlan scoffed. "Why shouldn't he be normal?"

"I don't know," Zemila said, taken aback by Lochlan's tone. "Just seems like you might lose some of that over time. You know? Like you would forget how to be . . ." Lochlan looked down to the textbook in his hands, and Zemila trailed off.

"It says here," Lochlan read, "that it is suspected that either Rakal or Rahor is actually Nefertem, son of the Egyptian Goddess Sekhmet."

"Does it say anything about a connection to Isis?" I asked.

"Not that I'm seeing." Lochlan flipped the page. "Are we thinking this is the same Rayyan?"

"Yes," I said. "And I'm sure she's still alive."

"How did a Vampire and an Ankhian get together in the first place?" Agatha asked.

"Yeah," I said thoughtfully. "I don't know."

How had that happened? Ankhians being of light. And Vampires needing darkness. Two sides of the same coin.

"Only one way to find out," Lochlan said, looking pointedly at me, knowing the full extent of everything I was trying to figure out. "You need to talk to your maker."

CHAPTER TWENTY-FIVE
2042

Over the next few weeks, Sahrias and I fell into a false sense of normalcy. I hated it. I also feared breaking it. What if I asked about Rayyan and Ankhians, and made it worse?

I hated that Sahrias and I were awkward around each other, when we had always been so at ease. I hated that it felt like I was lying to him by not telling him what I'd learned. I hated that all of this made me feel so alone and I still had no idea what this power was or how it worked.

Jab, jab, cross, slip, right hook. Duke held the pads, moving with me around the combat room.

I missed my friend, my brother, my father.

Jab, jab, cross, slip, right hook.

I wanted him to take the lead. I wanted him to bring up the Shield and explain this curse or power or whatever. I wanted him to want to help me understand.

Jab, jab, cross, slip, right hook.

But he didn't, and now he walks into my training session like everything is normal? Then he just leaves without a word? A joke? A playful taunt? Nothing!

Jab, jab, cross, slip—

"Woah," Duke said, as he shifted and my fist only landed a glancing blow. "Are you okay, Dyson?"

"Come on." My voice came out harsher than I'd meant it to. "Let's keep going."

"Umm, no," he said. "I am not trying to break an arm and you're starting to give off a glowy floaty energy." He waved a padded hand at me.

"Really?" I straightened. Duke and I had yet to discuss what happened and he'd never told me what he'd seen. I didn't want to push. It was weird, even by Luman standards.

"Not so much actual light, but your—" He paused, thinking of the word. "Your energy, the scent in the room maybe. The feel of the air. It changed when Sahrias walked in, and it changed again when he left. Intensified. Then kind of shifted."

I listened with rapt attention. I had no idea Duke's gifts extended to this, but I guess having heightened senses and being aware of the changes around you would do it.

"Tell me more," I said. The more I could learn about this, the sooner I'd be able to control it.

"Not much more to tell," he went on. "I noticed that shift last time too, but didn't think anything of it. Almost like a pressure change. I don't know how to describe it. What happened between you and Sahrias?"

"It's a long story," I grumbled.

"He hasn't watched a lesson in weeks." Duke removed the Velcro pads from his hands.

I did the same with my gloves. Looked like it would be a short lesson today. Maybe Zemila would want to wake up early and work out. I would see if I could find her before she went to bed tonight and ask.

"I think that was Si's version of an olive branch," I said, flopping down on the floor. A pair of teenagers popped their heads in.

"Yeah," Duke waved at them. "It's all yours."

They came in and started warming up.

"Olive branch for what?" he asked me.

"We haven't really spoken since." I nodded at his healed hand.

"It's been over a month!" he sat down next to me.

"I mean, we talk, but it feels off."

"Why?" he asked.

"You don't know anything about someone named Rayyan do you?"

"Does she go here?" he asked.

"No." I shook my head. "I read about her in an article after Marty mentioned—"

"Wait, wait, wait . . ." Duke narrowed his eyes at me. "You remember Roswell's? You were as sloshed as I was!"

"You passed out . . . in the bar. So, no, I was not as sloshed as you were."

"And then, you, who could barely sit up straight, had a full conversation with Marty, and remember it?"

"I wasn't nearly as drunk as you," I said. "I was exhausted, though. Marty gave me some coffee," I lied.

"He didn't offer you anything else?" Duke lifted his chin, showing me his throat. "I see the way he looks at you."

I laughed and spared only a moment thinking of the level of trust that action showed. A predator like him would not usually show a predator like me his throat. A sign of submission to some. A sign of trust to me.

"That would have really sobered me up," I said, zipping up my gym bag and standing. "But alas, no. Niloc mentioned her too, Rayyan, I mean. But I'm not sure I should ask him again. I feel like that's—"

"Going over Si's head?" Duke stood too. We waved to the kids who had started some kind of partner workout. They nodded back and we left.

"Yeah," I said.

"You'd be right. You shouldn't ask Niloc without talking to Si first."

The halls were relatively quiet for this time of night. We'd ended early and most students who were up were in class.

"Speaking of things, we should and should not be doing." I grinned up at Duke. "Have you seen Agatha lately?"

His eyes flew to the floor and his cheeks flushed.

I laughed. "Enough said. But you have to do it."

"I know I do." Duke's voice sounded small. "And I want to—I just don't know how."

"Yet again, I will come to the rescue," I said, in my most magnanimous voice. "Agatha, Mila, Loch, Nemo, and I, along with some of the other hospital staff, are going to Roswell's next week for the New Year's Eve party. I suggest you go with a few friends and, at some point in the evening, come on over, say hello to me. Then—"

"You know, Dyson," he interrupted. "We have had conversations before." We walked slowly through the wide hall. "I'm not just mooning over some girl I've never spoken to."

"I know that," I nodded. "She has asked you out multiple times and you haven't noticed."

"She has not," he protested.

"She one hundred percent has, she tells me every time you don't notice," I said. Duke opened his mouth, but I kept going. "When have you had a conversation in a social setting that might, ahhh . . ." I grinned. "Lead somewhere."

"Oh, hush." He shoved me a little. "I just don't know how to—"

"Leave the friend zone?" I supplied.

"Yeah." He ran a big hand through his hair.

"You were never in it, so you literally just have to ask her out. Or say yes the next time she asks you. You should Dyson-up and—"

"Dyson-up?" he repeated. We paused at the end of a hallway. I was turning left, back to my room. He was going right.

"Yeah, you know—" I brought my fist into the air, flexing my bicep. "Dyson-up! Be tough, brave, go after what you want."

"Oh," he said in mock surprise. "Is that what you do?"

"Well." I deflated a little. "I try."

He laughed and started to walk away.

"Next week," I called after him. "Roswell's. And no Moon for you."

"Never again," Duke called back. "Never again."

I went back to my own room to shower and change. It didn't take long for thoughts of Agatha and Duke to be overrun by Sahrias, Rayyan, and curses. Assuming his little visit to the combat room was an invitation, I went to Si's apartment once I was dressed.

He was sitting on the living room couch, waiting for me.

"Hello," he said. "How was your session with Duncan?"

I was frustrated with the odd formality between us.

"Good," I lied. "You didn't stay. I thought maybe you wanted to talk about. . ."

I didn't know how to finish the sentence.

"Indeed," he said.

"I have some things I want to talk to you about too."

"Please sit." He gestured to the couch across from him. I sat and we looked at each other over the coffee table. "Would you like to start? Or would you like me to?"

"I met an old friend of yours the night I was at Roswell's with Duke," I said.

"Oh?"

"Marty. I didn't tell you sooner because of everything." I waved my hand through the air. "I just didn't know how to bring up this other thing."

"Yes." Sahrias nodded. "That is understandable. And, yes, I know Marty. He has been around for quite some time. His kind age strangely."

I thought back to the age in Marty's eyes. I'd seen a similar age in Lochlan's.

"He said he is part Ankhian." I watched Si's face closely for a reaction.

"The oldest among all Luman," he explained. "Some say they walked with the dinosaurs, others start their creation myths with them."

"Marty said something about fate when he saw my tattoo. He told me to ask you about Rayyan. He said I reminded him of her, and that she is an Ankhian. A really old one."

Sahrias spoke his next words softly.

"You are nothing like Rayyan," he said. "You can't be."

"What happened with her?" I asked. "Does she have anything to do with this curse thing we have? Or why the Starlit Shield let you go?"

"Ha," he breathed. "You have been thinking about this."

"That thing," I said. "The glowing curse thing. It almost happened again tonight after you left." Sahrias looked up sharply. "I didn't feel it,"

I explained. "But Duke did and we stopped."

"That may have been a wise choice on his part," Sahrias muttered.

"I kind of agree. That makes it three times. Three times that this has happened. Today, the time I broke Duke's hand, and that dream."

I waited to see if he would say anything. If he would admit to his lie.

"It wasn't a dream, was it?" I asked

He shook his head.

"Is that why we left the mountains?"

He nodded. "I should have told you that night, or maybe the first night I met you. Perhaps the day you broke Duncan's hand, but certainly before now."

"About Rayyan?" I asked. "Or this glowy curse thing?"

"This will not be about Rayyan," he said, and I saw the depth of sadness in his eyes. "I will speak of her when I am ready, and though you deserve that story too, it will not be tonight. I am sorry. I—"

He paused.

"You may infer what you will from this conversation. You may infer a great deal." He gave me a small smile. "If you put together that she protected me from the Shield, I have no doubt you will."

"Okay," I said.

"Okay," he echoed, and took a deep breath.

"I learned the history of our line that night. Or at least the history as it had been told to Si. There was so much speculation, myth, legend. It wasn't until later that I learned the full extent of what happened with Rayyan. But that night, he told me what he could."

Thousands of years ago, a Vampire turned an Ankhian. It had never been done before, or since. If this was a forced change, or a desired one, the legend does not say. Either way, it had had unexpected consequences to the children of that line.

In very powerful Ankhians, a gift can manifest. It's very rare. The Ankhian at the top of our line was gifted. And so were the Vampires who followed. Or, at least, some of them were.

"I regret nothing," Dyson said, looking around the room. "Almost nothing."

She would be naïve not to recognize the effect it had had on their lives. Hers, Si's, and the lives of the ones they loved. Truth be told, the members of her line were—

"Cursed," she whispered. "Some were able to shape shift or fly or were exponentially stronger than their counterparts. Some were completely normal as far as Vampires go. Some fell in the middle somewhere. The only constant was the pull. The irresistible pull to someone who could live in the sun.

"Two sides of the same coin," Dyson said. "Darkness and light."

She looked down at the small ankh on the inside of her wrist. She'd always been drawn to the symbol. Even before she'd been turned.

Fate? She shook her head. Destiny?

"I hate that stuff," she muttered. "Destiny, prophecy . . . It makes me feel like I have no control, no agency."

The conversation with Sahrias felt like it had been just yesterday. If she closed her eyes and focused, she could hear his voice in her head.

"Sahrias told me that the consequence for the children of the Ankhian-Vampiric line was an irresistible connection to life, to one who was alive. That was how the Vampire compensated for being banished from the day."

Dyson remembered asking if it was the same as a soulmate.

"In the crudest explanation, yes," Sahrias had said. "But it is not love. It is obsessive devotion. It is not at all love."

Those words had come out cold. She hadn't understood why then. She did now.

"It wasn't a two-way thing," Dyson explained. "We were drawn to them. We—" She tapped her chest. "—the curse, or whatever it was. The mixing of Magics that shouldn't have mixed made us feel like we loved them. Like we needed them. They weren't drawn to us in the same way, or so Sahrias told me."

Dyson placed her empty glass on top of the broken piano and let it go. As soon as she did, it started to slide across the sleek dark wood. She could stop it if she wanted to.

But she wanted to watch it fall. She wanted to see it break.

The crystal shattered against the floor. The pieces caught the flickering light of a dying candle. It almost looked like stars.

"I thought they must love us." She shook her head. "Some of them must have loved us. If not, why was Rayyan with Sahrias for so long?

"Oh, Si," Dyson breathed. He was hurt and that's why he thought the way he did. "It all could have been so different."

CHAPTER TWENTY-SIX
2043

"THREE, TWO, ONE, HAPPY NEW YEAR!"

All around me, couples kissed their way into 2043. I saw Agatha and Duke share a very shy and very chaste press of lips. Nemo dipped his fling of the week, Jasmin, and kissed her with reckless abandon. Zemila had her arms around Trevor, who she'd started seeing about a second after she broke up with Driss.

Lochlan stood beside me, drink in hand, a wistful look on his face.

"Hey," I leaned over and bumped his shoulder with mine. "Smile, it's a new year."

He smiled. It was sad.

"Happy New Year, Dyson," he said.

"Happy New Year, Lochlan." I leaned over and kissed him on the cheek. We were the same height. All I needed to do was tilt my head. "She doesn't know what she's missing."

He flushed.

"Dyson, I—"

"Don't bother! It's a secret only to her. I think she wants it to be. I think . . . anyway." I tapped the side of my glass to his. "To a new year. To new things."

"A new year," he said. We both drank. "I'm going to leave before next semester starts. I've just . . . I . . ."

He trailed off and looked at the ceiling.

I knew something was going on with him. I also knew that bringing it up was a ploy to get me off the Zemila subject.

"You don't actually want to talk about this here, do you?" I asked.

"No," he shook his head. "I don't."

"Do you want to loosen up a bit?" I asked.

"Not particularly."

"That wasn't a no." I looked at him—not as a friend, but as a woman—for maybe the first time. He was so young when we'd met, it had never occurred to me to look at him like this way.

Bright green eyes looked out through dark square-rim glasses. He had a strong jaw and high cheekbones that I'd never noticed. He'd filled out over the years, and his broad chest was . . .

"Well, damn, Lochlan," I said.

"Dyson, I don't—"

"I know," I interrupted. "You and I are going to discuss that when we are not in a crowded bar. I'm talking about all this."

I waved a hand at him.

"All what?" he asked.

Now that I thought about it, Lochlan was very good at hiding "all this." I thought back to other nights out. He always seemed to find a shadowy corner to disappear into. He was present, but . . . unremarkable.

He made himself unremarkable.

"Interesting," I said with a wicked smile.

"What?" Lochlan lowered his drink, eyes wide. "Dyson," he said as I stepped forward. "Why are you staring at me like that? What are you—hey!"

I pulled his glasses off his face.

"I need those," he protested.

Sliding them into the pocket of his jacket, I continued my appraisal. All black was a pretty standard look for Lochlan. Lots of people wore all black but . . .

"Huh," I said again, realizing that was probably by design. His clothing, even tonight, was unremarkable.

"What?" he repeated. I ignored him.

He was dressed formally, like everyone else. Black suit, black shirt, black tie. And he had made intentional mistakes. His jacket was too big, it made him look thinner and more gangly than he was. It was also more grey than black—from wear, not design. It just looked faded and old. His tie was yet another shade of worn black and was tied a little too short.

None of it was overtly noticeable, but all together it looked sloppy. It allowed this tall, very attractive young man to be average. It let him fade into the background.

I stepped closer to him, unbuttoned his jacket and placed my hand on his tie.

"What are you doing?" His voice shook a little.

"A favor, Lochlan. Now shut up and stand still."

He did.

I removed his tie and stuffed it into his pocket next to his glasses. I unbuttoned the top few buttons on his shirt. Sliding my hands over his chest, shoulders, and down his arms, I removed his jacket.

"Wow," I said, feeling the hard muscle of his chest and shoulders.

"Dyson," he whined. I could hear his discomfort.

I threw the coat over my midnight-blue dress. I wasn't trying to impress anyone tonight. Curious, I pulled the shirt away from his body and looked down.

"Lochy, nice," I said with a smile, tapping his stomach.

"Stop it," he said, but he was smiling too.

"I mean it." I took a step back to take in the full picture I'd created. "Loosen up tonight. Have fun."

"Can I have my glasses back, please?"

"I know you don't need them," I said. "I'm going to keep them."

Worry crossed his face.

"I'll give them back to you tomorrow," I said. "You're safe here, Loch. You don't need to blend into the background right now."

Lochlan looked down. I couldn't read his expression.

"For me, no attention is better than, well . . ." He trailed off.

"You are not alone here," I said, fixing the collar of his shirt. "You never were."

When I looked up and my eyes met his, it was my turn to ask the question.

"What?" I said, wary. He was looking at me strangely. Then he closed his eyes, shook his head a little and the look was gone.

"Nothing. You just—" He paused.

"Tell me."

"You said something me and my brothers used to say," he explained. "That's all. I just," he took a deep breath. "I was just reminded of my brothers."

"You have family here too," I said, punching him lightly on the shoulder.

Really well-muscled shoulder. I grabbed it and squeezed a little. Wow, he hid that well. How had I never noticed Lochlan was a 10?

"Okay, last thing," I promised. I stepped close and ran my fingers through his jet-black hair. I played with it for a moment before moving away and admiring my work. "Would you stand up straight, please?" I said. "Would you hold yourself the way you do when no one is looking?"

His brow furrowed, like he was weighing the risk of being himself. The version of him I saw sometimes. The one who stood tall and exuded confidence. I saw that version when he cast and the odd time when I caught him alone. The times when he forgot to be invisible.

I saw it again now and I smiled. There was a slight energy shift in the room and a few eyes flicked in his direction.

"Well, damn," I winked at him. "You look good."

He smiled shyly, looked away from me and reached an arm up to scratch the back of his head self-consciously. It was one of those actions that, when done by a guy who doesn't know he's good-looking, was very, very attractive.

I noticed Lochlan making eye contact with a Shifter as she passed. The girl blushed and looked at the ground. Her friends giggled and whispered to her. Lochlan couldn't hear what they were saying. I could.

"Oooo." I dragged out the sound for effect. "She is into you."

"One night," Lochlan said, making eye contact with me. "Incoming," he nodded over my shoulder.

"Happy New Year!" Agatha shouted and threw her arms around me. Then she whispered in my ear, "Thank you, thank you, thank you."

"No problem," I said.

"Happy New Year, Lochl—wow." Agatha broke off, giving him an assessing look. "Were you wearing that before?"

"Dys," Duke wrapped me in a bear hug. "Happy New Year!"

"Happy New Year, Duke," I said. "You're crushing me, Duke."

"Oh, sorry." He jumped back.

Hugs were exchanged all around. I even caught Zemila giving Lochlan an appreciative look. Trevor quickly recaptured her attention.

The Shifter who had checked Lochlan out a few minutes before came over. Much to the amazement of the group, she asked if she could buy him a drink.

"Could we find someone to fix you up with for the night?" Duke said out of the corner of his mouth as Lochlan walked away, hand in hand with the Shifter. "I think Dean is single again. And Tobias has always had a thing for you."

"Bleah, not interested," I said. "My work here is done, and I kind of want to go for a walk. I've never wandered around the city before. I always just leave through the portal."

"You've never been in the city?" He sounded shocked. "You've lived here for like, ten years?"

"Five," I corrected. "And how much have you explored the school grounds? Ever climbed the rockface southeast of the building? Or seen the waterfalls? Or—"

"Yeah, yeah, whatever." He waved me off with a smile.

"That's what I thought," I grumbled.

"Have fun on your walk," he said, attention on Agatha. She was dancing with Zemila.

"Bye, Duke," I laughed and turned for the door.

Lochlan caught my arm when I walked by.

"Just a minute," he said to the pretty dark-haired Shifter. "You're leaving?" he asked me.

"Yeah, I just feel like a walk."

"Okay, well." He leaned in and spoke softly. "We can talk tomorrow? About . . . . other things?"

"I'll hold you to that," I nodded.

At the same time as I felt the tingling breeze lift my hair, I heard the jingle of a bell hitting the door as I left.

Light snow lay on the ground and rooftops. Up in the hills, buildings nestled in trees were dusted white. Never having gone in or out of Roswell's street entrance, I turned around, interested to see what the building looked like from the outside.

Oh. I looked at it, disappointed. Just a building.

It didn't vanish into the ones next to it or change into some new boring color. It was just there, protection spells keeping it safe.

I wove my way through the busy street as people cheered, screamed, and hugged. A few brave souls—drunk souls, I amended—were wandering around shirtless.

Lights twinkled like stars amidst the many-colored streamers tied high between the buildings. I smiled as I walked, feeling an odd peace with the world. I was happy to be around people who were happy.

Though I wasn't fully satisfied with what Sahrias had told me, it filled in a few blanks and somewhat bridged the awkwardness between us. Since that conversation a few weeks ago, we'd gone back to something I'd almost call normal.

The crowds thinned. I kept walking, thinking over everything Sahrias had and hadn't said. His sire, Yamini, had been linked to someone, and when he'd died, she'd gone mad. She'd pulled Sahrias into her madness, and Rayyan had pulled him out. He was adamant Rayyan hadn't loved him.

The way Marty had described them together, I wasn't so sure.

Maybe I would never know.

Then Rayyan had protected him from the Starlit Shield. How? I wondered. I found no information on Ankhians being part of the Shield. How was she able to protect him? Why would she hold any sway?

I let my feet guide me as my mind wandered. I had no idea where I was walking and I didn't care.

I wasn't sure if Sahrias would ever be ready to talk about Rayyan. That was frustrating. He knew everything about me, yet he guarded this part of his history. It didn't seem fair. There was so much of this whole thing I still didn't understand.

Rayyan, though part of Sahrias' life, was not part of mine. Knowing about her didn't help me control this cursed power or tell me how to stay off the Shield's radar.

And Lochlan. Lochlan was someone I was sure could help me control this thing. Or maybe he could help me figure out what it was. His connection to Magic was stronger than he let on. I was sure of it.

The foot traffic had all but disappeared. I longed for the jovial feel of the crowds, but not enough to turn back. Not just yet.

I will ask Lochlan to help me, I decided. And I will give Sahrias time. I won't ask about Rayyan again. When he's ready, he'll—

BANG!

It felt like a bolt of lightning. My body flooded with heat and light and connection. For a moment, I felt linked to every single thing in the world. Then the feeling narrowed, searched, found. Found something I didn't know I'd been looking for. Found something that fit perfectly into the empty space inside me. It made me fly.

I felt weightless as heat and light, lust and power, as connection and purpose coursed through my body.

I collapsed.

My hand found the ground for balance as one knee slammed into the dirt-packed road. I felt everything and nothing all at once.

A single tear slid down my cheek, landing inches from my hand. It shimmered gold in the dark night, creating its own light, and melting the snow around it.

In a moment, it turned clear, indistinguishable from the minute pool of water it had created.

As suddenly as the feeling had come, it was gone.

I was on my feet.

It happened again. But why? What triggered it this time?

I looked around. The street was deserted. All but for one person walking a zigzagged path away from me. A man.

Had I bumped into him? Had he bumped into me? Why would that have made . . . whatever happened happen?

No. Not now. Not when I had finally started to make peace with, well, not what was happening to me, but what I was going to do about it.

Just when I thought Si and I were going back to the way things were . . . I should go talk to Si now. I should leave now. I should turn around now.

But I didn't turn around.

I tried to want it. I tried to want to not follow that man down the street. I wanted to want to talk to Si.

But I didn't. I couldn't.

Questions chased each other around my mind. Only one thought broke the cycle. One feeling that was undeniable. One thing dragged my feet in the opposite direction of my maker. If I was sure of nothing else, I knew this without a shadow of a doubt, with the feeling that I was born for this purpose, for this reason alone.

I had to know that man.

"Si!" I'd fought every instinct in my body. Every fiber of my being. It had been hard, so hard not to follow the man into the apartment building he'd stumbled his way to. But I'd snapped out of whatever trancelike state I'd been in. I'd realized that I had been following this stranger for no reason.

And I'd ran.

I'd ran back to Roswell's, through the portal, to Si's apartment.

"Si, wake up!"

I was pounding on his bedroom door. There was no answer. I tried the handle. It was locked.

"Well, screw this!" I stepped back and raised my leg to kick in the door.

"That door," said a lazy voice from behind me, "is older than you are."

"Where were you?" I demanded. Sahrias was leaning on the front door frame.

"Having a New Year's drink with Niloc, thank you very much," he said. "I have friends too you kno—"

"Sahrias, something happened," I cut him off. The expression on his face changed as I rushed towards him.

"Tell me," he said, stepping into the apartment and shutting the door. He guided me to one of the couches, the coffee table between us.

I took a breath and opened my mouth to start speaking, but no words came. Trying to relive the experience was difficult.

"Dyson," Sahrias said. "You are scaring me. What happened?"

Maybe if I started from the party, I'll be able to explain it all.

I told him about the desire to explore the city and what I was thinking about as I walked. I was thinking about him, and Yamini, and Rayyan. I told him I didn't even know where I was walking. I was so lost in thought, then something happened.

I recounted the feeling of connection, of rightness.

"Maybe," I said, "maybe, I was drawn to that spot, to him. Is this what happened to you with Rayyan? Is that happening to me now?"

I looked up. Sahrias's stony expression told me nothing.

"Afterwards," I went on, "I went to him, bumped into him, whatever. All I could think of was going after him. Like I needed to know him, to make sure he was okay or something, I don't know. I don't understand. I followed him to a building and then kind of woke up."

I paused, hoping Si would speak. He didn't.

"I realized what I was doing and came straight here." I paused again. My eyes found the floor. "I feel connected to him, like I have always been connected to him. But I forgot. And now I remember. And I don't understand—what do I do?"

"Dyson, listen to me." Sahrias said. He sounded angry. "You must never," he paused to emphasize the word, "never seek out that boy."

"What?" I said. It hurt to think that. "You don't even know him."

Jesus, neither do I. Why am I being like this? Why does this hurt so much?

"Dyson!" he said again, this time in the voice of a maker speaking to their progeny. He spoke out loud, and in that voice I heard in my head, pushing the words with a touch of compulsion. "You must never seek out that boy."

"I don't—I don't know if I can do that."

"Dyson!" he stood.

"Tell me how to do that!" I yelled, standing too.

"You are stronger than some ancient story. Some fallacy of a curse that tells us we are slaves to someone else. You are stronger than any Vampire I have ever seen or heard of." He pulled my hands into his. "You can be the one who breaks this. Who survives. You can be the one, Dyson. You are strong enough to survive this."

Survive. But he had "survived," hadn't he?

"Si," I said. "I don't want to not see him. I don't want to stay away. I don't know how to want that."

"If you go to him, it will be a choice. Your choice. If you go to him, he will bring you unimaginable pain. And when he does . . . when he does," Sahrias repeated, squeezing my hands, "I will not help you."

No. No, he doesn't mean that.

Si dropped my hands and I sat down. Stunned.

He couldn't mean that. Sure, we had been in a bit of a rut, a fight, but in what world would Sahrias not help me when I needed it? If I really needed it?

But I could hear truth in his words. And it hurt. Almost as much as the idea of never seeing that man again. That man I didn't even know, but who I could still, now, miles away, who I could still feel. I could feel his life force as if his heart beat in my chest.

How was I supposed to be strong enough to ignore that?

I heard the soft click of a door closing. I looked up.

I was alone.

No. There is nothing so terrible, nothing I could do that would really make him abandon me . . . nothing.

"I was wrong."

CHAPTER TWENTY-SEVEN
2043

My alarm clock went off at 3:30 the next afternoon. I was exhausted and felt drowsy with the sun still up. Though I didn't want to be alone while I slept, I wanted to be out of the apartment before Si was awake. I dressed quickly and fled.

As I walked through the busy halls, questions ran through my head. Who was he? Was he safe? Happy? Did he feel me too?

Si's promise to abandon me if I went to this man echoed in my mind. Part of me still refused to believe those words.

"You are stronger than some ancient story. Some fallacy of a curse."

Was I?

"You are stronger than any Vampire I have ever seen."

He'd never said that to me before. He'd never said anything like that. It had taken me so long to get over my blood lust. It had taken me years to be able to control myself around Humans. I couldn't be strong if I was so behind, could I?

Moving slowly through the halls, I made my way to Lochlan and Nemo's room. I knocked. A moment later, Lochlan pulled open the door.

"Dyson," he said, shocked. Then he squinted at me. "Are you okay?"

"Here." I held up his glasses and jacket.

"Oh." He took them. "Thanks," he said. Then his eyes flicked down and back up to me.

"Lochlan," I heard from inside his room. "Who is it?"

"Shit," I said, eyes going wide. "Oh, God, I am so sorry. I didn't think—" I clapped a hand over my mouth, covering my laugh. "You sly dog."

He grinned.

"Where did Nemo sleep last night?" I whispered.

Lochlan shrugged. "At Jasmin's, probably. Give me five minutes."

"Just five?" I raised an eyebrow.

"Enough of that," he grumbled. "I'll meet you down the hall."

"Take your time," I said with a smile.

Under the circumstances, Lochlan was going above and beyond and getting the Gold Star Friend award. I needed his help. He must have been able to tell. I walked down the hall as my mind filled with unanswerable questions about the man last night.

But I had to put aside who he was and focus on control. I have to figure out what this weird Magical power surge thing was. That's what Lochlan could help me with.

"One crisis at a time," I whispered to myself.

"The first time you felt this was twenty-six years ago?" Lochlan asked as we walked a slow circle around the lake behind the school. We'd started our conversation in an empty classroom until the sun set, then made our way outside.

"It's a little fuzzy," I said. "I really thought it was just a dream. Lochlan, I was floating . . . in the air!" I raised my hands up to emphasize my words.

"Well, you've done that again, so it doesn't seem as bizarre if that is an extension of this, umm, curse?"

"I don't know what to call it either," I said. "I just want to understand it."

"Aye," he shoved his hands into his pockets. He wore a thin jacket and dark-washed jeans. His black t-shirt gave little protection from the cold, but he didn't seem to mind. "And why did you come to me?"

"I am so sorry about . . . what was her name?" I asked.

"Oh, Radi." He waved a hand through the air. "Don't worry about that. Not at all what I meant."

"Still," I said. "If you two were still in bed and it was almost 4 p.m., it must've been a good night."

He flushed. "A guy can't pine forever, you know?"

"I know," I nodded. We walked in silence for a while before I spoke again. "Hey, Lochlan?"

"Hmm." He looked at me sideways.

"You would tell me if you needed help, right?" I asked. "You know I'd help you any way I could."

"Do you need help, Dyson?" A grin pulling at the corners of his mouth. I noticed it didn't reach his eyes.

"Yeah, I do," I said. "But that's not what I'm talking about."

He raised an eyebrow at me.

"Well, this walk, yes. Right now, yes," I said. "But you've been off. And I know you don't want to talk about it."

His eyes went back to the ground. I stopped and grabbed both his hands with mine. I waited until his green eyes met my brown ones.

"I need to know that you know you can come to me. For anything."

"I know that," he said. "I'm trying to believe that."

I nodded, understanding what he meant. He didn't trust easily, and though rationally he knew I was there, emotionally he was still guarded. I knew that feeling all too well.

"Now," he said when I dropped his hands and started walking again. "Why did you pull me away from Radina? Just to talk? Which is totally fine, I just—"

"Radina," I repeated.

"She's a Panther Shifter," he smiled. This time it reached his eyes. "Very . . . lithe."

"Well, that's an overshare, but I am glad you had fun. Will you see her again?"

"Maybe." He moved his head from side to side. "Radi isn't into relationships. I don't know if I am either, right now. But we are getting off topic."

"Right," I said. "I need your help."

"Aye, I gathered that," he said. "With what?"

"Controlling these power flare-ups. This cursed Magic. Am I wrong to think you're the person I should be asking about this?"

"No." A dark shadow passed over his face. "No, you're not wrong at all."

We tried to recreate what had happened with Duke in the training room to no avail. I'd had no idea that Lochlan was such an accomplished hand-to-hand fighter. Duke was great, but Lochlan . . . he moved like water, smooth and consistent.

It was frustrating.

"This isn't going to work if you're holding back," he said.

"I could kill you by accident." I moved away from him.

He grinned. "You could try."

"I'm serious, Loch," I said, standing up straight. We were in a small clearing in the woods just inside the school's protective veil, but out of sight of anyone walking the grounds.

"So am I, Dyson," he said. "If the only way you know how to access this part of you is in an all-out fight, and Duke is going to back off when he senses a shift, then you're going to have to go all-out with me."

"Have you seen what Duke shifts into? His strength matches mine. Yours doesn't. I don't want to be responsible for killing one of my best friends."

"How can I prove to you—and I am not being arrogant here—that you cannot kill me?" Lochlan said.

"I could accidentally break your leg, or your arm, or your neck, and then where would we be?"

"Gods below, Dyson. We live at a Magic school. Agatha would heal me." He pressed his fingertips to his chest for a moment. "Narth-éascar."

"What was tha—hey!"

He advanced. Quickly. Quicker than I thought possible for him to move. After a short exchange where he pushed me to the edge of my Vampiric speed, I made a mistake. He caught one of my arms beneath his.

I tried to swing at him, it was stupid. I knew it was stupid. He caught that arm too.

"You've made your point," I said, both of my arms pinned under his. Our faces were inches apart.

"Have I?" he said. Then he headbutted me. Hard.

"Oww," I said as I stumbled back. "Seriously?"

I didn't have time to complain further.

Before I could get my guard up, he moved his shoulder like he was going to throw a punch. When I started to block him, he landed a vicious kick to the middle of my chest that I was totally unprepared for.

Flying backwards, I slammed into a tree.

"Uncle, uncle," I groaned, slowly getting to my feet.

"Nope," he said.

And we were at it again. It only took one more strong hit for me to get sick of him beating the shit out of me.

I don't know how long we fought, but I knew that when I started using my full strength and speed, it got a lot more fun.

I was able to focus.

It was better than with Duke. I wasn't holding back. At all. It was like the rest of the world went away and it was just us, and the fight. Until—

"Nasgadh!" Lochlan cried, raising his hand. "Fanaidh!"

My fist froze inches from his outstretched fingertips.

I was totally immobilized halfway to delivering a blow that would have killed a Human.

"Interesting," Lochlan said, straightening from his defensive posture and looking at me.

I tried to ask what was interesting, but I couldn't open my mouth. I couldn't even breathe.

It was a good thing I didn't need to.

He circled me. I couldn't shift my eyes to follow his movement. I was getting pretty pissed when he said, "Cagair."

I gasped for air that was more habit than necessity. I opened my mouth to rip Lochlan a new one, as I still couldn't move anything but my head, when he said, "I don't want to let you out of this hold because I think whatever I have captured here might dissipate."

"What the hell are you talking about?" I said, turning my head the little that I could. "I don't see anything."

"Let's try something," he said, and placed two fingers on my temple. "Aiteal-aire."

A strange heaviness came over my eyelids. It forced them shut, but was gone in a moment, and when I opened my eyes again, I was nearly blinded with a white-gold light.

"What the hell," I muttered as my eyes adjusted.

"You can see it?" he asked.

"Yeah, I can see it. What the hell is it?"

"I'm going to release you now, okay?" he said, one hand still in the air. It looked like he was struggling to hold whatever spell he'd cast.

"Okay," I said.

"Dúil-cagair," he said, lowering his raised hand and collapsing onto the soft earth. "Gods," he breathed. "I haven't had a fight like that in cen—years. It has been years."

"I don't think I've had a fight like that," I said, shaking out my arms. "And also, what the hell, Lochlan? You didn't want to let me in on your little plan? Or that you are some kind of ninja super soldier?"

"Magic," he said, raising his hand. Blue sparks danced between his fingers. "For strength and speed."

"Is there Magic for skill too?" I asked, knowing he wasn't telling me everything.

He huffed out a laugh.

It was decidedly not an answer.

"I didn't think I'd get an authentic reaction and display of your power if you knew in advance. It sounded like you were being pushed pretty hard when it happened before. Then something clicked in your head."

I flopped down on the ground beside him, and gazed at his neck before blinking. I shook my head. I was hungry.

"Yeah," I said, closing my eyes and trying to sense if there was any wildlife nearby. I wouldn't be able to focus otherwise. It was foolish of me not to have eaten when I'd woken up. "Can you wait ten minutes? I think I hear," I strained. "Maybe a bear . . ."

He waved a hand at me and I stood.

"Do what you need to do." Then he muttered something under his breath and snapped his fingers. A bottle of water and an apple appeared on the ground beside him.

"How the hell did you do that?" I said.

"Dyson." He looked at me, confused. "Magic."

"Oh, yeah . . . well, can you just get me some blood then? I won't have to hunt and I'll be able to focus on what the hell just happened."

"Sit," he said.

I did.

"I can't create something from nothing, mostly," he explained. "You have to show me where it is. You have some in your fridge?"

I nodded, and he put two fingers on my temple.

"Think of what you want," he instructed.

I had to work very hard to picture the bottle of blood in my fridge, not Sahrias's words, not the bright white-gold light, not the man from last night.

I heard a rustle and a snap.

"Here," he said, pushing a bottle of blood into my hands. "I'm exhausted."

He lay all the way down onto the ground.

"Thanks," I opened the bottle.

"There is a lot going on right now, Dyson," he said, his tone more serious than it had been a moment ago. "That Ankhian power of yours, Si, the man you were trying not to think about, and . . . well, and other things too."

"Are you okay?" I asked him again.

He sat up, but didn't answer my question.

"To me, it looked like energy," he said.

"What?"

"That white-gold light." He waved his hand at me. "I don't think it's light. I think it's energy."

"What kind of energy?" I asked.

"The kind that most people, no matter their power level, can't control."

My eyes went wide. Why would he think that? How would he know that?

"But I don't think you're most people, Dyson." He took a big gulp of water. "I don't think you're like most Vampires. They all felt different than you do. And it's not this energy. Now that I've seen it, I can separate it from you. And you," he put a hand on the side of my neck and took a slow, deep breath.

I felt a tingling wave of sensation run over every inch of my body. I shivered.

"You feel very different," he said. "They were old, yes, but you feel . . . ancient."

CHAPTER TWENTY-EIGHT
2043

Every evening, I woke up and met with Duke or Lochlan. Sparring or training to control this new power. Next, I would teach if I had a class or work a shift at Shine House. If not, I'd pray that Zemila was free and wanted a combat lesson.

The only reprieve I got from the thoughts of a nameless man came when I was teaching, fighting, or working with the kids. But every lull in conversation was time for worry, every pause in answering a question was time to wonder.

At the end of each busy night, I collapsed into my bed and hoped I was exhausted enough for a dreamless sleep. When I wasn't, the man was all I saw.

And I didn't even see him. I just felt him. His energy, his pull, his soul. Then I would hear Sahrias's voice in my mind.

"You are stronger than some ancient story. Some fallacy of a curse that tells us we are slaves to someone else. You are stronger than any Vampire I have ever seen."

Stronger than any Vampire he'd ever seen. I wished that were true, but it wasn't.

I wasn't.

Nothing had changed in the three weeks since New Year's Eve. Nothing had changed in how I felt. I rolled over in bed and hugged my pillow to my chest, willing myself to feel the sun's pull, hoping I wouldn't dream. Hoping that tomorrow I would still be strong enough to not go looking for the man.

Si was right. This was a curse. I hated feeling this way. I hated feeling pulled between a stranger and my father. I hated that Si had given me an ultimatum. I hated that I almost agreed with him.

And I hated even more that it didn't matter. I still wanted to know who that man was.

Rationally, I knew this wasn't love—it was obsession. For a moment, I allowed myself to imagine finding the man, knowing him, just being around him.

Heat and light and joy and lust seemed to course through my veins at the very thought.

Sahrias is right. I redirected my thoughts. I have to resist this pull. For this Human man's sake, and for mine.

I sat up in bed and held my hand out in front of me. Lochlan had been getting me to meditate. He thought it would help increase my control over these energy surges. For the first few tries, he had to cast a focus spell to help me. If he didn't, my thoughts drifted to . . .

"No," I said aloud to my empty room. "Stay on task."

I took in a slow deep breath, and let it out through my nose. I did it again, and again.

Focusing on the sound of my breath was the only thing that helped me if Lochlan wasn't casting.

In, and out. In, and out.

My breath was slow, even, and sounded like a faraway ocean. My hand started to tingle. I kept breathing. The tingle turned into a warmth. Soon there was a light glow surrounding my hand.

Tongues of white-gold energy licked my fingertips and I tried and tried to move it all into the center of my palm. I pushed and pushed at the glove of light surrounding my fingertips and—

"You look terrible," Zemila said, sitting down across from me in the library.

"Zemila," Agatha hissed.

"What?" she said. "She does! Are we still going to train today? Maybe you need a break."

"No." I tried for a weak smile. "No, I just didn't sleep well."

That was only half-true. I'd passed out mid-meditation.

"You and Lochlan have both been weird lately," she said.

Was that jealousy?

My eyes flicked to Agatha, who was hiding a grin behind a copy of *Pathopsychology and Latent Luman Ability*.

"What?" Zemila said harshly. "What?" she said again, snatching the pathopsychology book out of Agatha's hands.

Agatha burst out laughing.

"Shhhhhhh," hissed a student a few desks away.

"Oh, get a silence bubble," Zemila hissed back. "And a life."

"Mila," I laughed, my eyes going wide. "Teeth out today, huh?"

"I don't know what you're talking about," she said. "Your sleep-deprived brain isn't making any sense."

"Why did you snap at that poor kid?" I asked. "What's going on?"

She groaned, and spoke in rapid Serbian, then mumbled, "I didn't get in . . .

"Oh, Mila," Agatha said, her laughter dying away. "I am so sorry."

"You didn't get in anywhere?" I asked, surprised.

"No," she said. "I mean, yes, I mean—" She groaned. "I got into U Baltimore, and Temple University, a couple others."

"Mila, that's great," I said, a little confused.

"No NYU?" Agatha asked.

"No NYU," Zemila repeated. "No Columbia. I guess they were long shots."

"What are you going to do?" I asked.

"Cry a bit, then get over myself and be happy my skeeze of a father somehow got me an American passport," she said.

Zemila and Nemo rarely if ever spoke of their family. I knew their mom had gotten sick and died when they were young. They'd ended up in the system. They were almost as close-mouthed about their past as Lochlan. Zemila opened up more than Nemo, but it was rare. I think he had a harder relationship with their father than she had.

"That's not for a while yet. I might even defer a year and try to get into NYU again," Zemila said. "Anyway, I want to hit something. Or watch someone hit something. You and Duke sparring tonight?"

"No," I shook my head. "Not tonight."

"I hate watching you guys do that." Agatha scrunched her nose. "I never understood the appeal."

"I love it." Zemila laughed. "It's empowering or something."

"Hmm," Agatha said returning her scrunched nose to her book.

"Can we workout tonight, then?" Zemila asked me. "I need to get some frustration out."

"Sure," I said, happy for something to focus on.

That morning, I tried to meditate myself to sleep. I sat up in bed, breathed slow, and focused on pushing a ball of energy into the palm of my hand.

Nothing.

The day after that was the same. And so was the day after that. Every day I would toss and turn, then try to harness this new power, and every day I would eventually give up, flop down on my pillow, and think of the man.

Where was he? Who was he? Was he safe? And how could I ever stay away?

Every night I hoped I'd think of him less, and every night was the same.

After a couple of weeks, the control grew. I was able to call heat and light and energy to my fingertips. First, just for a second. Then longer— and sometimes not at all. And every night I didn't pass out from exhaustion, I would think of the man, Sahrias, and Rayyan.

Sahrias and I had fallen back into a false normalcy. It was stressful and strange. He was stiff and formal. He was cold. Just like he'd been when I'd been a new Vampire.

It made me wonder, had I been holding something together for him? Was I to him what he had been to Yamini? Did he think of Rayyan as much as I thought of this man?

God. That's torturous.

Sahrias was nothing like Yamini. I knew that. I knew he had deep scars from that relationship, and even deeper scars from Rayyan. Two women who he'd thought loved him. Two women who didn't.

I would not be the third.

But if his connection to Rayyan was only one way, why had she been with him at all? How could she have done that to him . . . if she felt even a fraction of what I feel for this man?

How could Sahrias have let go? If he knew how I felt, he wouldn't stop me. He would know that I just wanted this man to be safe and happy. If I knew that, I could leave him alone.

It must be different. I must be different.

But, no. I tried to stay rational. No, maybe this is exactly what he'd felt, and he still couldn't keep her. Maybe that's why Yamini went mad. Because she had loved like this and lost it forever.

Loved?

I pressed my face into my pillow. I was exhausted and I couldn't sleep.

Love was not what I was feeling, I reminded myself. I was still rational enough to know that this was obsession.

I wanted to be stronger, the way Si thought I could be. I tried to be stronger for him, and for myself. I was, for a while. It lasted just over a month.

Then I broke.

I walked through the portal to Roswell's, crossed the bar, and went out the front door. The jingle of a bell announced my exit and the tingle on my scalp told me I'd left the protection spell. It was only then that I realized I didn't know where to start.

Maybe if I just walk around? Like last time. Maybe I would find him that way?

It was worth a try. Anything was worth a try at this point. I couldn't think, I couldn't breathe, I couldn't do anything without the constant pull to find this man.

I started to walk aimlessly, wandering up and down the streets for what felt like hours. I searched for the rush of energy, the weightlessness, the feeling I'd had on New Year's Eve.

Nothing.

I tried again the next night. And the next. And the next. I started canceling on Zemila. I started canceling on Lochlan and Duke too. I did the bare minimum to not attract the attention of Niloc and Sahrias, and I walked the streets of the city.

Would I ever find him again? Was he lost to me forever? Was all I had of him this ache in my chest? This burn on my skin? A flare of anger at Sahrias for keeping this from me surged before despair set in. I looked down at my watch.

Only three hours tonight. I'd started late, having taught a class.

Maybe this is for the best. If I don't find him, maybe the spell will break. Spell, curse, story . . . whatever. I'll just go down to the end of this street and turn back.

As I walked, I tried to assess myself. Tried to gauge whether or not my obsession had lessened. I tried to assess my mental state.

I did that often. I was always left wanting. All I had was a feeling of incompleteness, disappointment, and disgust.

What am I doing?

I reached the end of the street. I turned and stared at the ground before starting back. Last week had been warm. I thought this might be the final snowfall of the season. I tried to only step in the footprints I'd already made in the light snow. It was oddly satisfying.

Twenty minutes later, I sat on a barstool at Roswell's. Marty took my drink order and walked off without chatting. He knew I was in a funk and had been for a while. Though he didn't know why. He slid a beer under my nose. I stared into it.

What am I doing? My chest ached with the question. How can I get over this? How can I get back to the way things were before?

The jingle of the doorbell broke my concentration. I blinked and looked at the ceiling trying to stop the sting of tears in my eyes.

The bell on the door rang out again as it was opened and closed.

Embarrassment washed over me at the thought of what Sahrias might say if he knew where I went every night.

Assuming he doesn't already know.

The bell rang again. Heat rose in my chest.

I really didn't want to cry in front of Marty. I closed my eyes and willed the tears away. I was lightheaded, weak. A tear rolled down my cheek. I covered my eyes with a hand to hide it.

The bell rang again.

"Can I help you?" Marty said.

I looked up. Was he talking to me?

"Can I help you?" Marty repeated.

The door chimed.

"I'll have to get someone here to update that protection spell," Marty muttered, turning away.

The clenching feeling in my chest began to subside at the same time as I saw a shimmer of gold turn clear on the countertop. I looked at my hand. I saw nothing but normal, clear tears. I ran my fingers along the bar. Had something caught the light? I found only a small circle of moisture.

I blinked furiously, frustrated with myself.

I wiped my eyes and got ready to leave.

Then I saw it. I saw a tear on my hand change from gold, to clear. I breathed slowly and looked up at Marty.

"Who was at the door?" I asked.

"I don't know," he said, walking over. "Some guy coming in and out over and over again. He seemed pretty wasted. He was Human, so I knew he was in the wrong place."

No. Marty didn't need to update the protection spell. It was the man. It was him. Sahrias was wrong. This wasn't just one way.

He'd found me.

CHAPTER TWENTY-NINE
2043

I rushed out the door. The street was empty.

He was here. He was looking for me. I was sure of it.

I tried to clear my mind. I tried to recapture the ache in my chest, so strong a moment ago. Now I knew why. He'd been close and his intention had been on me.

I could only hope that he could feel my intention now.

I took in a deep breath and tried to exhale away the worry of what this would do to my relationship with Si.

Inhale, exhale, right. My feet pulled me to the right.

I walked, trying to keep my focus. When it wavered, when I thought of Si, the pull stopped. I took in a deep breath, and centered my mind.

Forwards, right, forwards.

Walking in an awkward zig-zag down the streets. I soon recognized where I was going.

Of course I did. I would recognize every corner and every building after all of my searching. But this. This is where I'd first seen him, where I'd first started looking.

Stopping at the end of the street, I saw three figures standing together. They were speaking in a mix of Punjab and something else. Maybe Malay. I only caught a few words.

Two of them lifted—then roughly threw—a large duffle bag.

The bag was moving.

I stepped closer, trying to conceal myself in shadow. If they'd looked, they'd see me. I was lucky they weren't looking.

One of them knelt down beside the bag. "You brought this on yourself, David."

The words were heavily accented.

"David," I breathed. His name was David.

One of the men kicked the bag and laughed at the responding groan. Something inside me twisted.

I took a few steps closer.

"You can only run for so long," the kneeling man said. He raised his fist and drove it down hard. The answering grunt of pain made my decision for me.

I sprinted forward and knocked the two standing men off their feet.

"Ahh!" The man on the ground tried to scramble away.

As the other two were getting up, I weighed the risk of knocking them out. A hard hit to the head from one Human to another could kill or cause serious brain damage. With my strength, it was only too easy to end a life.

Lucky for me, they both ran.

I turned to the remaining man, still trying to find his feet.

Stalking forward, I felt a low cutting growl build in my throat. I pulled the man to his feet and felt my teeth slide from my gums.

"Oh, God," he said.

"Why?" I growled, lifting him off the ground. My eyes flicked to the duffle bag and back. "Why did you attack him?"

The man opened his mouth to answer. No sound came out. I lowered him. His feet touched down. He coughed and tried again.

"He owes money to the wrong people, I get paid to collect."

"For what?" I demanded.

"Lady, this isn't your—ghk—" I lifted him with my hand around his neck.

"For what?" I repeated.

"He—junkie," the man spat out. I lowered him. "He is a mess, not worth your time. Takes anything he can get his hands on," the man told me. "Started paying for drugs by working for some dealers. He did a shit job, lost some money, his boss found out and hired me. Now he can pay it back or be an example."

"Or I could just kill you," I said, showing teeth.

"Wo-wo-would make no difference," he stammered. "If he does not pay, there are others who will be sent. But please don't kill me. I have kids."

I rolled my eyes at the obvious lie.

"How much?" I said.

As much as I knew this guy was probably just trying to save his own skin, if David owed someone money, killing the messenger would do little to change that. I wasn't going to kill him anyway . . . but he didn't need to know that.

"How much does he owe?" I repeated.

"More than you can aff—ghk—"

I raised him off his feet.

"I'm going to ask you this one more time," I said as the man struggled to breathe. "I'm going to put you down, and if the next sound out of your mouth isn't a number, I will snap your neck like it was a twig under my boot. Do you understand?" He nodded as best he could. "All right then." I lowered him to his feet. "How much?"

There was a knock on my bedroom door. I'd gotten in just before the sun had risen.

"Dyson," I heard from far away. "Dyson, are you okay?"

"Lochlan?" I grumbled. My eyelids felt heavy.

"Dyson, I'm coming in," he said.

"What time is it?" I asked, after Lochlan mumbled a spell word and opened the door. "Why are you here?"

"We were supposed to meet at 4:30, Dys," he said. "I guess you slept in."

"Oh," I pushed up from the bed. "Oh!" I said, throwing my head into my hands. "Shit, Lochlan."

"Hey," he said, pushing me over and climbing in beside me. "It's all right. Nothing to stress about. Dyson." Lochlan wrapped an arm around me and let me cry into his shoulder. "Talk to me."

I tried to talk. I tried to formulate my words. But all that came out were more tears.

"I'm so sorry, Lochlan," I sat up and wiped my face on the blanket. "I am so sorry."

"It's okay," he said.

"No," I told him. "It's not. You don't know what I'm apologizing for."

He pulled back a little and looked at me through his thick-rimmed glasses.

"What are you apologizing for?" he asked.

I took a deep breath.

"I've been a bad friend to you," I said. "I know you are going through something. I know you're having a tough time and you want to leave. I know you've only stayed these past weeks because of me. I'm so sorry that I am about to make things worse."

"Not just because of you," he said.

"You know," I laughed a little, "you are a really good liar, Lochlan. But it doesn't work on me."

He took his arm from around my shoulders, took off his glasses, and rubbed his face with both hands.

"You have been helping me too," he said. "You calm something that I . . ."

He trailed off.

"Yeah," I gestured to my tear-stained face. "Calmest of the calm over here."

He huffed out a laugh. I knew he still didn't want to tell me what was going on with him, but I needed him to get over it.

"What do you mean worse?" he asked.

I sobbed again. "God, Lochlan, I fucked up, or I didn't, I don't know. I just know I need help."

"Dyson." He kicked off his shoes, and turned to face me. "What is going on? You're scaring me."

I took a deep breath. Let it out slow.

"I can do this now." I held up my hand and bright light licked up and down my fingers.

"Gods below, Dyson," he said. His eyes went wide. "Your control."

The light faded and I let my hand fall.

"It comes and goes," I said. "I've been practicing a lot."

"And this is why you're apologizing?" he asked.

"No." I wiped my nose. "Just delaying the inevitable, I guess. I went looking for the man last night."

"What?" Lochlan said, after I'd finished telling him about David. "I don't have that kind of money."

I stared at him, silently pleading with him to forgive me. Begging him to understand why I needed him to trust me right now.

"What?" he said again. "I don't."

"How old are you?" I asked.

His face drained of color.

"I—" He recovered poorly. "I don't—you know how old I am. We all went to Roswell's for my birthday in August."

"You are a very accomplished liar, Lochlan," I repeated my earlier sentiments. "But not to me."

I waited. He didn't speak. I asked again.

"How old are you?"

"Twenty-three, you know this." He stood up from the bed. "Dyson, I'm sorry, I have to go."

With two long strides, he was at the door.

"How old are you," I asked again, "Brother of Lugh?"

He froze. I waited.

"What did you call me?" he asked, hand on the doorknob.

"Brother of Lugh," I said, even though I knew he had heard me the first time.

Lochlan looked at me over his shoulder.

"Lugh is fairy tale, a myth," he said. "A character of legend."

"You're talking to a Vampire." My tone was dry.

"Lugh's brothers died," he said. "They were drowned at birth on orders from Balor, their grandfather. Lugh has no—" His voice cracked with a note of pain. "Had no living brothers."

"You and I both know that sometimes the storybook gets it wrong."

Lochlan turned quickly to face me.

"How long have you known this?" he asked taking a step back into the middle of the room.

"Not long," I said.

"How did you find out?"

"I started to notice small things." I gestured for him to come sit back down. "Then, when I was looking into Rayyan and everything that was going on, I went down a bit of a rabbit hole of legendary curses."

"Ha," Lochlan breathed, but there was no humor in the sound. "I've not truly thought of my brothers in so long." Tears fell freely down his cheeks; he took an unsteady step forward. "I have tried so hard not to."

He fell to his knees, hands covering his face.

"Lochlan—" I knelt beside him. "Lochlan, I am so sorry."

"I haven't been able to speak of them, to think of them." His breath was coming in rasps as he tried to breathe through his tears. "When Lugh died, we went into hiding. I mean," he sniffed loudly, "Llow and I were in hiding before but at least we were all together. I haven't seen Llowellyn in . . ." He shook his head. "It's been lifetimes."

"Lochlan," I said again, wrapping my arm around his shoulders. "I didn't realize . . . I didn't think."

I knew I would be pushing him by bringing it up, by telling him I knew who he really was. But I had no idea he'd been carrying this heavy weight alone, and how much it might hurt to think of it.

Selfishly, David itched at the back of my mind. I tried to push it aside.

"I didn't think it would cause you this much pain," I said. "I'm so sorry that I need your help like this, that I brought all this up. I didn't think—"

"Neither did I." He wiped his eyes and stood. I stood too. "Let's get out of here." He looked around my small room. "Let's go for a walk around the lake."

"So," Lochlan said as we circled the luminescent pool of water. He pushed his glasses up his nose. "Tell me how you found out."

"Well," I said. "I only really got confirmation about thirty minutes ago. Before that it was just a hunch."

"You're kidding," he said.

I shrugged, then I pulled the stone out from under my shirt. Lochlan's shoulders slumped like he knew what I was going to say.

"Niloc gave this to Si hundreds of years ago," I said. "The first thing that made me think you weren't all you said you were, that you were more, was that this thing reacted to you."

"You should keep that, and keep it safe," he said. I tucked it back under my shirt. "It is very old."

"Okay," I said. "I will."

"What else?" he asked.

"When you first met Tarin," I said.

"Hmmm." His eyes went down. "It felt wrong. Not to pay the proper respects when I knew how."

"Then you messed up by helping me with this curse thing." I bumped my shoulder into his.

"The fighting." He sighed.

The story he'd told us about growing up in the system and finding his way to Erroin was too mundane for him to know the things he knew.

Lochlan shoved his hands into the pockets of his jeans and started walking again.

"And my family?"

"Sahrias really likes to read," I said, walking with him. "He read me a lot of mythology and folklore when I was coming out of my blood lust. He also insisted I learned the history and mythologies of the places we stayed. I remembered something, and when I was researching . . ."

"Aye," he nodded.

"Irish folklore is weird," I said to Lochlan, the brother of a Celtic god.

"T'is. But in the old stories there is only one grandchild who survived."

"When did you go back to your true name?" I asked, glad he wasn't in pain talking about this. Maybe he was just hiding it better, but he seemed lighter.

"This is the first time in a very, very long time. It wasn't conscious really," he said, shoulders hunching slightly. "When I got here, Niloc asked my name. I said it before I could stop myself. Mayhap it was a compulsion on his part. He knows." Lochlan looked at me. "But I didn't tell him. He just knew."

"I thought he must," I nodded. "I found your name in a book."

"Which book?" His voice was deep.

"You will not destroy it. Burning books is bad," I chided.

"Just one page," he shrugged.

"I already did," I said. "Who do you think you're dealing with here? A girl who doesn't protect her friends?"

He smiled.

"A Vampire from a cursed line and the grandson of the King of Demons." I linked my arm through his and we walked in silence.

"Aye," he said, leading me to a pair of stumps in front of a wide oak tree. "Hell of a duo."

This tree was different than the others here. I'd never noticed before, but it looked a little out of place.

"I've been having strange dreams," Lochlan said. "Horrible dreams. In them, I'm—oh, Gods, Dyson." He leaned forward, elbows on his knees, and his face in his hands. "Dyson, I haven't felt like this since just after my brother died."

"You don't have to tell me all of it," I said. "But I think if you told me some of it, you might feel better."

"Yeah." He nodded, head still in his hands. "I think so too."

"Lochlan is a story in himself. He . . ." Dyson searched for the words. "What he went through after he left Erroin. And then what happened with Zemila. Gods, it was bad for a while. Really bad. He was strong, though. And they found each other in the end.

"You know what?" She turned and her brown eyes, no longer warm, met the stony grey gaze of the only person in the room. Other than the cold corpse of the soldier.

"That was because of you," she said. "I should thank you for him. Of all the misery you caused the world, you played a part in a beautiful love story."

Dyson threw her head back and sighed.

"Gods, why does it all have to be so hard? You." She pointed across the room. "You made it so hard for so many people. You and people who think like you. You, who—"

She cut off. They weren't at that part yet. That part would come later.

"Sahrias once told me that I would accumulate wealth over time. As old as Lochlan was, he had accumulated some serious wealth. He went above and beyond helping me, helping David. I don't think I would have survived without him. He said the same thing to me once. Funny how the world works."

With the bottle of oushifa in one hand, Dyson stood from the piano bench and stepped over the broken glass.

"I am going to take that gag out of your mouth, and give you some of this," she said. "I will give you enough to survive, or—" She looked from the bottle to blank eyes. "—I will only give you enough to make your death even slower. You will not speak as I do this."

She reached forward and pulled the bloody cloth out of the man's mouth. He sucked in a deep breath, glared at her, and opened his mouth.

"Good boy," she said as she replaced the gag.

CHAPTER THIRTY
2043

Last week, Lochlan had collapsed in the hallway in between classes. He'd played it off easily enough, but I knew he needed to leave. Still refusing to tell me the details, I didn't know exactly why. I just knew he needed out.

"The dreams are getting worse," he told me one night in my room. "I'm having them when I'm awake now. Something is wrong with me, Dyson."

"You can't be more messed up than I am," I said, leaning over his shoulder and looking at the projection as he typed quickly on an illuminated keyboard. "You're not planning to kidnap a stranger."

"I don't think I'm much better," he said. "And I don't know if he'll consider it kidnapping once he's home. Look here." He pointed at the projection. "See, there—every few weeks he tries to buy a ticket and the payment doesn't go through. He wants to go home."

Does he? This is all so crazy.

Loaning me the debt against David was only the beginning. Good with a computer, Lochlan got me more information than I could hope for. We were able to transfer the funds David owed without any in-person contact. Lochlan even went with me some nights to make sure he was safe.

'Safe' was a relative term. That guy was right. David was a junkie. It was a rare night that he was sober. But he was alive, and that was enough. For now.

The constant ache in my chest had subsided, and I was able to focus on other things again. It was as if just knowing that I was keeping him safe was enough for me to be who I was. It was like that empty space inside me had filled a little.

Like I wasn't so alone.

I was surprised at Lochlan's willingness to help my *Twilight*-level obsession. But more often than not, when I went to make sure David was okay, Lochlan would come with me. He would sit next to me across the street from the rundown apartment, judgement-free.

"Why aren't you talking me out of this?" I asked him, looking at the projection. "Why are you helping me, and not telling me how crazy I am?"

"We all have our issues, Dyson," he said, and his expression darkened. "We all have our . . . obsessions. At least this one is helping him."

"We've got to find a way to help you too," I told him.

"You're already helping," he said.

"My mere presence excluded." I grinned.

"Are you going into town tonight?" he asked.

"Going into town" was Lochlan's very tactful way of saying "going to watch a stranger."

"I don't want to sleep yet," he said. "Today was bad."

"The swim didn't help?" I asked.

He shook his head. A pained expression crossed his face.

"I'm afraid to sleep," he admitted.

"We've got to find a way to help you too," I repeated.

Like most nights, it was just before daybreak when I got in. Unlike most nights, Sahrias was standing in front of my desk, looking at something I couldn't see. I froze when I saw him, back turned and arms crossed.

Strange. He never just lets himself into my room.

"Hey Si," I said. "What's going on?"

"How is he?" Sahrias asked.

"Lochlan is okay," I answered, shutting the door behind me. "He has been—"

"Not Lochlan," he said

"I don't—"

"The boy," he cut me off again.

"I don't know—" I started to say, but I stopped myself. I was sick of the lying, all the sneaking around. I was sick of the secrets and the ultimatums. "I've never spoken to him," I said. "He's never seen me. He's just safe."

"So, you're stalking him," Sahrias said.

"Yeah." I accepted the harsh word. "Yes, I am."

"You must stop."

"I don't know that I can do that right now," I said, taking the few steps to my bed and sitting down.

He turned to face me. I expected to see rage in his eyes, on his face, but all I saw was pain. Pain and hopelessness.

It hurt to see. We stared at each other. I hated this. I hated having to choose.

"Go to bed." He started for the door but paused in front of me. "We will talk tomorrow. It's early." He leaned down and kissed the top of my head. "Sleep well, Dyson."

"Goodnight," I said.

Sahrias left my room and I turned to my desk to see what he'd been looking at. Beside my father's copy of *Carmilla*, the photo of Sahrias and Rayyan looked back at me.

I was awake when Niloc knocked on my door the next evening. I had been awake for some time, lying in bed and staring at my ceiling. I wanted to talk to Si, to finally be honest with him, but I was also afraid.

Would he really abandon me? Would he really not help if I needed it?

I don't need his help. I just needed him. I needed my father.

I swung my legs out of bed and got ready quickly.

"Good morning," I said to Niloc, a few minutes after he'd knocked. "Did Sahrias ask you to come collect me?"

"Good evening to you too." He laughed. It was a small sound but it never failed to make me smile. "I requested to talk to you first."

"What about?" I asked as we started to walk in the direction of his office.

"To tell you what Sahrias has been unable to—perhaps he is still unable. But I think if I start the conversation, he will finish it." Niloc sighed. "He needs a little help. Such is heartbreak, my dear, especially when we do not process our emotions."

"You're going to tell me what happened with Rayyan?" I asked.

"She is my cousin," Niloc said in answer.

This was the place to meet an Ankhian.

"Are you related to Marty too then?" I asked.

"Oh, yes," he said. "His great-great-grandfather was a good friend and opened the bar when I opened the school. But Rayyan and I haven't spoken much since she left, you see. Truth be told, she is my third cousin twenty-six times removed," Niloc admitted with another small yet infectious laugh.

"You are Ankhian." I stated. "Or part Ankhian."

"So, he has told you a little?" Niloc's thick eyebrows popped up in surprise.

"I found out a little," I corrected. "Asked around. Did some research."

"Medina," he muttered under his breath.

"Yes," I nodded. "He helped. Si did tell me some. About our line, our curse. Not about why he is so . . . him about it."

"People do tend to be themselves," Niloc nodded. "I'll let him tell you that part."

"You know what I mean," I said. "I found out that Rayyan was involved in an Ankhian civil war."

"You have done your research." He nodded.

"Sahrias told me that this curse, or connection, or whatever—" I still didn't know what to call it, "—that it only goes one way. That it is only us to them. They don't love us back."

I looked at Niloc. His eyes stared straight ahead as we walked. I gleaned nothing from his expression.

"I'm scared," I said. "I don't want to lose him."

"It will be all right, child," he patted my shoulder. "It will all be all right. There will be hard times and harder times, but, my dear—" He gestured to the stairs in front of us. We started to climb. "My dear, that is life. Without the hard times, we would never know how good it could be, hmmm?"

"I suppose," I shrugged. But I was still nervous. "They were together. She chose to be with him, right?"

"Oh, yes," Niloc said. "I dare say you know much more than I thought you did. More than Sahrias thought you did. He should have had this conversation with you long ago. But then," he sighed., "would you have understood?"

Would I have understood that I would be inexplicably drawn to a stranger? Sure. Would I have believed it? No.

"Marty told me she was happy when they were together." It wasn't really a question. I was grateful when Niloc answered anyway.

"They had a passion for each other," he said. "Sahrias was quite taken with her from the start, or so I was told, and for reasons beyond his control, of course. But Rayyan felt the same, that I know. She really did love him. I remember hearing about it." He whispered the next part. "It was hot family gossip at the time. I remember seeing it here. Whatever happened after, she loved him then."

"And they were happy?" I said, needing confirmation.

"For a time." Niloc nodded as we rounded a corner. I saw the study door at the end of the hall and could feel Sahrias's presence. "For a long time. They came here together, you know. She brought him here." Niloc sighed. "Well, of course, I was happy to have them. They both taught here for over sixty years before—"

He paused and stopped walking. We were just outside the study door.

"No doubt Sahrias has been listening," Niloc said. "No doubt he will tell you the rest. I wanted to get things started. Try to make things easier. They were together for a very, very long time." Niloc pulled open the door and we walked in.

Sahrias sat in one of four armchairs circled together near the fireplace, dancing with yellow and orange flame. I followed Niloc in and sat on one of the unoccupied chairs.

Sahrias stared into the flame. He seemed weighed down by time. By life. By hard choices and unspoken conversations.

"We were together for over seven hundred years," Sahrias said. "Then she left me for someone else."

Dyson took a deep breath through her nose and searched her senses. She could smell blood and fear, sour Magic, and fresh death. She could smell the sun ducking under the horizon.

She crossed to the balcony doors, wanting to see the dying light in the sky. She threw them open, stepping out into the cool air. She kept her eyes up, not looking at what lay below. Pinks and oranges and pale, pale blues painted the sky.

"A cruel joke," Dyson said. "I can almost see the sun. Almost feel its warmth. It's just enough to make you miss it more."

She turned her back to the blackening sky. It wasn't dark enough yet to see the stars and no darkness could hide the scene below. She almost looked over the large stone railing, but stopped herself.

She thought the air would smell better out here. And it did. Barely. The scent of fear was not as thick.

She inhaled.

No, she realized. It's just as thick out here.

"I understand now, why it was so hard for him to talk about it. He saw the woman he loved change into someone else and had to wonder if that's who she'd always been. He had to wonder if what they'd had was real. If she was the monster of legend.

"And, if she was, why he loved her anyway."

CHAPTER THIRTY-ONE
2043

"Rayyan is a part of the Egyptian Pantheon," Sahrias said. "Though she was written out over time. I suppose ruling was in her blood. Perhaps she felt that it was owed to her. She thought she deserved to be remembered.

"She got a letter one day from an old friend." Sahrias said the word "friend" in such a way that I knew they were something more than that. "He told her of his plans to reclaim the Ankhian birthright. That she would once again be worshipped as she should have always been."

"Who was he?" I asked.

"Another god. A lesser god, hungry, foolish. The son of a warrior of Ra. Fourth or fifth line." He stared into the flames. "I once thought love was the most powerful force in the world. I was naïve, weak, stupid." Sahrias's eyes glinted with unshed tears. "To believe that one would choose love over power."

I wanted to say something. Find some words of comfort—but none came.

"Seven hundred years," Sahrias said to the flames. "Nothing to someone as old as she. But how was I to know that? How was I to know that I was nothing but a schoolboy crush, a fling? Seven hundred years," he said again. "And it feels like just yesterday that she left me here. Left with him. When he came to collect her."

Bitterness tainted his words.

"She was the powerful one. Daughter of Isis and Osiris, she was a child of the First Line. He was using her. She couldn't see it. Or maybe she did and she just didn't care."

He looked up at me. "She destroyed me."

"Sahrias," Niloc said slowly, "you are not destroyed."

"I was," he said, still keeping his eyes on me, pleading with me to understand. "I was nothing. I wandered these halls an empty shell for ten years."

"I'm sorry," I said. I didn't know how to say this delicately. "But that doesn't mean that will happen with—"

"David," Sahrias spit out the name.

"Yes," I whispered.

"This boy doesn't know you exist." Sahrias's voice was furious. "This boy, who is mortal, will die. Even if he ever knows you, even if he loves you, you will end up alone."

I inhaled sharply. His words cut deep. The truth of any attachment to a mortal meant losing them.

"I don't need him to love me," I said. "I just need him to be okay."

"Okay?" he said with a mocking tone. "You want to follow this boy around, skulking in the shadows, making sure that he is 'okay,' for the rest of his life? You will spend your next sixty years stalking him."

"Maybe he'll—"

"Maybe he will love you?" Sahrias voice rose.

"Si," Niloc said, "Calm down."

"No!" he shouted and stood from his chair. "She must know, she must understand her choice. Maybe he will love you and then he will die!"

"Why are you being like this?" I yelled back at him.

"You think Yamini went mad for no reason?" He leaned toward me "You think she wasn't driven there by pain? By loss? You think that won't happen to you?"

"Why can't you just help me?"

I stood too. I was so sure that if he just helped me, it would be okay.

"I am helping you! I have been helping you!" he yelled. "From the moment that boy was born I have been helping you, trying to get you away from him, trying to protect you from him."

"What?" I said.

Sahrias stepped back, breathing hard.

"Oh, Sahrias." Niloc's voice was soft and sad.

"How the hell do you know when he was born?" I asked.

"She felt him then?" Niloc looked to Sahrias. He wouldn't meet his eyes.

"Don't give me that look, Niloc," Sahrias hissed. "You know as well as I do there was no other way. He was a baby. I was protecting him too. I still am."

"That's why we left the mountains," I said, putting the pieces together. "My dream, that dream of light." I worked through it out loud. "That wasn't a dream. That was—that was him being born?"

"And what should I have done?" Sahrias said. "You lived a good life, so did he."

"He's a drug addict with no future and debt up to his eyeballs without me." I couldn't believe what I was hearing. "How is that a good life?"

"A free life, then," Sahrias spat back. "What would his life have been if you found him at five years old? At eight? At sixteen? He had a choice in his life without a Vampire stalking him."

"I wouldn't have done that," I said, a sick feeling in my gut. "I wouldn't have done anything."

"You have no idea what you would have done. I do. And I know what I should have done. If I could do it over again, I would do the exact same thing, except I should have killed the child in his sleep first!"

"Sahrias!" Niloc scolded and something vital inside me snapped.

"Dyson, no!" Niloc shouted as I lunged for Sahrias.

Before I could reach him, he was lifted into the air by invisible hands. A barrier of soft light hung in the air in front of me.

"Niloc, put me down," Sahrias demanded.

Niloc lowered his hand, and Sahrias's feet touched the ground.

"It will be different," I said, "I am not you! He is not Rayyan! Maybe—maybe he will love me. Maybe I can turn him and—"

"And he would be of our bloodline," Sahrias cut me off. "He would be drawn to one who can survive in daylight, not you. And if another Vampire changes him, what will that do to your connection? When he can no longer walk in the sun, will you still care for him then? He turns, and your life together is over. And that is if he loves you," Sahrias said. "If."

"I don't care." Tears fell down my face. "I just want him to, to . . ." I searched for the words, but none came.

"Be okay?" Sahrias mocked. "This is not about me or Rayyan. Gods on High, if he were an Ankhian I'd be less concerned. Then all you'd have to endure after he casts you aside would be being an empty shell. Being cleaved in half and knowing all the while you loved him, you were just a plaything. Knowing that he didn't care one way or another if you lived or died.

"That, I know, is survivable. That, I have survived. But this? Dyson, he is Human. He will die. And when he does, the Shield will come for you. And they will compel me . . ."

He trailed off, squeezing his eyes shut.

"They wouldn't," Niloc said in horror. I turned to him and saw real shock in Niloc's eyes.

"Wouldn't they?" Sahrias whispered. "They've done such things before. You don't think they'd believe it a just punishment?"

He paused.

Maybe Sahrias waited for Niloc to tell him that he was wrong. I waited for Niloc to say it didn't have to be like this. That we could find a different way. But Niloc said nothing.

"I will not live the next sixty years watching you," Sahrias turned his searing gaze from Niloc to me, "stalk a human until he dies, then go mad with grief, only to have the Shield make me kill you. That, I could not survive."

"It doesn't have to be that way," I whispered.

"I was weak when I turned you." He shook his head and stared at the floor. "If I were stronger, I would have told the Shield to kill me—or I would have lived out my life alone. If I were stronger, I would have ended this blood curse myself. But I thought . . . I hoped—"

"So, it's not just David you want dead," I said, anger tainting my thoughts. "It's me too?"

Sahrias roared in frustration and lunged forward. He smacked his hands off the shimmering barrier Niloc still held between us.

"You understand nothing," he said. "I am the only one, Dyson, the only one in our line that hasn't been put down like a dog. I am the only one who hasn't gone mad with grief and gone on to terrorize thousands.

Just me. And do you know why? Because I am the only one who had the misfortune of being connected to an immortal."

I shook my head. I refused to believe it. I would never do something like Yamini had done. I would never hurt someone the way she'd hurt him.

Si is blinded by his pain. He can't see past his history with Rayyan to notice that I am saving David's life.

And I am doing that. I am saving his life. He will be okay because of me.

Just the thought of it filled a hole in my chest. Just thinking of how David would be able to live a real life because of me made me feel like I was less alone. It gave me purpose—and hope. Something I didn't have for Sahrias anymore.

I dragged my eyes from my maker to Niloc.

"Dyson," Niloc said, reading my expression. "Dyson, this does not have to be your path. You don't have to do this."

"I must," I said. "I must."

Sahrias looked back and forth between the pair of us. The hurt in his eyes broke my heart. I looked away from him.

"Thank you," I said to Niloc. "You have given me so much in my time here. Thank you."

"Niloc, take this down," Sahrias demanded, pressing a hand to the barrier.

"Dyson," Niloc said, ignoring Sahrias. "This does not have to be your path."

"I wish that were true," I said, swallowing the sob in my throat.

"Dyson!" Sahrias yelled, and there was a push to his words. The push of a maker speaking to his progeny. "If you leave now . . . if you go to him—"

"What?" I said. Hot anger burned in my chest.

Was he trying to control me? Like I was still a young Vampire, fresh from the earth? Like I'd learned nothing? Like I wasn't strong enough to push back when all I wanted was for him to love me enough to help?

"This boy will ruin you," he hissed. "He won't mean to, and neither will you. Maybe he will love you. Maybe you will be happy. But he is mortal. He will die. And you will break."

"I won't," I said stubbornly as heat grew in my hands and in my chest.

"You will have no choice," he said. "Yamini went mad, her maker went mad, there is not a single Vampire in our line that hasn't!" he shouted. "The only reason I haven't gone as crazy as them is that Rayyan is still alive. And whose responsibility will it be to kill you when you lose him and go mad!? Mine! It will be mine! They will make me do it!"

"Stop it!" I flung my arms out, palms open. A blast of energy surged from me. It shattered Niloc's barrier, hitting Sahrias and throwing him off his feet.

He looked up at me from the floor.

"I cannot watch you live a life I know must be ended by my hand," Sahrias said. "I cannot."

"We're through," I whispered. "I thought I needed you. Your support, your love." I turned away from him. "Tonight, you've shown me that no matter how much I love you, your baggage is more important to you than my future."

"You're wrong," he said.

"You have nothing for me now," I answered.

Then I turned and walked away.

I left Niloc's study. I went to my room to collect my first father's book and my second father's picture. I softly knocked on Lochlan's door, and together, we left Erroin.

We walked to the nearby town where David lived. We didn't use the portal. And with every step, I could hear the voice of my maker, my father, my brother, ringing in my ears.

With every step, I felt more and more like I was leaving a piece of myself behind.

"It feels like just yesterday," Dyson said, bringing a hand to her face. "But it has been lifetimes." She covered the tears that threatened to fall. A moment passed. Her hand went to the chain around her neck.

"There is a game I like to play," she said. "A thought experiment. What if you could go back in time with everything you've learned, and replace your younger self? If you could re-live your life, how far back would you go?"

She paused, not waiting for his answer but thinking of her own.

"I played this game when I was Human. Grade twelve. That's where I'd go. God, my hair was terrible then." She ran her fingers over her short curls, the rings on the end of her chain clutched tightly in her other hand.

"And you, General?" she asked over her shoulder. "Where would you go? Would you want to relive your years as a politician? Or maybe before that, in the war? Would you go back to the day you decided to pull on that string of hate and unraveled an unsteady peace? Or back to when you started to build your own little army?

"Or maybe you would just like to relive today."

Dyson turned and spoke to the dark sky.

"We would've ended up here." She felt a light breeze on the back of her neck. "You and I, in this room. No matter what, we would end up here. This room or another one just like it. I think no matter what we did, this was our path.

"If I went back to that night with Sahrias—if I was there, knowing what I know now—knowing what would follow my actions—the bliss, the agony, all of it . . . I would do the exact same thing."

A frown shadowed her face.

"But if I could go back to any day after, any day in the years that followed, I would go back, and I would reach out to him. I would try to make things right."

She took a slow deep breath, then let it out.

"Pride goeth before the fall," she whispered. "I barely noticed. It was a slow fall, an easy descent."

Lochlan's story continues in:

MAGIC REQUIRED

Enjoy a free preview now.

CHAPTER ONE

They decided water would be the way I died. But I swam anyway. It was my way of biting my thumb at them. At the Old Gods who made me like this.

To be honest, I hated the water. It scared me. I doubtless hated the fear more than the water itself, because I needed it too. It kept me centered.

I didn't use to swim. I didn't use to need to risk my life to clear my head. There was a time where singing did that for me. It still did . . . sometimes.

But not like it used to.

Not like before my eldest brother died.

My eyes flicked up to the clock on the wall. 5:37 a.m.

Twenty minutes.

The community center pool wasn't huge, but it was long enough for me to pick up some speed. With any luck, I'd have a lane to myself until just after six. Standing at the edge, I looked down at the rippling water and the only other person I ever saw swimming this early.

Tim.

Though he was likely in his early seventies, I could tell he'd been one hell of an athlete in his prime. I suspected a boxer. Or mayhap he reminded me of Muhammad Ali with darker skin.

He was here every day, without fail, right at 5:30, and he had the slowest front crawl I had ever seen.

Looking away from Tim, I positioned my goggles, filled my lungs and dove. Cool liquid engulfed my body and I felt the familiar jump of my heart.

That happened every time I was in the water. Blind panic rose up within me. But this particular brand of panic was familiar. With a practiced progression of thought and movement, I controlled it easily.

Tim and I were soon joined by the 6-a.m.-ers. Sharing the lane slowed my pace. I had no patience to swim slowly.

Not today.

I got out of the pool.

To say I was a little old for nightmares was a cosmic understatement, I thought as I stepped under the lukewarm water of the community center showers. Then again, the longer you live, the more you saw, so perhaps not.

I turned to let the water run over my face. When I closed my eyes, the young girl's lost and tear-stained expression was all I saw. I squeezed my eyes shut tighter, attempting to remember every detail of my nightmare.

I didn't want to remember, but it felt important.

Her crying seemed to flood my ears. She couldn't have been older than five. Why was she alone? The images of her wandering down an abandoned street flashed on the backs of my closed eyelids.

I saw her pass a sign. Fort Totten Park.

Her flushed cream-colored face was covered in blotchy red patches from crying. Dark brown hair stuck to her cheek where it had fallen out of her short ponytail. It was matted with blood from a cut on her forehead. The yellow tie in her hair matched the dress she was wearing. Both were discolored with dirt and grime.

I sighed.

There was nothing I could do for the imaginary girl, lost only to me.

I looked up into the small mirror in the shower. Bright green eyes stared back at me—green eyes that were the exact shape and color as those of my two brothers.

Someone had left a razor on the little shelf beneath the mirror. It reminded me I needed to shave before work. I ran my hand over the roughness on my cheeks and jaw, then through my short black hair that wasn't as short as I'd like.

And a haircut too, I thought as I stepped out of the shower.

"Hey Lochlan!" said the blonde teenager behind the counter on my way out. "How was your swim?"

I adjusted a thin chain under my shirt. The small stone at the end of it settled on my chest before I answered.

"Hi Ella," I said, ignoring her question. At 6:20 a.m., her cheeriness was unsettling.

"I noticed your membership is coming up for renewal," she told me with a bright smile. "Would you like to do that now?"

"No thanks," I answered, pausing briefly at the doors.

"Okay," she said, still beaming. "Have an awesome day!"

"Too late," I said under my breath as I left.

March air hit my face when I stepped outside the community center.

The swim hadn't rid my mind of the lost girl as I'd hoped it would, so I tightened the strap of my gym bag and ran home.

I took a slight detour on my way to pass one of my thinking spots. An old oak tree stood tall and proud not far from where I lived, and it reminded me of my homeland and of my brothers. The sight of it brought me peace, short-lived though it was.

Even with the detour, running cut a thirty-minute walk by a third of the time. When I rounded the corner of my block, I saw my elderly neighbor having an argument with the community mailbox. I ran past my house, only slowing once I reached her.

"Mrs. Abernathy," I said pushing my square-rimmed glasses up my nose. The glasses were thick and black. They helped me be less noticeable, more overlooked. I wanted to be invisible.

Society tends to ignore the impoverished, and today, in 2047, laser eye surgery was more affordable than ever, which meant glasses were a sign of poverty. I used this to my advantage and wore them every day, despite my perfect vision.

"How are you this morning?" I asked, waving to the small woman with dark-chocolate skin and grey-streaked curls.

"Oh, Lochlan, better for seeing you," she said, turning to look at me. My face broke into a smile. Mrs. Abernathy's southern drawl and kind face had a way of doing that to me. "You're up early," she said, adjusting her vivid green handbag on her shoulder and tucking a wisp of grey-black hair behind her ear.

"I went for a swim."

She returned my smile before grimacing at the mailbox.

I moved into the neighborhood almost three years ago. On my very first afternoon, while I was unloading the moving van I'd rented, I met

Mrs. Abernathy. She called me over, insisted I take a break and offered me some of her homemade sweet tea. Many a hot summer afternoon had been spent thus.

We both carried the accents of our homeland. It made the stories we shared all the better. She would tell me about growing up in the Deep South and I would tell her Celtic folktales. In reality, I was telling her about my childhood too. She just didn't know it.

"I don't know what it is with this darn thing," she said, placing her thumb to the scanner pad beside her mailbox over and over again, receiving nothing but an angry beep in return. "But it's not working."

"Why don't you let me have a look," I said, pulling my phone out of my pocket.

I worked for a technology and security company. That fact alone was usually sufficient explanation as to how I fixed things using my phone.

I didn't need the phone; it was a prop.

I'm a Caster, or at least that's what I call myself. Saying I'm a Demi-god, while accurate, would show hubris.

The bottom line was I worked with Magic.

Mrs. Abernathy stepped back, allowing me access to the box. I pretended to fiddle with the scanner pad while I muttered a few words under my breath and brushed the back of my hand over the black square.

"What was that, dear?" she asked from behind me.

"I think it was a glitch, why don't you try it again?"

She beamed at me and took a slow step forward.

Contrary to popular opinion, Magic and technology work brilliantly together if you know what you're doing.

And yes, Magic with a capital M because Magic is a name. Magic is alive.

"Oh!" she cried as the scanner turned green under her thumb. A door popped open to reveal several envelopes. "You fixed it!"

"Hardly," I shrugged. Seeing the multitude of letters she pulled from the small square, I said, "I can't believe you get so much mail. I'm jealous."

"Maybe I'll start writing you, shall I?" she said with a devilish gleam in her eye.

"With the price of postage these days, I wouldn't let you."

"And then you might not ever speak to me again, and you know how much I enjoy that."

"I do," I said.

If only she had heard me speak when I was in school five years ago. There, my thick accent was unremarkable. Here, it would get me noticed. I used to be able to speak without it completely, but for some reason it came back to me at school. I haven't been able to shake it since.

"Can I walk you home?" I asked her, offering my arm. "I'm going that way."

"Why thank you, dear," she said, placing her hand in the crook of my elbow after tucking her mail into her aggressively bright handbag. She walked at a brisk pace I was only prepared for because this exact scene had played itself out several times over the past few years.

Mrs. Abernathy filled me in on her favorite soap operas as we walked the half block to our side-by-side front doors. She lived in 34B and I in 34A.

After going up a few steps, she reached over the little wall that separated our respective porches and waved me towards her. Reaching out, she patted me on the cheek. If the wall were any higher, she wouldn't have managed it.

"You're a good boy," she said with a sad smile. "How come I never see you bringing any girls over?"

"Oh, ummm . . ." I didn't know what to say.

Sorry, Mrs. Abernathy, but any relationship I had would be built on the lie that I was Human. Been there, and I don't want to do it again.

No. I couldn't say that.

"Or boys," Mrs. Abernathy said, misinterpreting my hesitation. "I don't judge dear. In fact, I know of this wonderful bar—"

"No," I laughed. "I don't get out much is all."

"Oh, well try, won't you?" she said, stepping to her front door, punching in the unlock code and laying her palm above the doorknob. "Otherwise, as soon as they come up with some anti-aging technology I'll just keep you for myself."

"If only," I said, putting in my own door code.

φ

"Locherrrrrrr!" The familiar voice carried across the Tjart Tech and Security lobby.

"Jen," I replied to the twenty-something man walking towards me. "How are you?"

"One day I'm going to get here earlier than you," he said as he pulled the drawstring of his zip-up hoodie back and forth.

I gave him a wry grin. It was a bit of a running joke. I always seemed to enter the building steps ahead of him. Even on days when Jenner came in early, somehow, I would come in early too. It was something neither of us could explain.

"I'm good," he said as we walked to the elevators. "Better after I saw this gorgeous blond in the coffee shop around the corner."

"Did you ask for his number?"

"Madre de Dios, with eyes like that? He wouldn't give me the time of day."

Jenner wasn't unattractive. Confidence was his biggest problem. He was tall, only a little shorter than my 6'2". His warm copper skin hinted at his mixed heritage, and his puppy-dog brown eyes made him look nineteen when he was closer to twenty-five.

Jenner was my only friend in the city.

Well, that's not true, I thought. I guess I was friends with his sister, Cam. I made a mental note to call her.

"Anyway," he went on. "I saw him flirting with some skinny little muchacha who was flipping her hair like she had a tick or something." He moved his head back and forth in a jerky robotic imitation of someone brushing long hair over their shoulder.

"That seems like some misplaced anger, my friend," I said, stifling a laugh at the looks Jenner was getting from the people behind us.

The ding of the elevator sounded and we got on. In turn, everyone in the elevator pressed his or her palm to the scanning pad. After a few moments an automated voice told us we were going down.

The elevators are Tjart Tech only allowed five to ride at a time and there were no floor numbers to press. Instead, the system took you where you needed to go after it scanned your palm and looked up your file. No one ever got off on the wrong floor here.

"It's not misplaced anger," Jenner said, his light accent increasing with his irritation. "She was proudly wearing a Right Waters pin on her oh-so-lovely blazer."

I sighed while Jenner swore in Spanish.

Currently making headlines was the Right Waters Party. They were getting coverage because of their strong support of a new immigration bill. Though Jenner and his parents were born in this country, his ancestors had been immigrants.

Long before his mother's grandparents had walked across the border to find new life in "the land of the free," his father's side had been brought over in the belly of a crowded ship. As a result, Jenner kept himself well informed of the goings on in our nation's capital.

"Then she deserves your anger," I said with a serious nod.

"Okay," he said, throwing me a sideways look in exchange for my sarcasm. "Maybe not her specifically but I just, I just . . ." He abruptly switched to Spanish and I tuned him out. After three years of knowing Jenner, I knew once he got going, it was best to let him go.

The rest of my day passed without incident. My job of tech support was busied yet monotonous. It was more often a matter of resetting a system than fixing it. These days everyone and everything had a system. Unless you crossed the river into Lowtown, you'd be hard pressed to find a building that still used keys or a store that still accepted cash. Everything had gone digital.

Tjart Tech and Security took care of all things related to technological systems and private security. From phones to computers, banks to mail boxes, Tjart Tech did it all.

And yet somehow, in this age of technology, "Have you tried turning it off and then on again?" was the phrase I used more than any other.

Eight hours to the second after I had walked into the building, I was walking out. As I headed out of the front doors, I saw my bus nearing the stop at the end of the block.

Like so many times before, I had to make the split-second decision:

wait the nine minutes until the next bus came, or sprint down the street in a vain attempt to catch this one. It wasn't cold out, being the warmest March on record. Waiting wouldn't be so bad.

But who liked to wait?

I clutched my messenger bag and took off down the street. The driver saw me running and, with a vengeful grin, he closed the door and drove off as the light turned green. I got there in time to bang on the tail end of the bus as it passed.

I cursed under my breath and sighed. If there is one lesson a long life will teach you, it's how to let go of the little things.

Sitting down on the bench inside the bus shelter, I looked up at the images flashing across the glass wall to my right. Curious as to the time of the next bus, I stood and approached it.

The bottom half of the glass wall was a 24-hour news station with a ticker tape running across the top. Above that were tiny, flashing squares with rounded edges of blue, red or green. Each square had a number in it signifying a bus route.

I tapped twice on a blue square with a large 16 in the center. It revealed a drop-down list displaying the time of the next buses.

'*Delays*,' an automated voice intoned. '*Next trip: 21 minutes.*'

"Brilliant," I said.

The drop-down list disappeared. As I started to turn away from the screen, something caught my eye. I stared at the image of a smiling young girl with dark brown hair and a rosy complexion that had taken the place of the news anchor.

"I'm sorry." I'd bumped into a man when I took a step backwards to get a better look at the screen. He looked exhausted and made a beeline for the bench in the corner of the bus shelter. He sat so he could lean against two walls at the same time and seemed to immediately fall asleep.

I took another two steps backwards and sat beside him. At this distance I could better read the bold words written beneath the face of the girl who was the focus of my nightmare.

"What? No . . ." I muttered to myself as I read, "Fort Totten Park?"

"Oh, so sad," said the man beside me. I turned to look at him. "They found that poor girl's body."

"What?" I said again, shifting to face him. His skin had grey undertones and dark circles drooped under his eyes.

"Did you not hear?" he said, looking at me through one half-open, very blue eye. "The girl they thought had run away or been kidnapped or got lost or something. Melissa, Melinda?" he said, letting his eye close all the way as he struggled to remember her name.

"Melanie," I supplied, not knowing when I had learned that.

"Oh, so you did hear? Melanie, that's right. Melanie Connor."

"Yes I . . ." I stopped. I could hardly tell this man I had heard the girl's name in a dream. Luckily, he kept speaking and I didn't have to come up with a response.

"Poor girl," he said, his blue eye searching my face. "I feel for her family."

"Remind me of what happened?" I asked.

"She went missing a few days ago and they found her body in Fort Totten Park, oh," he said, peeking down at his watch, "maybe four hours ago. They say if they had found her even an hour earlier, she might have made it. No idea what happened."

"Gods," I said, not knowing what to say. "That's . . ."

"Yeah," the man said.

We sat in silence for a few minutes before he truly fell asleep. It was the snoring that clued me in.

Twenty minutes later when the bus arrived, I shook him awake.

"Thanks," he said, before stumbling onto the bus, finding a seat and falling asleep again.

The ride home was thirty-five minutes with a ten-minute walk on the other end. It took longer than that for my mind to attempt to make sense of my prophetic dream, if that's even what it was.

As soon as I got home, I started towards my office to look into the girl's disappearance. My single-mindedness was interrupted by an angry growl from my stomach. I remembered there was some leftover Chicken Thai soup in the fridge. I heated it in the microwave before taking it to my office.

I set the bowl of hot soup down on my desk, carefully avoiding anything that might make it tip over. Then I started my search.

One of the advantages of working for a tech and security company was there were few systems beyond my reach. And if there was one I couldn't get into, I would ask Jenner to hack it for me. I may be a Caster, but when it came to computers, he's the wiz.

It took me under five minutes to get into the city's police department system. Once inside, a quick search revealed the missing persons file I was looking for.

Melanie Connor, age five, disappeared from a friend's backyard on Saturday afternoon during a birthday party. It took anywhere from five minutes to two hours for the hosts of the party to notice her absence.

It's rare for a child to go missing. In the mid-2030s, it became commonplace for parents to have their children wear locators in the form of a bracelet or a necklace in case they got lost or, for some, broke their curfew.

Melanie's parents had told police she knew how to use the locator and how to set off the panic alarm. The locator bracelet was found on Sunday. It wasn't working.

Her body was found in a small patch of trees that bordered the southwest side of Fort Totten Park. There was no indication of abuse or sexual assault. The autopsy scan to determine the girl's cause of death was inconclusive and a true autopsy would have to be done.

"Gods below," I said, leaning back in my chair. I looked at the bowl of soup, forgotten. Picking it up, I brought a spoonful to my lips. It was cold. I didn't care. I ate it quickly.

Would I have been able to save this girl's life? Was I supposed to have figured it out somehow? How could I have known it wasn't just a dream?

Was this my fault? I asked myself. Could my soul bear the weight of yet another death if it was?

By the time I was done thinking myself in circles, I was mentally and physically exhausted. I went into the kitchen to wash the bowl and spoon from my soup.

I got ready for bed, thinking of Melanie and what I could have, or perhaps should have, done. It might have been minutes, or mayhap it was hours, before I fell asleep. Either way, I awoke the next morning, tired, blaming myself for the death of a young girl.

Lochlan's story continues in:

MAGIC REQUIRED

and

DOMINION REQUIRED

Find out more at:

www.hspaisley.com

@hspaisley